In Myrtle Peril

A MYRTLE HARDCASTLE MYSTERY

THE MYRTLE HARDCASTLE MYSTERIES

ALSO BY ELIZABETH C. BUNCE

In Myrtle Peril

Elizabeth C. Bunce

ALGONQUIN YOUNG READERS 2022

Published by Algonquin Young Readers
an imprint of Workman Publishing Co., Inc.

a subsidiary of Hachette Book Group, Inc.
1290 Avenue of the Americas
New York, New York 10104

LIBRARY OF CONGRESS CATALOGING-IN-PUBLICATION
DATA

Names: Bunce, Elizabeth C., author.
Title: In Myrtle peril / Elizabeth C. Bunce.
Description: First edition. | Chapel Hill, North Carolina :
Algonquin Young Readers, 2022. | Series: A Myrtle Hardcastle
mystery | Audience: Ages 9–12. | Audience: Grades 4–6. |
Summary: "Myrtle Hardcastle's search for a missing heiress,
presumed lost at sea, runs aground when a murder in plain
sight has no apparent victim"—Provided by publisher.
Identifiers: LCCN 2022011009 | ISBN 9781616209216 (hardcover) |
ISBN 9781643753317 (ebook)
Subjects: CYAC: Mystery and detective stories. | Inheritance and
succession—Fiction. | Shipwrecks—Fiction. | Murder—Fiction. |
Great Britain—History—Victoria, 1837–1901—Fiction. |
LCGFT: Novels. | Detective and mystery fiction.
Classification: LCC PZ7.B91505 In 2022 | DDC [Fic]—dc23
LC record available at https://lccn.loc.gov/2022011009

10 9 8 7 6 5 4 3 2 1

First Edition

In Myrtle Peril

A MYRTLE HARDCASTLE MYSTERY

1

EAR, NOSE, AND THROAT

Just as a crime can be pieced together by its component parts into a comprehensive whole, so is the human body a mystery that will eventually be solved by thorough Investigation.

–H. M. Hardcastle, *Foundations of Legal Medicine: An Introduction to Medical Investigation in Criminal Justice*, 1894

"You are behaving childishly!" My governess, the redoubtable Miss Judson, faced the bed, ominous brown bottle in one hand, spoon held aloft in the other, like a weapon.

Her patient glowered back, weak hand pushing the bottle away. "No moh me'cine." The words—if they could be called as much—scraped out painfully.

Miss Judson was without sympathy. "*If* you do not

take this, you will not get better. And *if* you do not get better, Dr. Belden will be forced to return. And *if* Dr. Belden returns, he will take you to hospital." She paused, a look of deliberation on her light brown face. "Perhaps that would be best." She moved to replace the stopper on the bottle.

But it was clear that she had won. The sallow hand withdrew, the feverish head nodded, and the spoonful of bitter tincture was administered—for all the good that it would do.

I beheld this exchange from a more or less safe position in the doorway. Father couldn't see me behind the tent of sheets and the steaming brazier set up in his stifling room. I twisted my fingers together and considered Miss Judson's words. Father was suffering his third bout of tonsillitis this winter, and that most dire of threats had been uttered. More than once. *Surgery.*

"*No,*" said a fretful little voice beside me. I scooped Peony to my shoulder, grateful for her soft warm fur and sharp claws digging into my neck. We had stood sentinel here more and more often lately, the room filled with steam and sickness. Dr. Belden was trying every treatment in his arsenal, with only limited success.

Her duty done, Miss Judson strode from the room, wheeling me and Peony into the hallway. "People do not die from tonsillitis," she said firmly.

"They *do* die from scarlet fever," I pointed out. "And erysipelas. And puerperal fever."

She could not keep her lip from quirking. "If your father contracts childbed fever, you two shall make a fortune from the publication of the case study."

"It's not funny! And I meant pyæmia." I had read all the horror stories; I knew how readily a minor illness could turn to catastrophe.

"Hush," she scolded. "Let him rest." She divested herself of apron and sleeve covers, bundling them into the laundry hamper. She tried not to show it, but I knew she was concerned as well. "I had my tonsils out," she said, false brightness in her voice. "And I survived."

Grudgingly, I turned my toe against the carpet. "Did Maman do it?" Miss Judson's mother was a nurse in French Guiana, endowed in my estimation with medical knowledge bordering on the superhuman.

"Hardly. A surgeon did it at the Boswell infirmary, and all the upperclassmen from the neighboring boys' school crowded inside to Observe."

Wide-eyed, I breathed, "Was that before ether?"

In return for that, Miss Judson set me an afternoon of study on the history of surgery.

Which was not, all things considered, particularly reassuring.

⁓

The latest treatment—a concoction of *Thuja occidentalis*, an American evergreen gaining popularity in that medical wilderness—seemed to help. Father rallied, improving enough to return to work, but that did not mean work was ready for him. After the murders at Christmastime had been so swiftly resolved, with the culprit sent to Broadmoor Asylum, Father's caseload had been surprisingly light, and he had taken to skulking about at home, getting underfoot. I had taken to scouring the newspapers—local, regional, and national—for the barest scrap of news that might turn into an Investigation, to absolutely no avail.

Miss Judson and I had likewise found little to occupy ourselves, beyond the conjugation of Greek verbs and the analysis of Lord Cardigan's actions at the Battle of Balaclava. (This was accompanied by rather gruesome illustrations of the casualties, Miss Judson being bored to distraction as well.) Winter is an uneventful time for criminals, Prosecuting Solicitors, artistic governesses, and aspiring Investigators. Even Peony was climbing the walls, leaving tiny shredded tatters in the wallpaper.

Which was why the post of Thursday, 25 January 1894, was so especially welcome. That dreary morning, cross and restless Hardcastles lurked about No. 14 Gravesend Close. After being banished from the schoolroom for suggesting that Russian Commander Liprandi ought to get a garment named for him too,* I sought diversion in Father's office. I found him at his

* Lord Raglan, Lord Cardigan, and Balaclava itself having had this honor already

desk, frowning slightly over a letter. That was a habitual expression, of course, and Peony bounded atop the desk with a curious "Mrrrw?"

Father swiftly tucked something away in a drawer, fastening it shut with a firm click.

"What's that?" I asked, closing the door behind me. "You have your Bad News Face on."

"I do not have a Bad—" Father stopped himself as a smile defeated the previous expression. "It's not bad news, exactly, just strange news. An old case." A steaming teacup sat on the desk, untouched. I caught a whiff of honey, which meant his throat was bothering him again.

"Unsolved?" I hastened to sit in the side chair, keeping an attentive and ladylike (one might say Professional, but in Father's presence it was *ladylike*) posture. "I can help." Our last Investigation had solved *three* murders, including one that was decades old. Not that anyone was keeping track. Or boasting about it.

"Not that interesting, I'm afraid. Just an old client resurfacing." Now he pulled a face I had no name for. "Unfortunate choice of words." He sat back, which Peony took as an invitation to climb into his lap, butting his chin with her forehead. He could no longer see the letter, so naturally I took advantage of Peony's cleverly timed diversion to examine it for myself.

It wasn't a new letter at all, nearly ten years old and addressed to the law firm of Ambrose & Belgrave, where Father worked before becoming Swinburne's Prosecuting Solicitor. Jonas Belgrave, Esquire, QC, the senior partner in the firm, had died long before I was born. I wasn't sure Father had even met him.

Dear Sir,

We regret to inform you that all inquiries on your behalf regarding the brigantine *Persephone*, her crew, passengers, and cargo, have failed to uncover the fate of the ship or the unfortunate souls aboard her. Agents dispatched throughout the Indian Ocean and our colonies in Australia and New Zealand have turned up no trace of the vessel, no sightings, and no evidence of her having reached any destination at all. It is therefore with much regret that we are declaring *Persephone* lost at sea, and would ask you to extend your prayers for those lost with her.

A settlement in the insured amount of £30,000 has therefore been issued for your firm to distribute among the heirs, creditors, and assigns as appropriate.

On a personal note, we understand that Viscount Snowcroft is not only a client but a personal friend, and we send our condolences

"Why are you looking into this now?" I asked. The fate of the *Persephone* was a promising mystery. She might have been deliberately sunk for the insurance money, captured by pirates, or any number of potential felonious fates.

Father tried to rearrange Peony, a challenge involving Immovable Objects and Irresistible Forces, but she turned herself to liquid and poured back into his lap. "Although the law firm has been dissolved,* I'm still the solicitor of record for many of these old clients. Including, it seems, the Snowcrofts."

One-handedly and blindly, he searched the desktop for another document and handed it to me.

This one was less promising. A railway now wished to lay tracks through the Snowcroft estate. They had reached out to Ambrose & Belgrave to handle the lease, and their letter had eventually made its way to Father.

"Do they want you to negotiate the contract?" That sounded dreadfully dull, when there were lovely, lively criminal trials to oversee right here in Swinburne. Or

---

* a consequence of a previous Investigation

there could be, but there hadn't been a single murder in at least a month, and barely any robberies or even Disorderly Conduct. Father had spent a great deal of time rearranging the furniture in his office.

"Mmph," said Father, which I took as an assent. At the rate Peony was going, she would smother him. Father was ridiculously indulgent of that cat—as I took pains to point out, since none of that indulgence passed to me.

Father shifted Peony to a more comfortable angle. "The real issue isn't the railway contract, it's that there are no Snowcrofts to make the deal with. Viscount Snowcroft passed away a few months ago—at the ripe old age of ninety-six," he added, "after a long battle with chronic pneumonia and a weak heart, so it was *unquestionably* natural causes."

"But—"

Father didn't let my objection in edgewise. ". . . leaving no heirs. So no one had a *motive* to kill him."

"Except these railway people," I pointed out hopefully.

"No, actually!" He sounded merry. "Without Viscount Snowcroft to sign it over, it becomes even harder for the railway to lease the land. And that's where we—er, *I* come in. I'm to track down the legal heir to the Snowcroft estate, and approach him with this railway business." He yawned—which turned into a wince.

"But that could be interesting."

"How? I'll be up to my elbows in old deeds by this time next week."

"It's a missing persons case." I returned to the documents from Albion Casualty. "Look, there are three missing Snowcroft heirs right here: Captain Andrew, Mrs. Audrina, and Little Ethel. Maybe somebody survived, and the ship wasn't lost at all!"

Father suppressed his smile. "There was a thorough investigation when that ship went down. It had members of the peerage on it, after all. I have the Board of Trade report around here somewhere."

"Where were they going?" My mind spun out all sorts of thrilling angles for this tale to take, where we might find the missing Viscount Snowcroft.

"Australia." Father shifted Peony to the desk. "Captain Snowcroft was going to take up some post with the colonial government. It seemed a better prospect, since his older brother stood to inherit here in England."

"What happened to *him*?" Perhaps there was foul play involved in that Snowcroft's demise.

"Got tired of waiting for his father to die, I expect." Realizing this was not a charitable thing to say, he added, "He died several years ago. A hunting accident, if I recall correctly."

"A shooting?"

Father was getting exasperated. "Thrown from his

horse, in front of six witnesses, and from what I heard, he had it coming. The horse was exonerated for self-defense, and now enjoys a happy retirement on the Snowcroft estate. Where Eastern Coastal Railways is champing at the bit to put tracks through the northern pastures, if I can figure out who to talk to on that account."

I posited a solution. "Do you have power of attorney? You could make the deal and simply set the profits aside for whoever turns up to collect."

Father looked like he couldn't decide whether to laugh or shake his head. "That is not without a certain legal elegance," he admitted. "Unfortunately, the way the estate is set up, it won't work. Any divestitures of the hereditary property—the lands originally granted to the Snowcroft family by the Crown—must be made by the Viscount himself, and approved by Her Majesty. I won't do, I'm afraid."

I was not put off. "It seems to me that the first thing to do is place an advertisement in the newspapers."

"For a new lawyer?"

I rolled my eyes. "For the Snowcroft heir to come forward. All you need is to advertise across the country—and Australia, too, I should think—and anyone who has information about the case can reply and let you know."

"And collect a reward, no doubt."

"You would discount the frauds and fortune seekers," I said. "Obviously."

"What a clever idea," Father said. "Why didn't I think of that?" He dug about on the desk and found a newspaper—last Friday's *Tribune*—turned to the personal notices.

I studied the inquiry he'd placed with approval. "Well? Has anyone answered?"

And *that*, it turned out, was why Father had had his Bad News Face on.

2
PATIENT HISTORY

The potential applications of forensic medicine to criminal Investigation should not be underestimated. The modern Medico-Legal Investigator is constantly devising new, and refining existing, methods of detection.

–H. M. Hardcastle, *Foundations of Legal Medicine*

"You're being terribly mysterious," Miss Judson remarked as Father helped her slip into her wrap. She wore an elegant gown of fawn-colored satin, which left her neck and shoulders bare and was guaranteed to sparkle in the candlelight of Magistrate Fox's drawing room. "Why does the Magistrate want *all* of us?"

"He's the mysterious one," returned Father—equally dapper in his own black evening suit, his usual tweedy waistcoat and battered homburg swapped for a fine white scarf and top hat. "The invitation mentioned you and Myrtle by name."

"*And* it was underlined." I twitched from foot to foot

with anticipation. Even I had been turned out nicely tonight, in a two-piece frock of dark green velvet and strange new pinchy shoes with low heels and too many straps. My hair was secured with so many pins the neighborhood hedgehogs would look upon me with envy.

In addition to the clothes, I had received a stern lecture on the expected behavior of Young Ladies of Quality who are invited to their fathers' employers' homes. It involved a great number of things *not* to do, including interrupting, asking questions, answering questions, and talking about autopsies.

On the outskirts of Upton stood Magistrate Fox's house, a half-timbered edifice in the Tudor style with imposing iron gates, a winding drive, and sculpted topiary. Father peered out the carriage window. "I feel like we should be on the lookout for wolves," he said. "Or Cavaliers."*

"Or drafts," said Miss Judson patiently, sliding shut the window. Snow clung to the topiary tops, and I scouted for paw prints along the frozen drive. (If I had spotted any, they would have been the handiwork—well, pawwork—of Magistrate Fox's several large and silly dogs.)

Inside, we were led into a Great Hall that was considerably less great than advertised, cramped and smoky and hung with drab tapestries. There wasn't even a suit

* I believe Father meant the supporters of King Charles during the Civil War, not the adorable little spaniels.

of armor, despite an alcove perfectly sized to receive one (it held, instead, a furry cushion). Still, it had its charms. There *must* be a very fine library of law books somewhere. Foxes had served as local Magistrates for generations, after all.

A butler took our coats and led us into the drawing room, where Magistrate Fox was waiting by a cheery fire. "Arthur! You've made it. And you've brought the family. Wonderful." He clasped his hands together with evident delight. "This must be the young lady I've heard so much about." He held out an arm, and I instinctively started to move toward him—until he said, "Miss Judson, you honor me with your presence."

I blinked, torn between confusion and pleasure. Father had spoken about Miss Judson? *Father* had spoken? About *Miss Judson*?

She stepped forward graciously. "Ada, please, my lord." She offered Magistrate Fox her gloved hand, which he lifted to his lips.

He beamed even more brightly. "None of that! I'm only *my lord* when I have the robes on. And this *can't* be Myrtle." Magistrate Fox pretended to regard me seriously. "There's no way this mature young woman is the impudent girl who interrupted my murder trial last summer."

I felt myself flush to the roots of my too-tight hair. "Yes, sir." That had been a singularly mortifying moment in my professional career. I was not proud of it.

"Keep us on our toes, young Myrtle! Don't you stop. In fact, I'm counting on you tonight."

"Sir?" That was Father, stepping in before I could spoil this evening like I had that trial.*

"You see, my dear"—he meant me this time—"we have a mystery on our hands. You remember my model ship?"

I turned toward the fireplace, the vaguest memory of a visit here when I was small rising through my embarrassment. Aboard a plinth sat a splendid miniature sailing ship rigged with tiny ropes of string and real linen sails. A coat of dust made it look like a ghost ship—which I realized was all too apt when I read the name stenciled on the bow.

"We're here about the *Persephone*?" How was Magistrate Fox involved?

Miss Judson joined me. "Did you build this, sir?" She brushed a finger against a white pennant displaying a stylized pomegranate.

"My son," he said. "Claims there's no room for it in his flat. But *Persephone*'s always been a bit of a personal

---

* The judge had declined to commit the defendants for trial—a matter which Father had never let me forget. Although I maintain to this day that my—er—outburst in the courtroom had not affected the outcome of that hearing one scintilla. Or mini-scintilla.

obsession. You see, my late wife's niece was on that ship when she vanished."

I took a moment to work this out, but Miss Judson beat me to it. "Mrs. Snowcroft?" she guessed.

"Well, Arthur, who's the detective in this family?" the Magistrate said. "I suppose it wasn't fair of me to say that I have a mystery. What I really meant is that I've solved *yours*."

"Sir?" Father frowned, but another voice broke in before he could say anything else.

"Oh, Uncle, don't tease them." This actually sounded more like, *Oi, Oncle, doin't tayse thim*, and all eyes turned toward the doorway. A woman and a girl stood in the threshold, the butler waiting to present them.

The Magistrate turned their way. "Now, now," he chided. "You must permit me my little indulgences. After all, it's not often one gets the better of the Hardcastle family."

"But we need their help," the girl said. Dressed in a black gown trimmed with crape* that just brushed the tops of her shoes, she was a little older than I, sturdily built with freckled cheeks, big brown eyes, and curly hair streaked with gold. In her arms she carried a frail white terrier with tearstained eyes and alert ears, one

* which is like *crepe*, only sadder

jauntily patched black and brown. An older woman in half mourning held her shoulder in a firm grip.

"Nonsense," this lady announced in an English accent. "He'll be thrilled to have our business, Ethel, dear. Well, Magnus, don't stand on ceremony—introduce your guests!"

"I was just getting to that. Mr. Arthur Hardcastle, may I present Mrs. Velma Dudley—"

"Of the Seaman's Widows and Orphans Benevolent Society," she inserted, somehow managing to fit all of that in the space of a breath. "SWOBS."

"Lest we forget," said the Magistrate. "And her companion is Miss—"

"Cooke," put in the girl hastily. "Sally Cooke."

Here the Magistrate and Mrs. Dudley gave her strange looks. "Are you sure, my dear?"

My brain was buzzing, all the pieces spinning about: Father's case, the model ship, the notice in the newspaper, Magistrate Fox's mysterious invitation, and what Mrs. Dudley had called her young friend. Suddenly they fell together with a bang.

"Ethel Snowcroft!" I cried—once again causing an outburst in front of Father's boss.

Magistrate Fox beamed. "Didn't I tell you? Cleverest girl in England, this one. As I was saying, Arthur, I've solved your mystery. I found the heiress to the Snowcroft Legacy!"

The Magistrate's declaration was received with a disappointing silence, and he frowned at us all. "Well, now, someone congratulate me."

Since nobody else seemed inclined to contribute, I wheeled round. Sally stood quietly, hugging her little dog to her chest, brown eyes wide and anxious. "Are you the missing Snowcroft girl, from the shipwreck?" (I didn't think this fell under the heading of *interrupting*.)

Patting the dog sadly, she said, "I don't know," just as Mrs. Dudley put in, "The very one! In the flesh, and ready to collect on her inheritance."

I glanced between them. "You must have proof."

Mrs. Dudley was ready for this as well. "Her birthmark," she declared, making Sally blush furiously red.

"Mrs. *Dudley!*" she mumbled into the dog's fur.

The Magistrate watched this unfold with undisguised amusement. "Of course she has proof. Go ahead, dear, run and fetch it." I heard the capital letter and italics in his voice: *It* must be a weighty item, indeed.

"Just—don't say anything else about birthmarks. Please." Sally set the little dog down on a plush settee near the fire, fussing over it for a bit. She gave us—me—a shy glance before running back up the stairs.

Miss Judson's eyes sparkled with speculation. She'd brought her sketchbook tonight, but the butler had taken it along with our coats, and I could almost see her fingers itching to record the scene: the wizened Magistrate by the fireplace, his model ship flickering in the shadows, the specter of Little Miss Snowcroft back from the dead.

"Magnus?" Rubbing his throat, Father tried to question his employer. "Where did you find this—young woman?"

"She found me," the old judge explained, looking serious for the first time. "Well, Mrs. Dudley did. But Arthur, she is the *very image* of her mother as a girl. It's like seeing Audrina alive again."

"How could she have survived?" I put in.* "Isn't it awfully susp—strange for her to show up just when the railroad started nosing around the Snowcroft estate?"

Father looked pained, but Magistrate Fox was nodding. "You see why I've called you here. We need all eyes on this case, believe me, Hardcastles. There's half a million pounds at stake."

"Not to mention your long-lost family," Miss Judson noted.

"What if she's an impostor?" I said, and the Magistrate's face went stony.

"Then we'll throw the book at her for the fraud she is. False personation is a felony, after all." The sudden hardness in his voice made me shiver. Clapping Sally with a life sentence of penal servitude seemed extreme (what would become of her dog?)—but he was right. If she was lying, that would be a serious crime.

---

* This may have qualified as an interruption.

Mrs. Dudley lingered by the roaring fireplace, fingering a jet brooch at her neck. Her gown was of deep aubergine taffeta, trimmed in black lace, and from this costume I deduced that she was a widow, though not a recent one.

Sally reappeared, bearing a small wooden case. "Here," she said, solemnly passing it to Magistrate Fox. He beckoned us closer, and we gathered at a table below a gas lamp, where he held the box up for our inspection. It was ordinary enough, approximately eight inches square, bound with brass corners. A tarnished nameplate adorned the lid.

Father leaned closer. "Does that say—?"

Sally finished for him. "*Persephone.*" As she tilted the lid, the nameplate caught the light and flashed it to all of us. The box contained a large watch—or a small clock—set in its wooden framework. "It's her chronometer."

"Is that real? Where did you get it?" I was unable to contain myself. If Father was frowning (he was probably frowning), I didn't take any notice.

Nor did Sally. "I found it in my father's things after he died."

Father regarded it with skepticism—no: he regarded *her* with skepticism. "But you believe it might have come from the ship?"

She met his eyes with a frank gaze. "What I want to know is, did *I* come from the ship?"

Mrs. Dudley gave her a bracing squeeze. "Of course you did, my dear, and he's going to prove it. Aren't you, Mr. Hardcastle?"

Father replied, "Er."

I interpreted this for the company. "If you're really Ethel Snowcroft, then of course Father will take your case." I gave him an encouraging look—but he was definitely frowning. At me. "*Can* you prove it?" My voice came out sharper than I meant.

Miss Judson took Sally by the arm and kindly walked her toward the settee. "Why don't you tell us your story, Miss Cooke?"

The Magistrate signaled his butler to bring coffee and cocoa as we all took our seats. Mrs. Dudley hovered behind us like a puppeteer. "Go on, dearie," she urged Sally. "Just like you told me."

"Well, I'm from Victoria," she began uncertainly. "Australia. We have—had a shop, in Melbourne. My parents, I mean." She turned a supplicating face to Mrs. Dudley. "Can't you tell them?"

"You need the practice."

"Practice?" Miss Judson's keen ear keyed in on this.

"For the stage, of course. Ethel's embarking on a lecture tour, starting this week." Mrs. Dudley spread her hands like a theater signboard. *"Little Girl Lost: Sole Survivor of the* Persephone*!"*

Father scowled, coughed, winced, and finally said gruffly, "Isn't that rather premature?"

Mrs. Dudley bestowed him with a Look that said he clearly was ignorant of the crucial workings of the English theater. "How else are we going to find witnesses who recognize her, or raise money for her legal expenses? Honestly, Magnus—I thought you said he was the man for Ethel."

"Oh, don't quarrel," Sally begged. "I can do it." She folded her hands around the chronometer and began a dutiful recitation in a clear, steady voice that would serve her well in court (though perhaps a bit wooden for a theater crowd). "It was just my father, my stepmother, and me. And Charley." At his name, the little dog thumped his stumpy tail. "At least, I *thought* he was my father." She regarded us with some urgency. "We were always happy, until my stepmother died. Then Father began to suffer these . . . bouts of melancholy. I thought he was mourning Mother. Now I'm not sure."

Mrs. Dudley gave her another encouraging squeeze, and Sally resumed her account. "Father passed away last fall"—which accounted for her somber attire—"and I had to deal with his belongings. This was locked away in a chest." She held the chronometer for our inspection, but it offered no sign that it was the lone witness to a mystery. It was keeping its own secrets.

"He might have acquired that from anywhere," I said. "A pawnshop or an acquaintance, or perhaps he was part of a salvage crew?" Or it could be a forgery, constructed for just this purpose.

Sally seemed doubtful. "But why should he keep it hidden all these years?"

"There's more," said Mrs. Dudley. "Show them!"

Sally reached inside her collar, withdrawing a long necklace. At the end was an unusual pendant—square, like the chronometer box, its warm, rosy gold surface delicately engraved. "Look." She undid a clasp, revealing a locket with a tiny magnifying glass inside, to enhance the contents.

She handed the piece around so everyone could study the miniature photograph within. I was more fascinated with the clever mechanism of the locket itself, but focused on the image of a gentleman with a prodigious beard, his plump and pretty wife, their serious toddler. Opposite the photograph was a curl of red-gold hair.

"This locket was in the chest with the chronometer. The little girl looks like me—the *woman* looks like me—but those aren't my parents. I mean the Cookes. Who are they? How did he get this?" Her voice rose with each question.

"This could be anybody," I said. But Magistrate Fox had an answer to that as well. He directed our attention to a portrait hanging opposite the fireplace, nearly invisible in the gloom.

"My wife had that painted after the *Persephone* was lost," he said. "From a copy of that very photograph. There's no question it's the Snowcrofts."

"Am I Ethel Snowcroft?" Sally said. "Did I survive the wreck of the *Persephone*?"

"If you are," said Miss Judson, "you'll inherit a substantial fortune."

"I don't care about the money. I just want to know who I am."

"That's exactly what an impostor *would* say," I pointed out, to a hearty laugh from Magistrate Fox.

"She has you there, my dear."

"Do you have any other evidence?" I asked. "Can anyone identify you from so many years ago?"

"Myrtle." Father tried to rein me in, but Mrs. Dudley was eager to answer.

"There's the birthmark, isn't there?" she declared in her forceful voice. "Show them, Ethel."

"The birthmark again," muttered Father.

Miss Judson came to Sally's rescue. "Don't feel you have to show us," she said.

"No, it's not like that. It's hardly scandalous. Look." She gently pushed aside her curly hair, revealing a pink blodge like a lopsided heart on the side of her neck.

I was still holding the locket, and I scrutinized the minuscule picture through the magnifier.

"I've tried that," Sally said. "You can't see anything."

"But everyone knows that Ethel Snowcroft had just such a birthmark," Mrs. Dudley said. "It was in all the papers, when there was still hope of finding you alive.

Along with little Charley, of course!" With a twittering laugh, she tousled the terrier's ears.

"But anyone could have a birthmark and a locket and a little dog. That's not proof—not really." It was plain how distressed Sally was, and no wonder. To live all your life thinking you were one person, one particular man's daughter, only to discover too late that everything you believed might be a lie? My heart went out to her.

"Father will help you," I said firmly. "Won't you, Father?"

"Yes, won't you?" Miss Judson had latched on to Sally's cause, too.

He shifted uncomfortably in his seat. "Well, technically I represent the Snowcroft estate," he said.

"That's Ethel," said Miss Dudley.

"Er, quite. That is, if the courts can affirm her claim to any Snowcroft property, then yes, I would be her solicitor, I suppose."

I glared at him. That was the most lackluster commitment imaginable. Was he feeling ill again? Or was he simply not interested?

"Audrina Snowcroft was my late wife's niece," Magistrate Fox said. "Which means that if this young lady is heir to the Snowcroft Legacy, she is my family." The pride and affection in his voice suggested that he'd already made up his mind. But he was also a shrewd jurist (he'd hired Father, hadn't he?), and no fool. I'd seen him in court several times: Magistrate Fox would require proof—irrefutable evidence that this girl was, in fact, Ethel Snowcroft—before he definitively accepted her as his own.

"I don't know who I am." Sally softly broke the silence, twisting the chain of the locket in her fingers. "But if I *am* Ethel Snowcroft, then why did Edwin Cooke have me? What became of my real parents? You see, Mr. Hardcastle, why I need your help."

3

PRACTICAL
ACOUSTICS

The anatomy of the human auditory system is
well understood, but the degree and accuracy to
which its use is practiced by witnesses can vary
considerably.

–H. M. Hardcastle, *Foundations of Legal Medicine*

"That went well." Miss Judson neatly arranged the
lap rug on our seat in the Magistrate's carriage as it
returned us to the railway station. "I think Magistrate
Fox was very impressed with Myrtle."

Before we departed, Father had drawn the
Magistrate aside for a private ex parte conversation,
and now he seemed wearier than ever. He scowled out
the window. "She's not supposed to impress him! She's
supposed to—to—" He crossed his arms in confusion
and defeat. "She was far too forward."

Miss Judson patted his knee. "That ship's not only sailed, it's run aground and sunk."

"I'm right here," I pointed out. "I can hear you."

But Miss Judson had detected something else in Father's tone. "Arthur Hardcastle, you are *not* going to tell me that you are envious of your twelve-year-old daughter."

I stared at her. At him.

"Of course not," he huffed. "It's just that—well, I'm the Prosecuting Solicitor!" He sounded so sulky that I knew it took every ounce of Exceptional Forbearance Miss Judson could muster not to laugh at him. But I sank into my seat, biting my lip and wondering.

"I don't understand," I complained to Miss Judson when we got home. I was curled up on the window seat in the schoolroom with Peony, who was trying to eat the ribbons on my bodice. "Why is Father upset with me *now*?" I had gone back over every moment of the evening and could find no transgression on my part. With the minor exception of some enthusiasm about the Snowcroft Legacy, I had been a perfect Young Lady of Quality, and the judge *had* seemed quite pleased with me. Father was the one behaving strangely—sneaking about and being unsociable to Miss Snowcroft.

Miss Judson sighed. "Men are sensitive creatures," she said, "their pride easily bruised."

"Well, that's stupid."

"You'll get no argument from me," she replied.

"*No*," agreed Peony, snuggling into my velvet lap.

❧

A few days later, Mrs. Dudley and Miss Cooke—with Charley the dog—called on Father at home. Magistrate Fox had given Father leave from the Prosecuting Solicitor's Office to handle the Snowcroft Affair exclusively. Father was not especially enthusiastic about this, grumbling things about being usurped and "losing his edge." It also meant that all of his work now occurred at home, making No. 14 Gravesend Close uncomfortably snug on weekdays.

Especially today, because we had one extra occupant, my friend Caroline Munjal. She was there ostensibly so Miss Judson could tutor her in French, but she'd arrived half an hour early, breathlessly shaking out her thick black hair. "Is it true?" she'd demanded, scarcely inside the front door. "Your father's representing Ethel Snowcroft?"

"Where did you hear that?" I peered past her, lest the press be lurking down the walk, ready to pounce.

"My father," she said simply, hanging up her coat. "Your father came by to ask him about medical ways to determine someone's identity." Caroline grinned. "It wasn't hard to *deduce* what they were talking about." Dr. Munjal was Swinburne's Police Surgeon, and he often worked closely with Father on criminal cases.

"Did he have any good ideas?" I asked. "All we have to go on is a birthmark."

Caroline wasn't listening. She craned her neck toward the stairwell leading up to Father's study. "She's here, isn't she? I spotted them getting out of the cab as I was walking over. Did she bring Charley?"

Running over was more like it. "How do you even know about the case?"

"Nanette," she said, freely implicating her elder sister. "She has clippings from back then, when the ship disappeared. There was a *Viscount* aboard," she added, as if this explained everything. Caroline opened her bag and produced a handful of the incriminating evidence. "Do you think I could get her autograph?"

Shaking my head, I grabbed Caroline by the arm and fairly dragged her to the schoolroom. "Try to be quiet," I said. "Father's in a Mood."

She clucked sympathetically. "His throat again? Tonsils are *awful*. Nanette had hers out and was a perfect beast about it."

I couldn't say which matter I least wished to discuss—Father's tonsils or the Snowcroft Legacy—so I merely shoved Caroline into the schoolroom, muttering, *"As-tu fait tes devoirs?"*

The lesson did not improve from there. Though clever, Caroline was a distracted pupil at the best of times, and it was clear even Miss Judson's mind was not on *du subjonctif.* She kept glancing out the schoolroom door, to Father's study across the hall. His door was firmly shut, and Peony had set up a plaintive vigil just outside.

Finally, Miss Judson set down her chalk and brushed off her hands. "This is an ideal time to study the science of sound transmission," she announced. "Caroline, Myrtle, each of you collect a beaker. Let us conduct an experiment."

We needed no further prompting, and a moment later, class had reconvened in Miss Judson's bedroom, which happened to share a wall with Father's study. Kneeling on the bed, we held our glass vessels to the creamy damask wallpaper, ears pressed against their flat bases.

"This seems unethical," I said, for the sake of covering all legal and moral angles. Not that I had any intention of stopping, mind you. "If not illegal."

"Nonsense. Science is morally neutral. We are studying how sound waves are affected by various media—such as plaster—and if we're not quiet, we'll miss the entire experimental stimulus."

"*Shh!*" said Caroline. "Ethel's talking."

I listened obediently, focusing on how well the glass focused and amplified the sound waves transmitted by the invisible vibration of the wall. Miss Judson was correct: a conversation among three parties made for an excellent experimental subject matter.

"Mr. Hardcastle, surely you can see what we're

asking is completely reasonable." That warm, treacly voice was Mrs. Dudley's. "Just a *small* advance on Ethel's legacy, enough to cover SWOBS's expenses. She needs a new wardrobe, for one thing—dispense with these dreary mourning clothes."

There was a muffled cough. "I'm afraid it doesn't work like that. We won't have access to the funds until the courts decide in Miss Cooke's—er, Miss Snowcroft's favor."

"Which they will do, of course, because *you* will have them convinced in no time, Mr. Hardcastle! I've been reading up on you, all your *clever* cases . . ."

"What are you doing?" said a new voice, entirely unexpectedly, at Miss Judson's bedroom door. In fact, what the voice said was, *"Watcher dewin?"* just before Sally-Ethel-Snowcroft-Cooke flounced right in, arms full of little Charley, and deposited herself among us on the bed. "Can I have a go?" (*Kinnaye ever gow?*)

Miss Judson stood upright in a flash, flushing—but it was far too late. Sally was laughing at all of us. "I've been at boarding school. I know all the tricks. Here—" She held out her hand for Miss Judson's glass. "Mrs. Dudley sent me from the room so they could talk about money. My money." She gave a little grimace.

Starstruck, Caroline nodded vaguely and scooted over, right into my lap. Sally squeezed in, and before I quite understood what was happening, we were *all* eavesdropping on Father and Mrs. Dudley. Except

Charley, although he could hardly disclaim knowledge of our actions.

"I'm the client," Sally said. "I've a right to know what my lawyer is saying about me."

What Father was saying sounded serious. ". . . caution that if we bring this matter before the court, and they fail to adjudicate in our favor—"

"Why can't he explain things in plain English?" Miss Judson complained. "I'm sorry, Miss Cooke. He's usually quite sensible."

"Shush." I loved it when Father said things like "adjudicate."

"—charged with impersonation for financial gain, which is a felony."

"A felony!" Sally gasped. "What does he mean?"

As if he'd heard, Father said, "It could mean prison time. Remember *Crown against Castro*." After a pause, he added, "The Tichborne Claimant?"

Miss Judson and I exchanged a Look of alarm. Decades ago, a butcher from Australia had turned up in England claiming to be the heir to a fortune—in a case very like Sally's, in fact. When his claim was thrown out, the courts turned around and charged him with perjury. He'd gone to prison, and his lawyer was disgraced. That mustn't happen to Father!

"Pish!" Mrs. Dudley could be heard even without the beakers. "That man was a common swindler. My Ethel is a Snowcroft. I'll swear to it in court, and I'll line up a dozen—two dozen!—witnesses to swear along with me!"

"You'll have to," Father said. There was a long pause, during which I pictured him drinking salt water or thickly honeyed tea to bathe his throat.

Sally set her glass on the bed and lifted Charley to her chest. "*You're* the only witness," she murmured to him. "The only one in the whole world who knows who I really am." Charley, all sympathy, licked her damp cheek.

Fraud wasn't Father's only concern. "We must address the matter of Sally's legal guardian. She won't be able to take possession of anything until she's of age—another seven years, correct? Er, Mrs. Dudley, will that be you, then?"

"Good heavens, that wouldn't do at all! I'm just a representative of SWOBS. I'm sure Mr. Fox will step in, as her closest living relative."

I glanced at Sally, but she wasn't listening anymore. "Magistrate Fox is a lovely man," I said, not terribly convincingly.

She started out of her thoughts. "Oh, I know. It's just—everything is so odd. Three months ago I was playing field hockey at Miss Fisher's Academy, and now I'm on the other side of the world, listening to strangers decide who should look after me."

Caroline hooked an arm into Sally's. "*We'll* look after you," she vowed. "Won't we, Myrtle?"

After Caroline (reluctantly) took her leave, Sally presented me with yet another surprise. "This is you, isn't it?" she said eagerly, producing a much-read and dog-eared copy of *Tales from the Red Graves* with a Mabel Castleton story in it—the penny dreadful tales penned by our neighbor, Priscilla Wodehouse.

I blinked at it. At Sally. All I could think to say was, "They have that in Australia?"

She grinned. "No, silly. I bought it at the news-agent in Upton. But this *is* based on you, isn't it? Uncle Magnus is very proud, you know. You're a real-life detective! Now I know why he picked you to help me. If anyone can find out who I really am, it will be you, Myrtle."

I took a page from Father's book. "Er."

∽

Sally wasn't the only Snowcroft claimant, of course. Over the coming weeks, Father had dozens of responses to his notice, and we were soon overrun with poten-tial Snowcroft heirs, all clamoring for a piece of the estate. As it turned out, it's much harder than you'd expect to prove—or disprove—someone's identity. They descended upon us with alleged birth records, marriage certificates, and affidavits of questionable authenticity, none of which could be proved or disproved outright, without thorough scrutiny and examination by the courts.

I Observed all this, thinking how helpful it would

be to simply take everyone's fingerprints at birth and keep a national registry of Bertillon body measurements, the admirable system used by the French police. (So far it only applied to people arrested for crimes, but expanding it to the population at large had obvious advantages.)

"That sounds expensive," Miss Judson said. "Not to mention concerns about privacy."

"Your *height's* not private," I retorted. "Why should anyone care about that? And you leave your finger-marks everywhere, so you can hardly turn around and complain, any more than if you'd signed your name or left your calling card behind." Thinking about what Sally had said to Charley, I wondered how one might prove a *dog's* identity. Perhaps his paw prints were as unique as human fingerprints. Or maybe some enterprising French veterinarian was already at work compiling Bertillon records of basset hounds and poodles.

"I believe there are subtleties here that you're overlooking." Miss Judson was shifting through the latest post, which had claims from as far away as Cornwall and the Orkneys—even one from Canada, where a Snowcroft Association had sprung up to share the expense and spoils (should any ever arise) among the so-called heirs.

"This one says his great-great-grandmother was secretly married to Viscount Snowcroft's illegitimate half nephew." She tipped that into the wastebasket, since illegitimate offspring have no claim in probate court. "Besides the obvious . . . generational challenges," she added, face twisted as she tried to work out how such a union was even mathematically possible.

Father had gone to Leeds to take a deposition from one of the claimants, and we weren't expecting him back until tomorrow, so Miss Judson and I had taken it upon ourselves to help with the overwhelming heap of paperwork accumulating thanks to the Snowcrofts. Magistrate Fox had been doing his best not to interfere, but he was understandably eager for word on Father's progress to ascertain the truth of Sally's identity.

Not all of the Interested Parties were so considerate. Mrs. Dudley had installed herself as a fixture in the case—in other words, our house—regularly popping by for status reports. That afternoon she arrived just in time for tea, the timing of which I found just as spurious as Sally's suspiciously opportune appearance from Australia. We obliged, with some hastily scraped-together biscuits and grumbling from Cook.

"As you know, the Seaman's Widows and Orphans Benevolent Society is *the* foremost organization of its kind," Mrs. Dudley reminded us, nibbling delicately at a ladyfinger (Cook had been planning to make trifle tonight, I thought regretfully).

"Among benevolent societies?" Miss Judson said, watching the ladyfingers vanish. "Or for orphans and widows?"

Mrs. Dudley went on as if she hadn't spoken. "And, of course, we've pledged to sponsor Miss Snowcroft's stay in England. Until her inheritance comes through, poor Ethel is all but penniless. Our benefactors have provided a little stipend, but the lecture tour is absolutely essential to raise money and support for her cause, in addition to everything else a girl her age needs." To say nothing of the dog. "And you can't imagine how many disreputable people there are out there, waiting to take advantage of someone like Ethel. Why, just yesterday a man telephoned to ask *her* for a donation, the nerve—"

"You have a telephone?" I interrupted.

"Well, of course, my dear. How else could I keep up with all my obligations?"

"Myrtle—" Miss Judson's voice was full of warning, but I ignored her.

"Father hasn't seen the need for one," I said, to Mrs. Dudley's horror.

"Oh, he simply *must* be brought into the Modern Age! Ethel's case is far too important. I shall have service installed immediately." Mrs. Dudley fairly dropped her teacup and rose to her feet, purple skirts rustling.*

"What—do you mean here? Right now?" Miss Judson looked alarmed.

"No time like the present! We'll have a direct line

---

* Miss Judson offers the following utterly extraneous detail: In addition to their advances in criminology, the French also have a word for the rustling sound made by taffeta: *frou-frou*. (It is an onomatopœia.)

put in from this house to—" Mrs. Dudley paused. "Is there an exchange in the village? Never mind, I'll take care of it. Tell Arthur not to worry about a thing—SWOBS are on the case!"

And she frou-froued from the house without a second look, leaving Miss Judson and me more than a bit bewildered. Peony appeared in the parlor doorway with a disappointed warble; Mrs. Dudley was known for leaving behind a splash of cream in her saucer.

⁓

True to Mrs. Dudley's word, the telephone arrived the very next day—before Father, thankfully. I was enraptured, Peony unhelpful, and Cook skeptical. Miss Judson reserved her judgment. There was no alcove for the unit in our house, much to the scorn of the workmen who came to connect it, so we directed them to Father's office. (My bid to install it in the schoolroom or my own bedroom went largely ignored.) In contrast to the devices I'd used before, like the bulky wooden box in the police telephone kiosk at the tram stand, ours was a streamlined, very Modern affair, with a slender black base like a candlestick, the earpiece suspended from a hook.

Before we had quite got used to that (there was no one to call to announce our good fortune, unless I wanted to alert the police. Which I didn't), another wonder arrived on its heels.

"A typewriter!" I exclaimed, as the deliveryman

unpacked the crate. It came with several marvelous accessories, including reels of ink and two reams of lovely, expensive paper. I fought the urge to cradle them to my cheek. Father had a typewriter at his office in town, but this was my own first opportunity to use such a device.

"Where do you suppose SWOBS are getting their money?" Miss Judson was examining the bill of lading. "This cost them nineteen guineas!"

I immediately plucked Peony from the desk, where she'd been sniffing hopefully at the ink ribbon. "Don't you dare," I said. It would take the rest of my life to save up that much money if she damaged it. I'd have to sell my microscope, my telescope, and all my clothes.

"Maybe they'll buy us a motorcar!" Miss Judson's eyes shone dreamily.

"Do you suppose we'll have to give it all back if they don't win the case?" I looked at the bounty, doubts rising. "Will Father think this is all a bribe?"

"Bite your tongue." Miss Judson had opened the manual to the typewriter, which was a work of art in itself, explaining everything from how to install the ink and advance the paper to the ideal posture at which to approach the device. She poked experimentally at a key, and a striker sprang up and tapped splendidly against the black paper-roller (which, according to the manual, was called the *platen*). "This will be a great advance in efficiency," she said. "Even your father can't argue with that."

Well, Miss Judson was mistaken. Evidently it had escaped her notice that Father made his living arguing, and that occasionally he forgot to leave his quarrelsome tendencies behind at the office. When he returned that day for elevenses, he was wearier and crosser than ever, rubbing his eyes and plainly Not Impressed by all the progress we'd made in his absence.

"I'm having some papers sent over—What is all this?" He dropped his brief-bag in the study doorway, not even doffing his coat. His scowl looked permanently etched into his features. "Where did it come from?"

"Mrs. Dudley sent them," I said proudly. "Aren't they splendid?"

"You spoke to Mrs. Dudley in my absence? What did you tell her?" Father stalked to the desk, where we had organized all his case notes by the relative merits of the claimants. "Who moved my paperwork? Myrtle, you know I don't like you playing in here."

"I wasn't *playing*," I said in a small voice.

"*No*," rejoined Peony.

Father shoved his chair aside and began rummaging through everything, not even noticing how nicely sorted it was. "That was two weeks of work," he muttered. "How am I going to find anything now?"

"We were just trying to be helpful!" I cried, eyes

stinging. I scooped up all the notes I'd taken and hugged them to my chest.

"I don't *need* your help! And I don't need any of this—" Father made a move to swipe the typewriter from the desk with his arm, when Miss Judson dived to save it.

"Enough!" Her voice was a thunderclap. "You. To bed. *Immediately.*"

He gave her a look of astonishment, and I had to bite my lip to keep from making any sound. I wasn't sure what would come out—but I daren't risk it. "I'm not a child," he growled.

"You might have fooled me," she snapped. "I won't hear another word of your nonsense."

Father glared at us. "I expect this room to be exactly as it was when I return." His voice was getting raspy again. "And send Cook up with something for my d——d throat! It feels like it's on fire." He stormed from the room, trying to slam the door, but it bounced against his brief-bag and swung to a sad, defeated halt.

Miss Judson gave me a look of concern and hastened after him.

After shifting Father's bag into the room and latching the door securely (so Peony couldn't eat anything), I followed them to the bedroom. Miss Judson had Father seated on the bed, mouth open wide. She was peering into his throat with a lamp and scowling.

"That settles it," she said grimly. "It's gone to quinsy.

Mr. Hardcastle, you can't go on this way! You *must* let Dr. Belden take them out. I'm sending for him this afternoon."

"Can't," he grumbled. "Have court."

"You are in no condition to go to court."

I gripped the doorframe with tight fingers. Quinsy was a dangerous complication of tonsillitis—this meant the inflammation had become an abscess, and Father was at risk of a systemic infection. I ran to fetch Cook and give her the news, and within forty-five minutes, Dr. Belden was closeted in Father's room while the rest of us waited anxiously in the hallway.

"I don't see why I can't be there," I said. "I'm his next of kin."

"Hush, you," Cook scolded. "Talking like he's on his deathbed, instead of just under the weather with a bit of catarrh. He'll be right as rain after Dr. Belden's done with him, mark my words."

She remembered as well as I did just how right as rain my mother had been after Dr. Belden's ministrations. I stomped into Father's room as he was putting his shirt back on. Peony stood atop his pillow and glared at the doctor, fur bristling.

"Arthur, this is ridiculous. Monday morning, I want you at the Royal no later than seven o'clock. Dr. Kinkaid can do the surgery that afternoon, and you'd be back on your feet and home by the end of the week."

I squeezed my fingers together. *Surgery?* "Can't you

do it here?" Only the very poor, eccentrics, and people dying from tuberculosis went to hospitals.

Dr. Belden, startled, turned toward the door. "Young lady, you should not be in here."

"It's *not* just quinsy, is it?" I crossed my arms, daring him to prove me wrong. "It's something much worse, and you're just not telling me."

Father's moustache twitched, but Dr. Belden's stern look only grew sterner. "Now, look here. I *never* hide the truth from my patients—or their daughters. You know me better than that."

"*No,*" said Peony.

Reluctantly, I nodded. I *did* know him better than that. When Mum was sick, he'd been frightfully open with us, although he'd tried to stay hearty and jolly almost up to the end.

He wasn't jolly now.

"You *would* tell me if it was something serious? *More* serious, I mean?"

Dr. Belden did not have a chance to answer, for in the very next moment—all in the *same* moment, from the best of my estimation—the doorbell rang, the front door sprang open, and footsteps thundered up the stairs like a herd of efficient stampeding cattle.

"Delivery for Mr. Hardcastle," rang out a voice—just as a shrill jangle erupted down the hall.

"That's the telephone!" I scrambled for the bedroom door, in time to run headlong into Cook coming the other way with the post in one hand and a pot of hot water in the other.

Dear Reader, I shall spare you the gruesome details, but that was nearly the end of Father's delivery, Dr. Belden treated the lad for minor injuries, and I never did discover who had placed the very first telephone call ever to the Hardcastle residence.

Father looked about, where a doctor, a cat, a daughter, a dripping Cook, a governess, a delivery boy, a puddle of salt water, and a ringing telephone all waited among the heaps of paperwork and law books demanding his attention. "A week?" he said, voice cracking with hope.

Dr. Belden answered sagely, "Perhaps *two* weeks would be best."

4
MATERIA MEDICA

Prosecutors make the worst patients.

–H. M. Hardcastle, *Foundations of Legal Medicine*

The cab trundled up to the wide iron gates of the Royal Swinburne Hospital, which stood open from seven a.m. to six p.m. on weekdays to admit the Unfortunate for care in the hospital's charity ward. Today a handful of ailing souls had queued up, wrapped in woolly shawls, collars pulled up against the frigid weather. Inside the carriage, Father sat heaped in rugs, looking more feverish than ever—pale and damp-faced, even his ginger whiskers limp. He'd barely tried to speak all morning.

We drove beneath a banner advertising HOSPITAL SUNDAY & BUILDING FUND, into a courtyard surrounded by the massive brick hospital. It was built like a castle rampart, a sort of square ring guarding an encampment of outbuildings. Sad little shrubs attempted to give the place a bit of cheer, but they only made it more depressing. It looked like a prison yard. Black-caped nurses and doctors strode briskly among the imposing pavilions.

Father caught my eye and tried to smile. "Hey, now," he said, "going to be fine. Be out of here in a fortnight, right?"

"And we'll be here every day to visit," Miss Judson added, too brightly.

I wouldn't look at either of them.

We jangled to a stop beneath a covered portico, alongside two porters in black uniforms and a tiny round dumpling of a woman, engulfed by her black cape and mantle like a plague doctor. On her head she wore a curious flat patch of lace with long lacy tails hanging down her back. The porters opened the carriage door and deposited us to the pavement.

"Mr. Hardcastle? I am Matron Finch." She had a high, tight voice. "Welcome to the Private Ward."

This was the person who would be taking care of Father for a whole fortnight? Sudden images of every story I'd ever heard about mistreatment in hospitals sprang to mind: ice-cold baths with strangers, being sloshed with caustic chemicals to kill fleas and lice, force-feeding of helpless patients strapped to beds.

"You're thinking of insane asylums." Miss Judson hadn't actually spoken aloud, but I was certain that was what she would have said to my parade of wild imaginings.

Father just nodded weakly, and Matron Finch snapped her fingers, conjuring two more porters from nowhere, who took Father by the arms. Miss Judson and I made to follow, but the matron swooped between us, blocking our path.

"Patients only beyond this door I'm sure you understand apologies good day." This was spoken through a rictus of a false smile, without pause or punctuation or the *least* measure of regret.

Miss Judson gazed down at her. "We're not leaving without seeing Mr. Hardcastle's accommodations and speaking with Governor Greeley, Dr. Belden, the charge nurse, the ward nurse, the surgeon who will be performing Mr. Hardcastle's surgery, and perhaps the night watchman. I'm sure you understand."

Matron Finch's closed expression never faltered. "I'll let the duty surgeon know to expect two cases of frostbite this evening, then." She turned in a whirl of black cloak and floated like a specter past the tall, barred doors, which the porters swung solidly shut behind her.

"Miss!" I cried.

Miss Judson stood mute, looking around the portico as if she couldn't recall how we'd come to be here. Soon her vague gaze became calculating—and then angry. She marched up to the doors and gave them several firm bangs with her fist.

Nothing happened.

"But—"

She held up a silent and forestalling hand, then banged once more on the intransigent portal. Finally, it swung open a crack, and Miss Judson slid her foot into the gap before the porter could slam it in her face. For a moment it looked like an Epic Battle might ensue, and I nearly told the porter to alert the Casualty Ward—but evidently the man's duties did not include clobbering governesses into submission, so he fell back, releasing the door. Miss Judson clasped me by the hand and shoved inside.

"I'm afraid there's been a misunderstanding." Her voice was completely flat, leaving no room for doubt that there was not, in fact, and never had been any such misunderstanding, yet Miss Judson was giving the staff of the Royal Swinburne the opportunity to correct themselves before she unleashed her wrath upon them. "We're with Mr. Hardcastle. You may have heard of him."

The porter paled. "There are no visitors in the Private Ward on Mondays, Miss. No exceptions."

Miss Judson sized him up with her steady gaze. "We're not visiting. We are Inspecting these facilities for their suitability to treat Swinburne's Prosecuting Solicitor. Did I say Hardcastle?" She glanced at me for confirmation.

"You did, yes."

"Excellent. This way, then?" And without further commentary, she breezed us right past a deserted reception desk.

In any other circumstance, I might have found the interior of the Royal Swinburne Hospital to be a marvelous specimen of modernity. Wood floors shone under a polish of wax and disinfectant; green-and-white-tile walls sparkled with cleanliness. At the end of the corridor, a massive window admitted the weak sunlight, augmenting the artificial lighting overhead, and brass fixtures of every description studded the walls: bells, speaking tubes, signal buttons, and still more I could not identify.

Two nurses flitted past, clad in identical pale lavender frocks and crisp white aprons, caps, and sleeve protectors. Farther down the hallway, a cluster of young men gathered before a set of doors—the Operating Theater, I noted as we rushed past; they must be a class of medical students here to watch a procedure. Not Father's, I hoped. Some of their fingernails looked grubby.

Miss Judson barely paused in her march down the corridor, and I noticed ours were the only footsteps audible: her telegraph-tapping boots, and mine scuffing along in her wake. Another pair of nurses—did they *come* in pairs, like lovebirds?—turned and gave us reproving looks.

"Rubber soles," one of them said sternly, her voice low. "The patients are resting."

"Are you supposed to be here?" said the other. "There are no visitors on Monday."

"We're here with Arthur Hardcastle," I said.

The older nurse softened. "Oh, is he your father, then? Agnes, show Miss Hardcastle and—Mrs. Hardcastle?—to the Ward. I think Dr. Belden is with him."

"Right this way," Agnes said, her voice brisk and cheery. Her wide, dark eyes and glossy black hair made a striking contrast with her lavender uniform. "I'm Probationer Ling."

"What's a Probationer?" I asked, alarmed. It sounded like she was an inmate on loan from a penitentiary.

"It's my last year of training. You can recognize us by our uniforms. Probies in lilac, duty nurses in green. If you have a question, ask a duty nurse. If you need something, tell a probie."

Probationer Ling led us to a set of swinging doors, stained green. "This is the Men's Ward." She backed through the doors, skirts swishing professionally. A blast of freezing air greeted us. A dozen or more beds lined the walls of a lofty space more corridor than room, and between every bed, vast windows stood open to the elements—the February elements of cold, cold, wind, and cold. How was this helpful?

"Fresh air is critical to prevent infection," Probationer Ling explained. "We follow Dr. Lister's methods* here, you know."

"I didn't realize Dr. Lister advocated hypothermia," Miss Judson said mildly—to a clap of laughter, hastily stifled, from Probationer Ling.

"Well, Dr.-Lister-as-Interpreted-by-Matron," she clarified. "Dr. Belden, I found some unattended valuables in the hallway. I believe they belong with your patient?"

Father had changed out of his street clothes into white flannel pyjamas and a dressing gown with green piping. He was tucked into the bed (window open behind him), with the blankets pulled up to his chin and a swinging bar suspended above his head—a device for weakened patients to pull themselves upright.

"They'll have you fixed up in no time, Father." My voice sounded stiff and false.

"Indeed we shall," said Dr. Belden. "Dr. Kinkaid is one of the best surgeons in England."

"And Ireland," came a cheerful voice from the end of the ward. Miss Judson and I turned to see a tall, handsome man about Father's age, with a dark beard and dark hair, strolling our way. A coat of starched white cotton flared behind him as he walked.

---

* The Right Honorable Joseph Lister, Father of Germ Theory, had revolutionized the treatment and prevention of infections in hospitals, and been made a baron as a result. Which was not as reassuring as you might suppose.

"Good morning," he said. "I'm Russ Kinkaid. Which of you is Arthur?" He turned to inspect each of us. "You?" He proceeded to peer into my ears—and against my better judgment, I giggled.

"Oh, dear," Dr. Kinkaid said. He had an easy, lilting voice. I'd expected someone from Ireland to have more of an accent, but he sounded as English as anybody. "We can't have *that*. Excessive levity is a symptom of a much more serious condition than I'd been led to expect. Belden, what have you been giving my patient?"

Even though he was being silly when he ought to have been looking at Father, even though I knew perfectly well he was doing it to dispel the tension and make all of us (notably me) relax, I couldn't help myself. I liked him instantly.

"Dr. Belden's explained your case," the surgeon said, "and I've read your file. But before we proceed, I'll need to examine you myself. Is that all right, Mr. Hardcastle?" He *said* Father's name, but I had the most curious feeling he was actually speaking to me.

Father released his death grip on the sheets. "Of course." He tried to use his Courtroom Voice, but it dissolved into a painful cough.

Dr. Kinkaid handed him the glass of water from the bedstand. "None of that, now. We want you back in the courtroom sounding out doom and gloom to Swinburne's criminals." He waved to Agnes. "Probationer Ling, please take the patient's vital signs. So, Mr. Hardcastle: you've an Irish doctor and a Chinese nurse. What do you think of that?"

His voice was still friendly, but I detected an undercurrent of challenge in it. I looked anxiously at the nurse, but if the comment made Miss Ling uncomfortable, she gave no sign of it.

Miss Judson answered for Father. "He thinks it's brilliant," and Father nodded emphatically.

Probationer Ling whisked out her thermometer and thrust it between Father's lips, then proceeded to take his pulse.

"Blood pressure?" Dr. Kinkaid instructed, and the nurse produced a curious apparatus with a leather strap, a dial, and an India-rubber bulb like for a camera shutter.

"Keep that in," she commanded, as Father fidgeted and tried to return the thermometer. "Three minutes. You've a hundred and twenty seconds left." She fastened the leather cuff about Father's left arm.

"Miss Hardcastle!" Dr. Kinkaid barked, making me jump. "What is the name and function of that device?"

"Er—" I searched my memory of Mum's old notes and equipment. A word popped into my head—I was quite proud of it, actually. "A sphygmograph?"

"A *sphygmograph*? What sort of institution do you think this is? Are we barbarians? Is this the Dark Ages?"

"If you ask my mother, it is,"* Miss Judson said.

"This is a sphygmomanometer." Dr. Kinkaid brandished the leather bulb. "Which is *obviously* better than a sphygmograph, because it has more syllables."

Father let out a gasp as Probationer Ling finally withdrew the thermometer. "One hundred one point two," she said, dutifully recording it in her black notebook.

"Very good, Ling. Thank you."

"Yes, Doctor. Anything else?"

"Go make yourself a cup of tea. You look done in."

She hesitated. "But Matron—"

"Won't hear it from me. Off you go."

"Thank you, Doctor!" She sped away before anyone else could find something for her to do.

"The probies here are positively run off their feet," Dr. Kinkaid said. "Now, then, Mr. Hardcastle, Prosecuting Solicitor, what *are* we going to do about these inflamed tonsils of yours? Like a couple of overripe strawberries in there, if you ask me." I watched and listened rapturously for the rest of Dr. Kinkaid's consultation with Father.

"As your chronic condition has developed an acute complication, we'll need to resolve the quinsy before we can remove the tonsils."

* Maman's reaction to the prescription of *Thuja occidentalis* had been singularly unimpressed, and included some Strong Words about the primitive state of English medicine.

"Resolve?" Miss Judson turned her most critical gaze on the surgeon. "Clarify."

"Gladly. First, I'll—" Dr. Kinkaid's eyes lingered on me. (They were green. Which I note solely for accuracy's sake.) "You sure, then? This bit's a bit graphic."

It was hard to tell who uttered the strangled laugh, quickly stifled, but Miss Judson merely said, "Carry on."

"I'll begin by irrigating the abscess with a solution of salt water and carbolic. We'll give you a hearty whack of morphine beforehand, but I won't lie to you— the irrigation isn't pleasant."

"None of this is pleasant," Father grumbled.

"Is he always this cheerful? I'll have you know, Mr. Hardcastle, that Matron Finch prides herself on having the happiest patients in the British Isles." This was directed at the very personage herself, who had descended upon us soundlessly, like a miasma.

"Dr. Kinkaid, we have rules."

"I am explaining the patient's procedure, *Sister.*"

She was unmoved. "We Have Rules."

Dr. Kinkaid was now writing in his own notebook. "You know, Sister, I believe I spotted a nurse having an unauthorized tea break," he remarked—at which Matron Finch's hackles rose. She spun on her silent heel and vanished.

Miss Judson and I exchanged a frown. He'd just promised *not* to tell on Probationer Ling! My opinion of him slipped a bit. Maybe more than a bit.

The surgeon went on as if he'd never been interrupted. "Now. If the irrigation goes well, we'll be able to perform your surgery this afternoon."

I crossed my arms and glared at Dr. Kinkaid with all my professional might. "What safeguards will be in place during the procedure?"

Dr. Kinkaid crossed his own arms. "Safeguards?"

"Against infection. You won't be operating in a crowded public theater with all the germs coming in off the street, will you?"

"And here I was thinking of doing it outside in the gutter, after washing my instruments in old dishwater. How's that sound?"

I gave him my most withering scowl. "Not very funny."

"Miss, I've performed this procedure many times, and—"

"How many?"

He blinked at me. "Nineteen—on humans."

"How many *successfully*?"

"Nineteen. I'm sorry to say one of the experimental subjects didn't make a full recovery. Frogs are hard to predict that way."

"Myrtle." Father gave a little croak, reminding me all too keenly of the unfortunate frog. "You're scaring me."

"But—"

"You're scaring the doctor." Father reached out and squeezed my arm. "I will be fine."

"Miss Hardcastle, I can't promise that your father will come through this without harm," Dr. Kinkaid said frankly. "There are no guarantees in medicine. But I can swear to you, on my honor as an Irishman, that I will give him my very best work. And my best work is very good indeed." He held out a hand.

I hesitated. "As long as you acknowledge that any malpractice on your part could make you and the Royal Swinburne Hospital subject to a lawsuit."

Now Dr. Kinkaid couldn't hide his smile, and he tossed back his head in a hearty laugh. Even Father joined in, raspily.

Dr. Kinkaid grabbed my hand and shook it firmly. "Aye, then. It's a deal."

5

Primum Non Nocere

Fully expecting to spend the remainder of that day in an unproductive tedium of *waiting*, Miss Judson and I returned to No. 14 Gravesend Close. She paused at the foot of the walk, and I hung back as well. It felt as if even opening the door might somehow bring some unspeakable catastrophe upon us, upon Father, and we could avoid it by lingering here forevermore. At long last, however, she gave me a bracing nod and unlocked the front door, whereupon we were greeted by a notable and curious Absence of Peony.

Miss Judson was hanging up her coat when Cook's voice lifted up from the kitchen. "Ada? Young Miss? How is Himself?" She appeared in the corridor, worrying her apron. Her grease-stained trousers and heavy leather work gloves told us she'd spent the morning taking out her anxieties on the kitchen appliances. There was a gas jet she'd been eyeing with deep distrust, and she'd recently entered into uneasy negotiations with our boiler.

"He's all settled in, and they'll do the surgery this afternoon."

"Thank Providence!" Cook relaxed. "There's been a delivery. I had it sent up to Himself's study."

Miss Judson sighed. "Thank you, Cook. We'll look at it later. Is there any tea?"

"If you don't mind, I think you'd best handle it direct. He's been waiting up there for hours, now."

"You don't mean you left the delivery boy upstairs all this time! Cook!" Miss Judson summoned reserves of preternatural energy and surged up the stairs. Since our last deliveries had ended with Father being sent to hospital, I straggled after more reluctantly. But cheery voices greeted me, and I cautiously poked my head round the study door.

"Hullo, Stephen!" A curly-headed young man sat at Father's desk, with Peony draped about his neck like a ridiculous furry ascot. (I wondered, briefly, if what was commonly reported about dogs and loyalty might be true.) It was our good friend Mr. Blakeney. "I thought I could lend a hand while your dad's—on his holiday."

"Right," I said slowly. "His *holiday*."

"Well, Miss J. tells me I'm not supposed to know

that he's really in hospital, so I most certainly do not know any such thing, and I *certainly* wouldn't say anything about it. How is the holiday going, by the way?"

I couldn't help grinning. Mr. Blakeney's silly ways made everything seem easier.

"The surgery's this afternoon," Miss Judson said, doing her best not to betray any anxiety.

"Well, they know their stuff there," he said. "Fixed up Genie's ankle—she's nearly back to her normal, mischief-mongering self." Imogen Shelley Blakeney was Mr. Blakeney's twin sister, a reporter for the *Swinburne Tribune*. A recent injury she'd incurred while pursuing a story had only briefly dampened her Incorrigible Spirit. "She also claims they stole her favorite fountain pen, but you know Genie."

Mr. Blakeney was a law clerk, and we'd often had cause to call upon his professional expertise—which made his appearance this morning doubly welcome. "Figured since the mess from Ambrose and Belgrave was mine to clean up, I might as well pitch in. I'd no idea things had gone this far."

He shook out an envelope full of aged, brittle clippings and what appeared to be the fragments of an embroidered handkerchief. "*To whom it may concern,*" he read, "*Please accept the enclosed materials as proof of my connexion*—misspelled—*to the Snowcraft*—also misspelled—*lineage.*" He examined a leaf that had fallen out of the letter. "Compelling."

"It's hardly your fault," I said. "This all happened long before you worked for the firm."

"All the same, it looks like there's more work here than one chap can handle—even a Hardcastle. Besides, let Mr. H. have all the fun? Perish the thought!" He gave the carriage return lever on the typewriter a thwack, sounding the bell.

Miss Judson fairly wilted into a chair, looking relieved for the first time in weeks. "Mr. Blakeney," she said, "we would be eternally grateful."

The four of us dug into the piles of paperwork that had accumulated, and three of us were reasonably productive. Mr. Blakeney did the heavy legal lifting, sorting the claims with at least superficial merit from those that were most obviously spurious, and answering a couple of letters from the courts (he was a surprisingly able typist). Those would require Father's signature when he returned, but even my critical eye could not find fault with Mr. Blakeney's work. Miss Judson and I followed up on Father's notes, looking up obscure inheritance laws he hadn't got round to consulting yet. Peony contributed by eating the leaf from the Snowcraft correspondent and rendering her own judgment on the matter.

Father's study was one of my favorite places in the whole world, and I often came in here while he was gone, breathing in the Fathery scents of leather and tea and moustache wax. But today its smells were all unfamiliar and wrong: typewriter ink, Mr. Blakeney's damp coat, and a lingering air of hospital disinfectant. I twitched in my seat, unable to settle.

"So this Sally Cooke's the favorite, eh?" Mr. Blakeney was studying one of the documents Father had produced in an effort to authenticate her claim. "That's what the papers are saying, anyway. She's got quite the following now. And little Charley's a verified celebrity."

"*No*," Peony yawned. (She remained Categorically Unimpressed by Charley.)

"What *Genie*'s saying, you mean?" Miss Judson's voice was teasing.

"Well, she does know how to pick a story," he said. "And what a tale! Lost on the high seas, only to emerge from obscurity in Australia, of all places, ancient little dog in tow?" He whistled. "It has all the makings of a music-hall production. Genie claims she's found a source that'll throw the whole thing open."

"What source?" I demanded. "Who is it?"

"No idea," he said. "You know how she is. But supposedly this fellow—or lady—can prove whether the girl's an impostor or not."

"Well, have her send him over when she's done with him," Miss Judson suggested. "We'd love to know, too."

Concentrating on the work helped, a bit, and around four o'clock, Cook delivered us a bolstering tea, even staying to hear some of Mr. Blakeney's recent exploits. By the time the telephone rang—startling us all out of our brief distraction—we had begun to feel somewhat cheered.

Miss Judson answered, and a tense hush fell over the room. "Good afternoon, Hardcastle residence."

The horrible pause that followed made me fidget.

Finally, Miss Judson's face relaxed. "Yes, I see . . . What a relief, thank you, Doctor. When can we come in? . . . First thing in the morning sounds fine. Give him our lov—our best." She replaced the handset with great ceremony, and we let out a collective sound that was half sigh, half cheer.

"Another round of biscuits, I should think." Red-faced and blinking, Cook hurried from the room.

Mr. Blakeney rose from his seat, looking a bit stiff. "Well, I suppose I ought to head out." He winked at Miss Judson. "Give Mr. H. my love, too."

If Miss Judson blushed, it was too dim in the room for anyone to see.

☙

Long after midnight, the bells on the new telephone jangled again, rattling me from sleep. I didn't even realize telephones worked in the middle of the night—I thought the exchange would be closed, the operators all at home and snug in their beds. Unlike me. I groggily made my way to Father's study, tripped over Peony, and was caught by Miss Judson, coming down the hall from her room.

I reached the device before it finished ringing and

yanked the speaking apparatus up to form the connection. My heart was clattering, so I gave myself a moment to catch my breath before speaking.

"Ahoy-hoy," I said in my most professional voice. "Hardcastle residence, Myrtle Hardcastle speaking." Many people were not accustomed to telephony, so presenting a calm and confident demeanor was key to fruitful communication. Miss Judson motioned for me to pass the set to her, but I didn't. I couldn't. A raspy, frantic voice on the other end of the line held me captive.

"Muhrl! Lis'en—I saw 'em—"

"Father?" Alarm turned my voice to a squeal, and I beckoned Miss Judson closer. She hastened to my side and we tried our best to listen together. "Father, where are you? How did you get the telephone?"

"Can' talg. Had to sneak . . . nurses' desk . . . comig bagh." That was delivered amid a torrent of gaspy breaths and painful whispers, Father forcing words past his ravaged throat.

"Mr. Hardcastle, return to your bed this instant!" Miss Judson fell back on her most practical advice.

"Shh!" Father hissed. "Lissen—someone choked. Wigh coadh. Widow—they're comig!—"

"*What's* happened? What are you saying? What white coat? Father? Father!"

But the line had gone still, just a faint, haunting crackle, like his handset had been dropped and left swinging from its cord.

6
NON COMPOS MENTIS

A witness's state of mind must be given due consideration by Investigators. Untrained amateurs may lack the skills and experience to report their Observations accurately.

–H. M. Hardcastle, *Foundations of Legal Medicine*

I stared at Miss Judson in a panic. But she merely lifted a finger and took the handset from me, replaced it firmly in the cradle, waited a moment, lifted it again, then turned the crank to initiate the connection with the exchange. "The Royal Swinburne Hospital, please. Yes, right away. It *is* an emergency, thank you."

I let my breath out. While I'd been listening to Father rave, she'd been formulating our next steps. Her expression told me to wait in silence, but it was an agonizing few moments before someone at the hospital picked up.

"Yes, hello. This is Ada Judson 'phoning from Arthur Hardcastle's residence. He is currently a patient in your Private Ward. Could someone find him and return him to his bed? I beg your pardon—I *am* most certain that he is indeed 'out wandering the floors' . . . How? He telephoned us . . . Well, I'm afraid it *is* possible, Nurse." There was a longer pause. "Yes, I'll stay on the line. Thank you."

She gave a faint, pained smile as we waited. I stood dumbfounded, my whirling thoughts tying up my tongue. Peony spoke for us, anxiously twining around our legs and meowing at the top of her voice—meows that were all wrong (they sounded like *meow*). I scooped her to my shoulder, but she peeled out of my arms and onto the desk, scattering papers everywhere.

Finally, Miss Judson stiffened slightly. "Yes, I'm here . . . I see. Do try to keep him there, won't you? We were given to expect a very different standard of care, you understand. I hate to imagine how Matron Finch will take this . . . Oh, you may *certainly* expect us first thing in the morning." She hung up the handset with a decisive click.

"*Now?*" demanded Peony, but I knew not to press her. Miss Judson rubbed the bridge of her nose and sighed.

"Apparently he escaped"—her voice caught dangerously on the word, like she was suppressing a hysterical laugh—"while the duty nurse was changing his chamber pot. He has been safely returned to his bed, with an extra dose of laudanum." She shook her head.

Cook lumbered down the corridor in her striped pyjamas, paisley dressing gown, and frilly white cap. Miss Judson explained the situation, and Cook said, "Cocoa, then, Miss Ada?" She looked at the clock on Father's wall. "And toast, perhaps? Come along, you." This was directed at Peony, who had decided that since we were all up, breakfast should naturally be forthcoming, despite the fact that it was only one o'clock in the morning.

Miss Judson still rubbed her forehead. "I suppose none of us is getting back to sleep now."

"We should work on Sally's case," I proposed.

"I have a better idea," she lied—and steered me into the schoolroom to resume our analysis of the Crimean War.

It did the trick, and within the hour, thanks to the lecture and Cook's cocoa and toast, we were warm and sleepy and bored enough to go back to bed.

⁓

The next morning at the hospital, we were painfully delayed at the reception desk, now manned by a brusque nurse who made us sign the visitors log and issued us tickets, like we'd arrived at a carnival. The name badge pinned to her apron identified her only as Woolley, and she was a veritable font of helpful information.

"Good morning. We're here about Mr. Hardcastle." Miss Judson's voice was sunny, but Nurse Woolley only stared back blankly. "There was a disturbance in the night?"

"I wouldn't know anything about that. Would you care to make a donation?" A great glass jar was stationed at her elbow, half full of coins, labeled HOSPITAL SUNDAY FUND. Beside it was another one, practically overflowing: SWOBS FUND FOR ETHEL SNOWCROFT.

Miss Judson tried again. "We'd care to learn the status of a patient."

Nurse Woolley never looked up. "You'll need to ask the duty nurse. Sign here, please."

Hospital staff bustled about, wheeling patients in bath chairs, toting armloads of laundry, and casting wary glances our way. My fingers cramped as I scrawled my name in the log. It felt like everyone was staring at us.

Finally, Nurse Woolley tore our passes from the book—crisp sheets of perforated paper declaring the date, our names, and the patient we had come to see. "Those are *nontransferable*, mind." I nodded mutely; Nurse Woolley did not seem the sort of person you wanted to cross.

The Men's Ward was still bright, cavernous, and chilly, and still guarded by Matron Finch in her perfect green frock and frilly headpiece. "If you hadn't come, we'd have had to sedate him." She sounded smug. Or disappointed.

"What happened?" I demanded, not caring I was rude. "Why won't anyone tell us anything?"

"Why, *nothing*'s happened," she said. "Although I doubt that's Himself's version." When Cook called Father Himself, she meant it with fondness and respect. The way Matron Finch said it, it sounded like she was speaking about a spoiled child.

But the matron had met her match. "Is it your custom to misplace surgical patients in the middle of the night and let them wander about unattended? What if he had hurt himself?" Miss Judson's calculating eyes scanned the shining floors and walls and fixtures, Matron Finch's uniform, starched hem to lace lappet. "As you are aware, Mr. Hardcastle is a solicitor." The threat of a lawsuit—perhaps even criminal charges—hung unspoken.

Matron did not flinch, but I Observed her narrow eye get even narrower, a faint bleaching of the color in her florid cheeks. "I'm sure nothing like this has ever happened before on one of *my* wards," she said. "Your Mr. Hardcastle has been causing mischief since he got here." She swung open the door to the Men's Ward. "See for yourselves."

Down the endless room we went, hastening to Father's bed. He was upright and looking feverish again—eyes too bright, skin flushed and damp.

"Father, what's wrong?" I cried.

He waved his hands for me to shush, which only

made me more concerned. Looking furtively around the Ward, he crooked a finger at us, beckoning us even closer. "I—" he croaked, then shook his head in frustration, waving at his throat. Of course, after yesterday's "unpleasant" procedure, not to mention his exploits overnight, he could not speak.

Miss Judson put a very forward hand on his damp forehead, which he shook away. "Where is Dr. Kinkaid? Dr. Belden?" She glanced about the huge room, but this early in the morning it was populated only by efficient nurses tending to their patients. "Nurse—"

Father grabbed at her arm, face contracted in an exaggerated scowl, shushing her too.

I was seized with inspiration. "Give him your sketchbook!" Miss Judson carried one almost everywhere.

Father snatched the book and pencil from her hands. He scrawled frantically, then held it up for us to see—six frenzied letters carved into the page:

MURDER!

For a moment, Miss Judson and I merely stood beside Father's hospital bed, looking at him, at the paper he was waving at us. Father stared back impatiently, waiting for us to react.

Miss Judson managed a single word—"That's"— before giving up. "Are you feeling quite well?"

Perhaps Father was joking; he wasn't entirely

humorless, after all—not that any of the character evidence supported that conclusion. He shook the book at us once more. I took it from him and flipped it over, looking for the rest of the joke. Father glared at me, then turned to point out his huge drafty window.

"I don't understand," I said helplessly.

He snatched the sketchbook back and scrawled again.

I SAW A MURDER!!!!!

Miss Judson had gone for help. Father's color was high and his eyes alight, like when he got done with his vigorous morris dancing, but he didn't exactly look ill. He laid a finger against his lips and scribbled a few more notes.

"I—we won't tell anyone," I said, heart banging. "What should we do?"

He didn't have a chance to tell me anything else, for Miss Judson had returned with a doctor. More or less. He seemed frightfully young (he still had spots). Father shoved the sketchbook under his blankets.

"And you are . . . ?" Miss Judson's voice was pitched so it was impossible to ignore.

"Stewart," the doctor squeaked. "Alfred Stewart. Resident. Er—house officer, that is."

"Are you familiar with Mr. Hardcastle's case?" A

medical chart was hanging from a clip at the foot of his bed, and Miss Judson handed this to Dr. Stewart.

"Er, no—not exactly. That is, I saw him last night during rounds. HOW ARE YOU, MR. HARDCASTLE?" Dr. Stewart nearly shouted.

"He can't *speak*," I said. "His hearing's fine." Or was it? I couldn't honestly swear that anything about this situation was operating at peak efficiency. My mind reeled—Father had witnessed a murder? Here, at the hospital?

Miss Judson was clinging to practicality. "What drugs was he given last night? It says *morphia.* That's a narcotic, yes?"

Dr. Stewart looked terrified, as if Miss Judson had appeared to give him a surprise practical exam on Father's case. "Er, yes, that's right. It dulls the perception of pain."

"And causes hallucinations."

Father made a sound like someone had stepped on Peony—a wordless exclamation of affront and disbelief.

Dr. Stewart's eyes flashed to Father's face but swiftly returned to his Inquisitor. "Well, no, not generally."

"Muh!" Father uttered a triumphant syllable.

"And vivid dreams?"

Now Dr. Stewart nodded emphatically. "Oh, yes. That's very common. It is derived from opium, after all." His scientific certainty was not especially convincing.

"I see." Miss Judson directed this comment at Father, who glared back sullenly. She fixed Dr. Stewart with her most placid expression. "You've been on duty all night, Doctor?"

Dr. Stewart hid behind his clipboard, nodding.

"Was there any sort of disturbance here?"

"Last night?" Dr. Stewart looked around in a panic. "Here? A disturbance? Like—like what?"

"Anything out of the ordinary," she said. "Perhaps involving the police?"

He relaxed. "Oh, no, I should say not. They have their own doctor—chap called Munjal. Don't see much of them around here, thank goodness!"

A terrific crash from Father's bedside made us all jump. Father was glaring at us, and the contents of his bedstand—water carafe, metal tray, and a tiny potted fern—had all mysteriously ended up on the floor.

It brought Matron Finch running. "Mr. Hardcastle! What is the meaning of this? *Ling!*" she barked. "This patient will need to be sedated." She loomed in, grasping Father by the arms.

Father made it worse by struggling, and for a terrifying moment I thought Matron Finch might resort to violence, but Dr. Stewart stepped in and together they soon had Father pinned against the mattress. Probationer Ling hastened over, and Matron Finch snapped at her to clean up the mess Father had made.

Standing to her full height—nearly as tall as I, Dear Reader—Matron gave us a deadly look. "You. Out."

"We're not going anywhere!" I said, but Miss Judson seized me by the arm. Holding me in a grip like iron, she drove me from the Ward, into the corridor, down the stairs, and out into the teeth-freezing air of the courtyard. (It was actually warmer than inside.)

"I knew this would happen!" I cried. "I was afraid of this!"

Miss Judson regarded me patiently. "You were afraid your father would witness a murder while in hospital?"

"You needn't be so literal. I knew *something* would happen. That surgeon was far too cavalier* about Father's treatment, and now he's delusional! What if—" I could hardly bring myself to *think* the words, let alone give them life. What if they'd somehow made him mad—*permanently* mad? Such things happened. I'd read all about them. I stomped across the cobbled paths. We would have to visit Father in a sanitorium, with the horrible cold baths and force-feeding. I spun back.

"And what if word gets out? The press are just waiting for the latest news on the Snowcroft Affair—they'll eat Father alive if they find out he's gone barmy! We'll have to move out of town, change our names . . ."

Miss Judson crossed her arms, head tilted to the

* absolutely *not* the little dogs

side, waiting while I paced and ranted. After a moment more, she said, "Are you quite finished?"

"Not nearly." I kicked the uneven cobblestones. "What are we going to do?"

"Well," she began sensibly, "I don't know that there's necessarily anything *to* do. To be done, rather."

"We have to take him out of here."

"Don't get carried away. He's just had surgery. He needs proper medical care, which you and I and Cook are not equipped to provide. And furthermore, you are leaping to exaggerated conclusions based on no evidence."

"Am I?" I countered. "Either Father really saw a murder, in which case he's in danger from the killer—"

"Presumably why he was so circumspect in his report of the crime."

"—or he *didn't* see a murder, which means he's having some sort of horrible aftereffects from the surgery. In either case, he's safer at home." There. Let her argue with that logic.

She did not argue. Instead, she put her hands on my shoulders. "Breathe," she said. "As you and I know, a murder is not an easy thing to erase from existence. There are witnesses, evidence . . . a body."

"Good," I said, fixing on this last detail. "Let's go find it."

"Find—" She raised an eyebrow.

"The body! The victim of this so-called murder!"

"And how do you propose we do that?" A moment later she would have cause to regret that ill-considered query, for I wheeled round and pointed across the courtyard, to a stolid brick building that had caught my eye on our first trip through this setting, thanks to its sober iron signage.

"There's the morgue." Most murders didn't conveniently happen in proximity to a facility ready to receive a corpse. A hospital, however, was ideally situated for such an eventuality.

Miss Judson was skeptical. "Bodies don't just show up there unannounced. There would be all sorts of paperwork. You saw the forms your father had to fill out. He had to sign them for the surgery, to allow the probationer nurses to treat him, to permit us to visit, and for his menu preferences. I'm sure the morgue here has just as much red tape."*

"All the more reason to subject it to a thorough inquiry," I said. "I'm sure they'll want to know if something suspicious is happening." With that unassailable speech, I set off, with no small thrill of anticipation.

Shaped like a hybrid of barn and church, the building had two stories, a sloped roof, and shuttered windows. I knew that it contained the Anatomy Theater, where medical students—like my mum, once—could attend dissections. The heavy outer door stuck,

* probably not the menu preferences

but wasn't locked, which I took as a sign that the public were welcome. It admitted us into a long, somewhat less welcoming corridor, older and darker than the rest of the hospital, lacking the huge windows and sparkling tile. The stone floor was cold underfoot, and oil lamps hung from hooks in the ceiling, casting their sickly light against brick walls the color of dried blood. How could anyone do proper anatomical work in these conditions?

"Look!" I tugged Miss Judson into the plentiful shadows.

Dr. Kinkaid had beaten us here, striding up the long passageway from the other direction in a manner that was *definitely* suspicious. I was less impressed with the Brilliant Surgeon by the minute.

"I'm sure *he* has a perfectly good reason for being here," she murmured. Louder, she called out, "Good morning, Dr. Kinkaid!"

He froze, startled. In this light his green eyes did not look quite so lively.

"What are you doing here?" I asked him. *Instead of in the Men's Ward, looking after Father.*

His scowl deepened. "I believe that's my line. You've rather lost your way, I think."

"Not at all," Miss Judson said. "Myrtle is a very inquisitive girl, as you've noticed."

Dear Reader, it took a great deal of squirming not

to protest this outrageous (and yet accurate) statement. I also noticed how deftly her "explanation" failed to actually explain our presence here in any satisfactory manner.

"The morgue doesn't have visiting hours," Dr. Kinkaid said. "But I don't suppose you'll bother the occupants." He depressed a buzzer affixed to the wall beside the inner door, and we heard its resulting tone even from without—a sort of low, mournful groan. A moment later a head appeared around the doorframe.

"Who summons me?" A stout, bearded young man in a rumpled suit regarded us with surprise. "Kinkaid, back so soon? And—you brought me girls? Live ones?"

I peered round him eagerly—or I tried to. He stayed wedged in the doorway, and there was no way to see past him.

"Davis, my good man. How are things in the morgue this fine day?"

"It's been dead around here," replied the man. No one smiled.

"May I introduce the family of one of my patients, Miss Judson and Miss Hardcastle?"

Mr. Davis blinked. "Hardcastle? As in—?"

"The very same." Dr. Kinkaid's voice was smooth. "You know the routine."

Mr. Davis abruptly stood up straighter, tugging on the hem of his jacket. He put an anxious hand to his hair, which looked like he'd forgotten to comb. I was glad to see how much respect everyone—well, present company and Matron Finch excepted—had for Father.

"Ladies, explain to the nice man why you're here."

"We're looking for a body. Obviously." I knew that sounded pert. I still hadn't forgiven Dr. Kinkaid for whatever he'd done to make Father think he'd seen a murder. "Why are *you* here?"

"I work here. Allow me to demonstrate: Davis, cancel my anatomy lecture this afternoon. Something's come up."

Mr. Davis nodded. "Do you want me to save the subject for you?"

"Does she have somewhere more pressing to be?" Dr. Kinkaid was sarcastic. "Her family signed the forms, didn't they?"

"Right." Mr. Davis's brow crinkled. "That's it, then?"

"Well, to tell you the truth, I find myself rather *inquisitive* about the business that brings these ladies here this morning." Dr. Kinkaid leaned casually against the brick wall—although I sensed there was nothing really casual in his demeanor at all.

Miss Judson took pity on the morgue attendant. "Mr. Davis, we're just making certain that your facility has the proper complement of bodies."

"All right." Mr. Davis blinked myopically, like he wasn't accustomed to callers. "Er, why?"

"Well, it's professional curiosity," Dr. Kinkaid said.

"This must be, what, the fourth time this week some-one's come in off the street asking about bodies in our morgue?"

"There's no need to be rude," I said. "It's a simple question."

"It's a strange question, and I'd like to know why you're asking. Oh, but I forget!" Dr. Kinkaid tossed his hands toward the ceiling. "It's a *Hardcastle* asking, so of course we must all hop to."

Now Miss Judson and I were openly gaping at him. "Dr. Kinkaid," she said with genuine curiosity, "have we done something to offend you?"

"Don't mind him," Mr. Davis put in unexpectedly. He grinned, showing crooked yellow teeth that made him look even more friendly. "All surgeons think the world revolves around them, and they're always sur-prised to discover it doesn't. You're looking for someone in my morgue, you say? Anyone in particular?"

"Someone who arrived unexpectedly in the last twenty-four hours," I said. "Maybe murdered?"

Dr. Kinkaid dropped all pretense of good humor. "You'd better explain what this is about. Now. Hardcastle or not."

Before Miss Judson could intervene with a softer, subtler version of events, I blurted it right out. "My father says he saw a murder last night."

"*Murder*, he said?" Mr. Davis glanced up and down the hallway.

Dr. Kinkaid pulled back. "That's rather the opposite of what we do here, you know."

"We're still trying to ascertain the details," Miss Judson said.

"Let me get this straight." Dr. Kinkaid studied me. "Your father experienced some disorienting side effects while recovering from anæsthesia and on narcotic pain medication, and your first reaction was to check a hospital morgue for murder victims."

"Of course not! Our first reaction was to check with you," I snapped. "But you weren't there. So naturally we did the next most sensible thing."

"Naturally." Dr. Kinkaid looked over my head at Miss Judson.

"Once you know her, it makes sense," she said.

Dr. Kinkaid knew when he was defeated. With a sigh, he said, "Davis, do you mind if we take a look at your records for the last day or so?"

Mr. Davis was not so sure. "Russ?"

"Just to reassure some nervous family members. No breach of the rules."

"We're not nervous!"

"We are, perhaps, *impatient.*"

Mr. Davis slipped farther out into the hall, face flushed with excitement. "Has something really happened out there? A murder?"

"Of course there hasn't been a murder!"

Mr. Davis scratched his scruffy hair. "A hospital has always struck me as the ideal place to commit murder."

"Me, too!" I liked Mr. Davis. I wondered how one got a job supervising a morgue.

"There are so many ways to do it and go undetected. You have poison—ingested, injected, applied topically. The wrong dose of medicine, and—" His fingers flicked like a puff of air—or a soul—dissipating. "Or a patient just slips away during surgery." Mr. Davis looked knowingly at Dr. Kinkaid. "Too much ether, no one the wiser."

"All right, that's enough of that," said Dr. Kinkaid, but Mr. Davis hadn't finished.

"A heart attack's easily induced," he continued.

"Digitalis!" I said, and he grinned.

"Exactly! Or arsenic—there are tests for it, but we never do them. It always looks like cholera or gastritis. Heavy metal poisoning, although that takes time . . ."

"Strangulation?" I said, still thinking about past cases.

Davis waved a dismissive hand. "Impossible to pass off as accidental. You'd have to hide the body, and why do that, when it's so easy to make a death look like natural causes?"

"I said *reassuring* the family, Davis."

Oddly, however, Mr. Davis's take on the scenario did make me feel better. Whatever Father thought he'd seen seemed less probable the more we learned. Still, I wouldn't be doing my duty as an Investigator if I didn't insist on a closer examination of the witness. "And you're sure there have been no unexplained deaths? Perhaps we could see for ourselves."

Davis looked surprised—or pleased. "Inside the morgue? I don't get many visitors . . ." He smoothed his unruly moustache.

"I think this has gone far enough," Miss Judson intervened, although we hadn't examined Mr. Davis's paperwork yet.

"I couldn't agree more," said Dr. Kinkaid. "Ta, Davis."

"Absolutely," he said. "Everyone's welcome here."

I shook his hand, trying to conceal my disappointment at not getting even a *glimpse* inside the morgue. I was sure the police surgeon's carriage-house laboratory could not compare to the modern, generously funded facilities of the Royal Swinburne.

Dr. Kinkaid broke into my thoughts. "What are you waiting for, a souvenir? Let's leave the poor man be. He must be exhausted from the company."

Mr. Davis paused on his way back inside the morgue. "Say, Russ—"

"Aye?"

"I'd steer clear of the Guv if I were you. He's in a fine dander about something today. Heard him yelling at a nurse about her uniform earlier, of all things."

"Dr. Greeley?" Dr. Kinkaid frowned. "That's not like him. T'anks for the warning."

Out in the courtyard, Dr. Kinkaid looked bored. "Well, that was my good deed for the day. I trust this puts this murder business to rest?"

Miss Judson forestalled my reply. "Certainly. Thank you, Doctor. We shall leave Mr. Hardcastle in your capable hands."

I watched him leave with a scowl fierce enough to burn holes in his polished white coat. "Do you really feel the matter is put to rest?"

She didn't turn her gaze from the surgeon's departing back. "Not even remotely."

ⸯ

Back at the Men's Ward, Father was quiet. He wasn't exactly asleep, but he seemed drowsy and dreamy, and was no longer trying to communicate so urgently. The mess of his overturned bedside table had been cleared away, even the tiny fern replaced. It was almost as if the disturbance we'd all witnessed this morning had never happened. Dr. Stewart, too, had vanished.

"I've given him some laudanum to calm him," Matron Finch said. "Now, Mr. Hardcastle, will you apologize to the ladies for your outburst this morning?"

Father nodded sleepily. "Beg y'r pardon," he mumbled.

"And we'll have no more of that behavior?"

He shook his head.

"And you'll mind the doctors and stop scaring my nurses? Good." She brusquely tucked the already tucked sheets, giving the foot of the bed a sound slap with the flat of her hand. "I have a Ward to see to. You're not the only patient here, you know. If I hear any more reports of unruly behavior, we'll have to restrain you. We have Rules."

As she floated away, lappet bouncing behind her, Miss Judson's gaze grew keener. "Now," she said briskly. "Let's get to the bottom of this. My sketchbook?" She held out an expectant hand, but Father only stared at her.

"I gave it to you," she said.

"You hid it under the blankets," I reminded him.

Father shook his head slowly, eyes growing wilder. He reached both hands beneath the tidy bedding, and I could see them rustling, searching more and more frantically. Peony would have been in ecstasy trying to attack them. Finally, he threw back the covers altogether, revealing his white hospital pyjamas and a shocking view of bare feet.

The sketchbook was gone.

7

Nullum Corpus, Nullum Crimen

> The modern hospital offers the Medico-Legal
> Investigator several invaluable perquisites, in-
> cluding access to staff, equipment, and facilities.
>
> –H. M. Hardcastle, *Foundations of Legal Medicine*

I instantly leaped to the most dire conclusion. "They
stole it!" I cried—but softly; Matron Finch still hovered
nearby. "They're trying to cover it up."

Father nodded as emphatically as the laudanum
would allow, but Miss Judson was skeptical. "Cover
what up? We don't know what you saw." She gave him a
pointed look, urging him to elaborate.

"Bald?" he rasped.

"Are you still disturbing my patient?" The matron
rematerialized at the foot of Father's bed. "I'll have to
insist you let him rest now."

I was desperate not to abandon him. "Father, are you in danger?"

"Is he what? Are the lot of you mad? Get yourselves gone before I set the porters on you!"

Father shook his head sleepily, waving a vague hand at us. "Mmfine." The laudanum was taking its toll, and we'd exhausted Matron Finch's patience, such as it was.

"I suppose we might as well let him rest." Miss Judson sounded uncertain, but I let her lead me away again. Our footfalls clattered louder than ever, and nurses glared at us. Had one of them swiped the book? Had one of them *killed* somebody? It was too fanciful to believe—and yet I couldn't help shivering. Could all this sparkling scientific order truly conceal such a dastardly crime as murder?

We passed a nurse with an armload of laundry, whose narrow gaze lingered on us a moment too long. Behind her, porters with green bunting paused in their work, burly hands clutching hammers. A finely dressed lady and her daughter chatted at the reception desk, dropping coins into Nurse Woolley's jars. The *clink-clink-clink* stopped abruptly as we went by.

Once out of earshot—I hoped—I burst out, "We can't leave him here! He's completely at their mercy. They could do anything."

"What they will *do*," Miss Judson said darkly, "is give him the Excellent Care upon which the Royal Swinburne Private Ward prides itself." That sounded like a threat. "We needn't assume that anyone here means him any harm."

"What about the sketchbook? That's proof he's on to them."

She sighed. "It's my book, and you and I are known to have been involved in several local murder investigations. Those could be *my* notes, about an entirely different matter."

I was not appeased. "If there's a killer lurking about the hospital, he's not going to take the risk of Father exposing his crime. We need to know what else he wrote down."

"What crime?" she said. "We haven't the faintest idea what he thought he saw—"

"Because we couldn't get any details from him!" *Bald*, while intriguing, didn't exactly give us much to go on.

She went on as if I hadn't interrupted her. "And if something *had* happened, don't you think the hospital would be crawling with police?"

"You heard what Mr. Davis said. A murder at a hospital could easily look like an ordinary medical happenstance. Do you want an Ordinary Medical Happenstance to befall Father?" My voice had gone shrill.

A flutter of well-oiled wheels heralded the passage of a nurse pushing a patient in a bath chair. An elderly man I recognized from Father's Ward turned a shifty gaze our way as they rolled by. *Not bald*, I noted, as Miss Judson maneuvered me out of the path of traffic, not that it was much comfort.

"In the *Highly Unlikely Scenario* that there is a killer on the premises," she said, voice low, "that person is hardly going to risk even more exposure by doing something to Swinburne's Prosecuting Solicitor. That really will have the police descend, not to mention two rather Irrepressible amateur Investigators who will raise a holy fuss should anything untoward occur."

"We're not amateurs," I protested.

"I don't recall receiving a cheque from any grateful parties," she reminded me. "One thing is certain, however. Your father clearly expects us to investigate this matter."

"How?" I said. "How do we even begin such an Investigation? We don't know who was killed, or where, or even when." Or even *that*, I added silently.

"That's where you're wrong," she said. "We have a limited window of opportunity in which the crime might have occurred. We last saw your father before nine a.m. yesterday, and he telephoned us at approximately twelve-forty-five this morning."

"That's sixteen hours!"

"Ah, but we can refine it further." She began to pace, neat skirts swishing against the polished floor. "In all likelihood, it happened after your father's procedure, subsequent to the administration of the morphine. I was able to determine from his chart that the surgery occurred at three p.m., and he received another dose of morphine at nine." Hands clasped at her waist, she waited for my reply like an eager schoolgirl.

"I suppose," I said. "But that means we only need to question everyone who was in the hospital from three p.m. until one a.m." That was dozens—if not hundreds— of doctors, nurses, porters, maids, patients, and other assorted murder suspects.

"We've worked with less," she said blithely. Was *she* hallucinating now? "Wait—where are you going?" She scurried to catch up with me.

"To start questioning witnesses, of course. We need to find someone who was on duty last night." And if a witness didn't turn up, I could at least track down who-ever was responsible for letting Father out of their sight and give them a piece of my mind.

Frankly, the errand felt increasingly futile and ridiculous. As my feet grew wearier, Father's fevered claims seemed ever more far-fetched. The halls of the hospital were spick-and-span, the staff as efficient and disciplined as Her Majesty's Army. Even the patients seemed unnaturally healthy for sick people. I could hardly imagine the Royal Swinburne *allowing* a mur-der to be committed within its well-ordered Wards.

We searched for Father's nighttime nurses first. We were directed to the Nurses' Sitting Room by a helpful porter who had evidently heard of Miss Judson from his colleague, for he stepped into a doorway and hid behind his mop as she whisked by, and didn't say a word about her heels leaving streaks in his floor wax.

The Sitting Room was on the same floor as Father, on the other side of the ring of buildings, almost exactly opposite the Men's Ward. We had left the patient side of the hospital behind. The floors were the same polished wood, but the tile walls had been supplanted by dark wainscoting—very sophisticated—and offices declared themselves with brass nameplates: FLORA FINCH, HOSPITAL MATRON; TRUSTEES' ASSEMBLY ROOMS; JULIUS GREELEY, GOVERNOR; and on one glass door, neat letters read SURGICAL LABORATORY, R. KINKAID, M.R.C.S.*

Across from the laboratory, a door labeled NURSES' SITTING ROOM was just swinging open.

"Oh, Hardcastles!" That came out like an interjection—an exclamation of surprise and dismay, like she'd dropped a tray of biscuits. Probationer Ling stood in the threshold, uniform draped by a black mantle with lavender piping. "Wh—what are you doing all the way over here?"

"Looking for you, in fact," replied Miss Judson.

Nurse Ling's hand fluttered to her throat. "Me? Oh, I'm off duty now." She tried to move past us, walking

---

* Member of the Royal College of Surgeons, an advanced certification beyond mere physician. (Evidently they prefer to be called "Mister," instead of "Doctor," having achieved the royal stature of gentlemen. Most people ignore this, which must be annoying.)

swiftly toward the exit. Miss Judson kept pace, falling in beside her.

This seemed to make the young nurse nervous. In a tight, false voice, she asked, "And how is Mr. Hardcastle this morning?"

I wanted to shout, *They've sedated him!* or *He's delirious!* but Miss Judson smoothed past the question. "Matron Finch is with him now."

"He couldn't be in better hands, I'm sure. She'll have everything sorted out in no time."

"What exactly?" I asked sweetly (well, I tried).

"What's that?" Probationer Ling walked steadily down the corridor, focused on the exit.

"What exactly will she sort out? What's happened?"

"Nothing." She hunched into her cape and hurried on. "I'm sure your father was just anxious. Patients get that way in hospital, you know."

We'd arrived at the door to the stairwell, and Miss Judson put out a hand to hold it closed. "Probationer Ling, did you happen to see any sort of disturbance last night?"

This made her laugh. "Ha! A disturbance in the Private Ward? Matron would never allow it." And somehow, I believed her.

We let her go after that. It was plain she had nothing more to tell us—or nothing more she *would* tell us. "She was lying," I said, watching her black mantle disappear down the stairwell like water draining away.

"Well, I suspect she was not entirely forthcoming," Miss Judson agreed, provisionally. "Unfortunately, that tells us very little."

"It tells us she was *lying*."

Whatever reply Miss Judson was about to make got cut off by parties clambering up the stairs. "Ho there! Make way!"

A moment later I found myself pinned behind my governess, holding open the stairwell door to admit a porter hauling a laden handcart up the stairs. He was followed by a spring-heel'd surgeon barking orders.

"Careful, man! Those are live specimens. You're already a day late with them—if there are not a dozen happy, healthy *Rattus rattus norvegicus* in those crates there will be he—eaven to pay." Dr. Kinkaid's rant ran out of steam when he spotted the figure holding the door.

Unfortunately, the lapse in his attention was nearly disastrous, for the crates wobbled wildly on the porter's dolly. "For pity's sake!" Dr. Kinkaid bellowed. "You're doing more harm than good! Clear off. I'll handle this. Go!" He shooed the porter away—who was only too happy to oblige. The words the man uttered on his flight to the stairwell were not intended for the ears of a Young Lady of Quality.

Dr. Kinkaid was as pleased to see us as we were to see him. "You two again? What do they say about bad pennies?"

"I beg your pardon," I said, affronted.

"Well, you may as well make yourselves useful." Dr. Kinkaid dug in his coat pocket and withdrew a ring of keys. Before I was quite prepared, they came sailing over the handcart right toward me. I am pleased to report, Dear Reader, that I acquitted myself quite admirably, despite Sport not being among Miss Judson's academic foci for me.

"Run along, then, open the lab." Dr. Kinkaid stationed himself at the dolly's handles, Miss Judson stood guard over the cargo, and I scurried down the hall and, with no little thrill, unlocked the door to Dr. Kinkaid's laboratory.

It was just as impressive as you would expect. Rows of fine wooden workbenches filled most of the space, with shiny brass microscopes, gas Bunsen burners, and racks of glass vials at every workstation. Canisters of chloroform and carbolic stood at attention near the doors, and the room was full of the Royal Swinburne's trademark smell of fresh air.

"What are you waiting for? Get the lights on. Why the blazes is it so cold in here?"

"Dr. Kinkaid, may I remind you there is a child present. Please moderate your language."

"I'll moderate whatever I like, thank you." Dr. Kinkaid shoved the handcart—none too gently—into the laboratory, as I looked for matches. I pulled open a drawer in the workbench and found a box of Vestas.

While I was searching for a gas fixture to light, a fizzy crackle sounded and light sprang into the room from a row of bulbs overhead. "Electricity," Dr. Kinkaid said dryly. "All the rage."

I did not moderate my tone when I slammed the drawer shut.

But Dr. Kinkaid had already forgotten about us. He was unpacking the cart with a fervor. "Crowbar!" He held out a hand to me, gestured impatiently, and then snapped his fingers. "Crowbar—you don't know where they are. Sorry." He shoved a rueful hand through his dark hair. "You're not my surgical dresser, either. Though you would make a fine one, I suspect."

I softened a bit. I would be a good surgeon's assistant. I am patient and precise and not the least bit squeamish. While Dr. Kinkaid rummaged through one end of a workbench and found hammer and crowbar, I looked around the laboratory. His huge windows looked straight across the courtyard, and I could almost make out the movements of people in the Ward opposite.

"Sorry I was short with you earlier." (He did not specify if by "earlier" he meant a moment ago or this morning at the morgue.) "This whole place is at sixes and sevens today. My delivery's late, the Guv's in a mood, and *why* is this room so cold? I'll have to get Maintenance in before my new subjects freeze to death, making mine the shortest study in the history of

English medicine." He said this while huffing and shifting about the crate, pulling all the tacks out. "Aha!" All at once, the planks of the crate fell away, like a magician's trick.

"Rats!" I let out a little gasp of surprise and pleasure, then scurried over to inspect Dr. Kinkaid's new delivery.

"Aye," he said fondly. "The Norway rat. It's me versus the Vikings, and this time, boyo, the Celts have the upper hand."

Dr. Kinkaid's rats didn't look much like the vermin in cellars and alleys. They had lovely soft tawny fur, pink paws and ears, and clever little whiskers, and were putting up an unhappy, squeaky racket in their cramped cage. One of them came forward to sniff my fingers. Miss Judson, I Observed, was far more circumspect in her admiration, standing some distance away and studying the ceiling.

"The Guv has ordered a study on the long-term effects of temporary starvation," explained Dr. Kinkaid. "The Trustees are oddly persnickety about experimenting on the patients."

"You're going to starve them to death?" Of course, I knew the fate of laboratory subjects was seldom kind, but this seemed cruel even by scientific standards.

Dr. Kinkaid actually smiled. "What good's a study on the long-term effects of something if the subjects don't stick it out for the long term? I'm to keep them here for the whole of their natural lives. These lads just became the luckiest rats in England."

"How very fortunate you all must feel." It is sometimes difficult to tell when Miss Judson is making a joke.

As we helped Dr. Kinkaid make room for the rats, he quizzed us about Father. "What you said earlier, about Mr. Hardcastle, were you serious?"

Miss Judson's smile seemed forced. "Mr. Hardcastle broke out of the Men's Ward last night to gain access to a telephone and report a murder." She carefully omitted the fact that Father had not managed to communicate anything useful during that fateful call.

Dr. Kinkaid stared at us a moment, green eyes agog. "I'll imagine that caused a bit of a stir. Patients on morphine . . ." He shook his head.

"We can't rule out his claim without a thorough inquiry," I said stiffly. My loyalty to Father outweighed scientific probability. Barely.

"I thought that's what we did this morning."

Miss Judson let out a pitying laugh. "Oh, Doctor, we haven't even *begun* to Investigate matters."

"Your windows are directly across from the Men's Ward," I pointed out. "Whatever he saw, it must have happened close by. Maybe even in this very room."

Dr. Kinkaid took several easy steps across the laboratory to look out his windows. "Aye, I can see him over there, sleepin' like a wain.* Well, let's have a proper look, then." He eyed me sidelong. "Excuse me, I mean a *t'orough inquiry.*"

He took a slow circuit of the room, glancing carefully into corners and inside cupboards. He might have been trying to help—or he might have been attempting to sweep the crime scene for any evidence left behind. Perhaps *he* was our culprit. I hastened to his side to be certain he did not secret away anything incriminating, but he merely tested the lock on the door (sturdy), checked the latches on the windows (firmly affixed), and took a swift decisive inventory of his equipment (everything present and accounted for and properly arranged. *Beautiful* goes without saying). He stood at one end and surveyed the scene, eyeing it like a patient, trying to diagnose its condition.

"Tell me again what happened."

Miss Judson swiftly outlined the barest framework of Father's story, which was all we had: white coat, choked, and widow.

"Don't forget *bald*," I said.

"Bald?" Dr. Kinkaid scratched at his beard. "Who was bald—the killer or the victim?"

"The victim," I said automatically, just as Miss Judson said, "The killer."

---

* This turned out to be Irish for "child"—and made far more sense in context than my first thought, a wagon for carrying hay (like in the painting by John Constable, of which Miss Judson was particularly fond).

We shared a Look, and Miss Judson, sounding apologetic, said, "I'm afraid we don't know."

"Maybe they were both bald."

She tossed up her hands and said a few Choice Words in French. "English! Such an imprecise language. In French, we would know. *Le chauve*—one man is bald. *Les chauves*, both."

"Or Irish," agreed Dr. Kinkaid.

I let them carry on the linguistic debate as I continued my examination of the scene—assuming this *was* the scene. Assuming there was a scene at all.

The laboratory floor—lino this time, in a pattern of green-and-white checkerboard—was spotless. I was becoming convinced that a hospital really was the ideal place to commit a murder—or any crime—because of the splendid cleaning that got done here. Even Cook would find it unassailable. But among the shadows of the stools, stuck into a crevice between floor and workbench, I spotted the smallest gleam of something bright and glittering. Thinking it just a lost brass screw or lid to a tiny jar, I squeezed between the legs and pried it out with my fingernails.

It was immediately clear that it did not belong in the laboratory. I withdrew myself from the workbenches and held the item up, where it shone in the chill morning light.

"Dr. Kinkaid, do you have pierced ears?"

I heard a chuckle from beyond the workbench. "Aye, what?"

I showed him and Miss Judson my find: a cold, small hoop of gold. An earring.

8

Pas de Nouvelles, Bonnes Nouvelles

The forensic surgeon must be prepared to deal with oversight from his colleagues in the constabulary, who will continually demand that he do more work in less time with fewer resources and better results.

–H. M. Hardcastle, *Foundations of Legal Medicine*

"How do you explain this?" I demanded.

"Ah." Dr. Kinkaid suppressed a knowing smile. "You've cracked it. Mystery solved."

"What do you mean?"

Miss Judson, for her part, had gone silent, lips pressed together in a disapproving line.

Dr. Kinkaid strolled back to the windows and viewed the laboratory from that vantage. "Your father—under the influence of heavy medication—witnessed two people locked in a struggle . . ."

I nodded warily.

". . . or an *embrace*, perhaps?" he said. "It would seem that my laboratory became the site of an—erm"—he glanced at Miss Judson—"an illicit assignation. This sort of thing has happened before, I'm afraid."

It took me a moment to realize what he meant, and my cheeks got hot. I turned to Miss Judson. "Is *that* what Father saw?"

Miss Judson failed to respond for some time. "I would hope even your father would recognize the difference between . . . amorous advances and a murder."

Well, considering his track record with Miss Judson, I wouldn't bet on it.

"Thank you, Doctor. I believe we've taken up enough of your time." With satisfaction, Miss Judson swished from Dr. Kinkaid's laboratory to the Men's Ward, down the shining hardwood floor to the very edge of Father's bed. I followed more grudgingly.

Father was sleeping, but Miss Judson gave the bed a none-too-gentle shake. He roused, blinking grumpily. "Myrtle, the earring."

"Father, we found this—" I held it out to show him, but Miss Judson plucked it from my fingers.

"Your report has received a thorough inquiry,

and we are pleased to assure you that there has been no murder." She handed the earring to Father, who scowled at it. "Behold: the evidence, merely, of some late-night peccadillo."*

He crossed his arms and his scowl deepened. He didn't need a voice for us to know what he would say: "I know what I saw."

"Father, we *Investigated*," I insisted. "We've been all over the rooms across from you"—I waved at the windows—"inside Dr. Kinkaid's laboratory, and even to the morgue." Well, we'd been just outside the morgue. "There are no missing patients or doctors, no reported injuries, no unexplained bodies."

"I trust this puts the matter to rest." Miss Judson's voice was dark with consequence.

Father shook his head emphatically, making himself wince. Miss Judson gave him a sip of water from the cup beside his bed.

"Father, you must be careful," I said. My voice was hoarse and low, since a simmering Matron Finch lurked nearby, overhearing every word. "You can't go running about the hospital accusing people of murder! It's—" I glanced at Matron, who was pretending to be busy with another patient's chart.

---

* When I was small, I supposed this must be a fascinating sort of North American mammal. Imagine my disappointment to learn that it is merely yet another euphemism for the silly things adults get up to.

"Unseemly?" Miss Judson suggested. "Irresponsible? Antisocial?"

"I was going to say *dangerous.*"

"Buh—" Father croaked.

"No *but*," I said sternly. "You are not here to solve a murder. You are here to recover from tonsillitis. Is that understood? Good." I leaned in and fluffed his pillow and adjusted his blankets. "Now, Miss Judson and I are leaving you to rest. We will be back in the morning, and when we return, there shall be no more talk of murder."

We left the Men's Ward, leaving a baffled Father staring at us in perplexity.

႟

I was not as relieved as I ought to have been, walking away from Father's bedside, leaving him behind in hospital where, we'd determined, there had not been a murder. Worry still squirmed in my chest. I tried to tell myself that No Murder was a good thing—an excellent thing! But that meant that Father had imagined something horrible—and what that meant was too horrible to contemplate.

"We ought to have stayed and helped," I muttered, not sure I meant Miss Judson to hear me or not. We stood at the crossing, waiting for an omnibus.

"Don't be disappointed." Miss Judson patted my hand absently. "I'm sure there will be other murders."

"Miss?"

Realizing what she'd just said, Miss Judson grimaced. "It's been a long day. Let's just get this next errand over with, so we can get home and have some tea and a monthlong nap."

"What errand?" I said warily.

"I promised your father we'd pick up the latest replies to his notice from the *Tribune*."

"He's supposed to be resting," I said.

"Yes, well, no one said what *we* were meant to do in the meantime, did they?"

The omnibus deposited us a block or so away from the newspaper offices, and I was glad for the fresh air to cool my swirling thoughts. In the excitement, I'd nearly forgotten the *other* matter currently preoccupying the Hardcastle household. Perhaps that was what had driven Father to hallucinate a murder—stress brought on by the Snowcroft Legacy. It had hastened his physical illness, after all. I squared my shoulders, more determined than ever to shield Father from strain and overwork.

Before we even reached the brick edifice of Swinburne's daily newspaper, it was obvious that was easier resolved than accomplished. A newsboy hawking the morning edition was surrounded by a throng of people. Someone in the crowd had a wandering eye, which fell on Miss Judson and me.

"Look!" I heard a cry. "That's them! You there—

you're Hardcastle's daughter and nanny, aren't you?" A man came running toward us, muffler flapping behind him. He nearly lost his derby hat in his rush to overtake us.

"Governess," I muttered, stepping smack into Miss Judson, who had stopped suddenly, glancing calmly about for an avenue of escape.

"Don't speak to them, Myrtle," she commanded—unwisely.

"It *is* them! Where's the Prosecuting Solicitor? When is he coming back to court? The Snowcroft Legacy must be settled!"

"Hmm." Miss Judson made a sound like an idling steam engine, not that she was audible above the chants of "Snowcroft! Snowcroft!" and the hum of questions peppering us like hailstones.

Suddenly, a hand reached out and grabbed me by the arm, making me squeak.

"Hist," said a familiar voice attached to the arm, coming from a jauntily dressed young woman with loosely knotted hair, spectacles, and a crutch she was using to gesture with. "There's a side way in. They'll never find you." Genie Shelley, *Tribune* reporter, ferried Miss Judson and me down an alley, where we disappeared into a doorway before the crowd realized we'd gone.

"Field hockey," she said, brandishing the crutch like her hockey stick. Her foot was still in its cast, which she largely ignored, hobbling about with vigor. (I knew for a fact that she had shamelessly used her temporary infirmity to gain sympathy to secure access to news sources—such as probate hearings that were not technically open to the public—and I rather doubted she would give up the useful accoutrement once it was no longer medically necessary.)

Genie prodded us into a corridor lit by a low gas flame, and then to a room familiar from our previous Investigation—the newspaper's marvelous (if curiously named) morgue, an archive housing back issues and other research materials. "What brings you two down? Silly question—and a *casual* one," she added. "Not an interview. On my honor." She held up her hands in a gesture of surrender, but I think she was trying to remember how someone took an oath in court.

"Thank you," Miss Judson said formally. "We are much obliged." She put a hand to her forehead, which was uncharacteristically damp.

"Well," said Genie, pulling out a chair at a long table laden with books and newspapers and notepads, "who knew probate law could be so fascinating! You'd think the Snowcroft Legacy was the only thing happening in England right now."

Miss Judson picked up the morning's *Tribune*, whose only other story was about a rugby match between England and Ireland. "I can't imagine why."

I was dying to blurt out what Father had told us—but

Genie was probably the last person in Swinburne I should mention it to. I could tell Miss Judson was thinking the same. She slowly unbuttoned her ulster and draped it on the back of the chair, folding her gloves neatly into its pockets.

"I hope you're having a better day than I am." Genie sounded cross. "I was supposed to have an interview this morning, but it fell through."

"With your source on the Snowcroft case?"

"That came to nothing. He never showed." She shrugged. "It happens—people think they want to talk to the press, then someone talks them out of it, or they have an attack of conscience." Her mouth flattened. "Or they get a better offer from Gray Baker at the *Upton Register.*" She flung down her copy of the competing newspaper in disgust.

"Do I detect a professional rivalry?" Miss Judson did not quite suppress her smile.

"He's a hack," Genie said with some heat. "The one I really want to talk to is Ethel herself—but that manager of hers, that Dudley woman, won't let me near her. The *Trib* isn't a big enough paper for them. Say—" She eyed us with consideration.

"Don't even think about it," Miss Judson said severely.

"Just tell Miss Snowcroft that we're friends?" Genie tried to look winsome, and it made Miss Judson laugh. "Here. As a gesture of goodwill, I'll let you see my latest research." Rummaging through the stack on the table, Genie unearthed her notes. "Back in '85, a cove called Edwin Cooke applied for a permit to open a haberdashery shop in Melbourne."

"That's Sally's—er, adopted father," I said.

"Right," said Genie. "But there's no record of him before that. It's like he just popped up out of Botany Bay one day."

"Port Phillip Bay," I corrected. "Botany Bay is near Sydney." (I had looked this up myself, Dear Reader.)

"Whatever," Genie said. "The point is, your Sally's da's a ghost. There's no Cooke on the *Persephone*'s manifest, so I figure it's one of three things." Warming to her theory, Genie perched on the edge of the table, cast swinging. "Either the whole thing's made up—Cooke gets the chronometer and locket from somebody else—"

"Who?" I broke in.

"Who cares? Won 'em in a poker game, took 'em as collateral to pay off a debt, found 'em while beachcombing. Doesn't matter. That trail's long cold." She waved that aside. "Or second, Cooke's an alias adopted by a crewman after a mutiny on the *Persephone*."

"Hmm," Miss Judson said.

"Oh, it's possible," Genie said. "Snowcroft was a scoundrel—known for sending crews down in coffin ships just to rake in the insurance money. Or third," she continued, "Cooke's like a million other Australians—one of the old convicts who changed his name when his term was up, started a new life. Either way, he's a dead end."

"So in your estimation, Miss Cooke is unlikely to be the heir to the Legacy."

"Well, now, *she's* an interesting case." Genie scooped up another pile of notes and handed them to me. "She first shows up on a lease in Melbourne, just down the street from the shop, along with Edwin and Martha Cooke. No birth certificate or adoption records. She just springs into being at exactly the same moment as Edwin Cooke. And look—" She reached over and shuffled through the pages in my hands until she found a reproduction from a Melbourne newspaper, showing a young family outside a tidy storefront called COOKE'S SUTLERY. A tired-faced woman held the shoulders of a small girl standing before her. The girl wasn't looking at the camera, but at something that had distracted her in the street behind them—

"Have your magnifier?" asked Genie, so I fished it out and peered closer at the image.

"She has the birthmark!" I cried. "Well, there's a blotch of some sort there, anyway." I showed it to Miss Judson, who subjected it to her own scrutiny. "So this proves Sally was in Australia in 1885. Just like she claims. How does that help?"

Genie deflated. "It doesn't. Not *yet*. I'm still working on it. And that"—she nodded at an imposing stack of newspapers, journals, telegrams, and books piled precariously on the edge of the table—"is every known report of shipwrecks from 1875 to 1890. If anyone survived the *Persephone*, they should be in here." Her stack looked about as easy to sort through as every person in a hospital in a sixteen-hour period.

Trying not to let her discourage me, I riffled through the other materials: the *Persephone*'s manifest, a gushing statement from Mrs. Dudley about SWOBS (with a sketch of a respectable white-columned edifice captioned *International Headquarters of the Seaman's Widows & Orphans Benevolent Society, Liverpool*), and a letter from a supposed Snowcroft cousin proposing marriage to Miss Snowcroft, in lieu of having the estate signed over to him. I sighed.

"So," said Genie. "Fair's fair. I've shown you mine. What have you got?"

"Not a chance," Miss Judson said with a grin, just as I said, "No comment."

"Well, tell Mr. H. to hurry and wrap the case up," she said. "I'm not sure how much longer this can last."

"Don't you want the story to go on for weeks?"

Genie's expression turned grim. "You saw the crowd out there. They're starting to get ugly. And some of the letters we're getting feel downright threatening."

"Threats? Against Sally?" I frowned. "Against *Sally*, right?"

"What? Oh—no, nothing against your dad, don't worry." Genie gave my knee a friendly squeeze that did nothing at all to reassure me. "Rubbish like this comes in all the time. You should see *my* collection!" For a moment her eyes sparked with pride. "But Sally's just a kid. Even if she turns out to be an impostor, she doesn't deserve this." She shuffled her stack of papers, tapping their edges against the table.

"Wait, what's that?" Among the clippings, something caught my eye, and it was not *Snowcroft, legacy,* or *Persephone.* Below the news about Sally, a Manchester newspaper reported a much different story.

ANNIVERSARY OF GASWORKS TRAGEDY

Honoring Constables Killed by Fenian Bombers
Family members and friends gathered today to remember the dastardly and deadly bombing of the Manchester Gasworks in December 1883, which killed two Manchester Constables and one Fenian and caused countless injuries, terror, and damages. The Manchester Ladies Auxiliary Committee has planted a tree in memory of the victims of this terrible crime.

"What's a Fenian?" I asked, and Genie looked at me, shocked.

"Sure and you don't know what a Fenian is? Ach!"

"The Irish Republicans," Miss Judson explained, somewhat more helpfully.

I remembered now. Protests against British rule in Ireland had led to some violent conflicts. In the 1880s, radical supporters of Irish independence had set dynamite off in places all over Britain to prove their devotion to a free Irish Republic. There were still grumbles of discontent, and even I was aware of tensions between Irish people and the English. Perhaps that explained some of Dr. Kinkaid's curious behavior.

I pulled the clipping from the stack to see the photographs of the bombing victims: two young constables in their black uniforms and domed helmets—and one handsome young man with dark hair and twinkling eyes . . . and a vaguely familiar face.

Michael R. Kinkaid, age 25, it said, is believed to have constructed the device that caused so much devastation in our city. His fellow collaborators in the bombing have never been brought to justice, but his death put an end to his career of violence and terror.

Miss Judson's eyes met mine. "Dr. Kinkaid!" we cried.

9

AD HOC

The forensic surgeon's equipment includes a
variety of specialized tools, including measuring
apparatus (for length, weight, and volume); knives,
saws, and scoops for accessing the evidence; and
magnifying devices to examine the findings in
minute detail. His most important tool, however,
is his skill at Observation.

–H. M. Hardcastle, *Foundations of Legal Medicine*

We finally made our escape from the *Tribune*—
thankfully without revealing to Genie where Father
truly was or how he'd been spending his Mysterious
Hiatus. "You *will not* use that as a headline," Miss
Judson said.

"Get me that interview with Ethel, and I'll consider
it!" Genie sneaked us out another back way, into the
twilight, past the mob who'd got bored and gone home
for tea.

That night Miss Judson made good on her plans

for her monthlong bath, leaving me and Peony to fret over Father's murder and Sally's inheritance and the ravenous crowd clamoring for updates. At least they hadn't followed us home. It felt like my worries were all tangled up around the wrong things, but I wasn't sure I wanted to worry about the right ones.

Instead, I dug out my notebook to make notes on the case—not that there really was a case. It just gave me something useful to do. "It wouldn't hurt, would it?" I asked Peony. "Maybe Father really saw something. Or he didn't and we'll all have a laugh about it when Father's recovered and Sally and Charley and Mrs. Dudley are out of our hair."

Dear Reader, you might be able to predict Peony's response.

The problem was, there wasn't much to go on. Miss Judson's missing sketchbook was strange, and Probationer Ling's behavior was suspicious, but other than that, we had nothing. No body, no crime, no evidence of anything untoward occurring at the Royal Swinburne Hospital. Except Father's testimony, that is. And as much as I *wanted* to believe him, I couldn't ignore the evidence. Or more to the point, the lack thereof.

With a sigh, I shoved my notebook aside and picked up the newspaper. Maybe someone had mislaid a bald widow in a white coat, and advertised.

The paper was full of Sally: her picture, her locket, her lecture tour, the funds raised by her ardent supporters, her charitable spirit (how anyone knew *that* about her, I had no idea), her dog. A livery company in Camden had changed its name in his honor, and a yacht launching from Falmouth was newly* christened the *Ethel Snowcroft*. I wondered what Sally thought of this. Was she taking it all in stride, or was she knotted up with worry?

I studied the picture of Sally in her black crape dress, clutching Charley. How brave she'd been, to sail halfway around the world after losing her father—the man she believed was her father. How could she stand it? And to have gone through it not once, but *twice*? (Even if she couldn't remember the first time.) I only had one father—thank goodness—and the idea of losing him was unthinkable. Now Sally was willingly subjecting herself to the scrutiny of the nation and the judgment of the courts, all to find out if her father was really her father, or if he was just a stranger who'd been lying to her for ten years.

My fingers crimped the edges of the paper. Father didn't always tell me everything, which occasionally forced me to take circuitous action to obtain certain vital information—but I didn't think he'd ever lied to

* not to mention inauspiciously

me about anything really important. I couldn't imagine it. Nobody was more devoted to truth and justice than Arthur Hardcastle. I tried to picture someone else in his place, another man teaching me about law, scolding me for unladylike behavior, letting Peony nibble on his beard . . . but the images just wouldn't come. Father was *Father*.

I turned my pencil against the paper until the lead snapped. "Would we turn our backs on Father if we learned he'd . . . been wrong about something?" I asked Peony, and her response here was predictable as well.

"*No*," she said, punctuating it with an extra-loud purr.

"You're right," I said. "We'll stand by him—no matter what crazy stories he tells us."

～

First thing Wednesday morning, Miss Judson telephoned the hospital and ascertained that Father had just received his morning dose of morphine and was expected to sleep until after lunch. So that afternoon we trekked back to the Royal Swinburne, which was even more abuzz with activity than usual. In the courtyard, porters were hanging green-and-white bunting under the supervision of a small, neat man in a dark suit and homburg hat. We paused long enough to make out the words as the banner unfurled: WELCOME, LADIES HOSPITAL COMMITTEE!

"What's a hospital committee?" I asked.

Miss Judson resumed her brisk stride toward the Private Ward. "I believe that might be one of your aunt's Causes."

Father's aunt Helena (my great-aunt and the source of my first name—which I *never* use, for obvious reasons) was always sticking her nose in other people's business. What had the sick people of Swinburne done to deserve her? Weren't they suffering enough already?

Arriving on Father's floor, we were greeted with a familiar sight. "There's Caroline," I said. Mrs. Munjal and her daughters wore green-and-white rosettes pinned to their collars, and the girls waved eagerly.

"What brings you here?" Miss Judson asked.

"The LHC," Nanette replied, in a voice that was not quite a groan.

Caroline showed me her jar of coins. "We're collecting for Hospital Sunday." All of Swinburne turned out for this annual event to raise funds for the hospital, paying sixpence for tickets, plus extra for food, games, and Amusements. A carnival at a hospital doesn't *sound* terribly entertaining, but you would be surprised. Last year there was a horse who could do sums.

Caroline added, "Your aunt's around here somewhere, too."

Now I not-quite-groaned (not quite). That's all we needed today. "Don't let her see Father," I whispered to Miss Judson. "She'll want to start Investigating, too!"

I did not think I could keep an eye on two wayward Hardcastles of the elder generation at once.

"We tried to visit your dad, but that matron wouldn't let us in," Caroline said. For once, I was relieved by Matron Finch's draconian* Rules. The last thing—well, second-to-last—we wanted was for the Munjals to get wrapped up in Father's delusions. Nanette passed me an armload of spiky white flowers wrapped in tissue as Mrs. Munjal led them away. "For your father. Mother finally got her forsythia to bloom."

As we were disentangling ourselves from the Munjals and the other Committee Ladies and their flowers and donations, we heard voices in the stairwell. Sound carried splendidly in the brick towers anchoring each corner of the hospital, spilling out whenever the heavy doors swung open. One of these particular voices was readily identifiable as Matron Finch's.

"A little bird told me you spoke to the Hardcastle family yesterday without permission."

Gasping, I yanked Miss Judson over to the stairwell door. Through the gap in the door, we recognized Probationer Ling.

"I didn't tell them anything! I didn't see anything, I swear."

"See anything?" Matron purred. "I wonder what you could possibly mean."

* named after Drakon, an ancient Greek official who was especially fond of handing out demerits. And the death penalty.

Nurse Ling's alarm was palpable. "I—nothing!"

"I won't have disobedience or gossip on my Wards, *Miss* Ling."

"Of course not, Matron. I wouldn't think of it."

"There aren't many hospitals in England that would hire you, you know. Governor Greeley has given you a marvelous opportunity—if you're wise enough not to squander it."

"I am," Nurse Ling said. "I won't. I promise."

Clearly, Matron Finch was not convinced. "This is going on your record as a demerit." She stroked her notebook, relishing the process of writing up a subordinate. "And you're being transferred to the Charity Ward. See that you keep in line down there. We would hate to lose such a promising nursing candidate, Ling."

Nurse Ling's face fell at this obvious demotion. "Yes, Matron."

"Collect your things from the Sitting Room. You may retain your room in the dormitory. For now." As Probationer Ling fled, Matron watched with satisfaction, red hands folded happily at her middle.

When she emerged from the stairs, it was to come face-to-face with my governess. Her nasty smile spread. "Well, if it isn't the Hardcastles again." I bristled; I could tell she was just itching to give Father—and us—demerits, too.

Miss Judson was ready for her. "Matron. And

how is Mr. Hardcastle this morning?" (Only the very Observant would note the faint sharp edge to her voice.)

"As you can see we're very busy today, and I haven't had a chance to personally look in on every little patient."

"It's your job to check on them!" I said, with an emphatic flourish of forsythia.

"I have a competent nursing staff. He is being well looked after."

"Oh, like the one you just sacked?" Miss Judson's voice was sweet.

Color—or perhaps alarm—flashed in Matron's eyes. "That is none of your concern."

"You said *our* name!"

Matron fixed her beady eyes on me. "I see the apple doesn't fall far from the tree."

I never got a chance to reply to that outrageous statement—or, more importantly, figure out what she meant by it—because we were interrupted by the arrival of a marginally less unwelcome personage. Clomping footsteps, the thump of a walking stick, and a loud, haughty voice sounded round the corners and down the corridors, causing everyone to turn and stare.

"Now, Julius, Viscountess Snowcroft is the *ideal* guest of honor for this year's Hospital Sunday. Think what she'll mean for the Free Surgery Fund. The Hardcastles are *close personal friends* of the Viscountess, you know." The person attached to the voice and the feet and the walking stick and the hyperbole was none other than my very own great-aunt Helena.

"It's too bad Mrs. Dudley's not here," Miss Judson murmured. "Those two would get on like a house afire."

"Don't even think about it," I said. "They'd wind up pulling poor Sally apart, quarreling over her." Which was all too accurate, given the claims to her fortune.

It was impossible to tell what Aunt Helena's companion thought about her Brilliant Plan, because she didn't give him a chance to respond. She'd spotted us. "Julius, I want you to meet my niece and her governess, who have taken dear Lady Ethel under their wings. Helena Myrtle, Judson, say hello to Dr. Greeley, the hospital governor."

Governor Greeley turned out to be the man we'd seen in the courtyard overseeing the bunting (he still wore his homburg hat). As Miss Judson pulled me over, I caught the look on Matron Finch's face: she was gazing at Governor Greeley with admiration. She almost looked pleasant.

"Well, now." Dr. Greeley had a serious voice, but kind eyes. "So these are the young ladies who've been causing so much mischief in my hospital." By my reckoning, *Father* had been causing the mischief, but of course we would be blamed for it. "I would like to assure you that the . . . incident has been looked into, and nothing of the kind shall happen again."

He was a fussy-looking fellow in a fastidious suit,

with a lean, clean-shaven face and small sharp eyes behind rimless spectacles that put me in mind of the Norway rats. He didn't look like a doctor, in the sense that I couldn't imagine him up to his elbows in messy body parts—he looked like the sort of man you'd entrust all your important documents to, particularly if they involved calculations and accounts and sitting patiently for a long time under a lone lamp. Which was probably what he did here, as the governor of a hospital.

Miss Judson's "Hmm" probably didn't convince Governor Greeley. "And how is Mr. Hardcastle today? No further 'incidents,' I hope."

"You don't mean, Arthur is *here*? In hospital? Oh, my poor dear boy!" Aunt Helena clapped her gloved hands to her generous bosom. But an instant later, her gaze bored into Dr. Greeley. "It's nothing *serious*, I trust."

And just like that, the hospital governor had three Hardcastle Ladies lined up and staring him down—and we can be a formidable committee indeed, Dear Reader. The poor man didn't stand a chance.

Dr. Greeley hesitated a moment too long.

Aunt Helena sniffed. "I can see I'll need to look in on him myself." Nobody would miss the edge to *her* voice.

"That's hardly necessary!" Matron bustled over. "He's only had a tonsillectomy."

Aunt Helena regarded Matron through her lorgnette. "And *you* would be . . . ?"

We were fated never to witness that confrontation play out, alas, because a moment later, footsteps—definitely *not* silent—pounded down the corridor from the office wing, and a red-haired nurse burst upon us, followed by Probationer Ling.

"Dr. Greeley!" the unfamiliar nurse cried. She halted when she realized the hospital governor was not alone. "Sir—that is—well, it's Mr. Hardcastle again, and you told us—"

"Yes, yes," he said impatiently. "What seems to be the difficulty? These ladies are Mr. Hardcastle's family—you may speak freely, Pethwick, Ling."

Neither Nurse Pethwick nor Probationer Ling seemed inclined to do anything of the sort. But they didn't need to. I had a sinking feeling I knew exactly what the difficulty was.

"You've lost my father again, haven't you?"

10

GUARDIAN AD LITEM

Before the Anatomy Act of 1832 legalized human dissection, medical schools often resorted to unsavory methods to acquire their teaching specimens, including robbing graves. Some entrepreneurial criminals made quite a thriving business out of providing cadavers to surgeons.

–H. M. Hardcastle, *Foundations of Legal Medicine*

"Helena Myrtle, don't be pert."

"I'm terribly sorry, Governor," said Nurse Pethwick. "He just—slipped away."

"Now, girls," Dr. Greeley said. "I'm sure you've done nothing wrong. From what I've been hearing, Mr. Hardcastle is quite the handful."

"Not usually," Miss Judson murmured.

"The most important thing right now is to find our wayward patient and be sure he's not hurt himself, yes? Chin up, Ling. Everything's going to be fine." Probationer Ling was staring at her hands, which she'd clamped together so tightly they were turning blue.

"What happened?" I demanded. "I thought he'd been sedated."

Dr. Greeley gave a pained smile. "Evidently your father does not respond in the typical way to opiates. Occasionally they agitate our patients instead of calming them. We may have to resort to—other measures. But first, let's track him down, shall we?"

That was all too easily accomplished. Commotion had upset the office wing, and panicked nurses fled the suite across from Dr. Kinkaid's laboratory. From their Excited Utterances, I had the impression that a wild animal—a tiger or an Orang-utan perhaps—had somehow got loose within.

I was not far wrong. A wild creature had, in fact, invaded the sanctuary of the Royal Swinburne Hospital Nurses' Sitting Room, and was tearing up the place with abandon. It was no animal escaped from a zoo, however, but a frantic patient escaped, yet again, from his bed.

"Oh!" exclaimed Aunt Helena. "What have you done to my poor boy?"

"For pity's sake, you're all nurses!" Dr. Greeley directed Nurses Ling and Pethwick back into the fray, like Lord Cardigan urging his doomed troops toward the Valley of Death. This inspired the rest of the force, and soon Pethwick and Matron had the intruder firmly in hand. Magazines were strewn everywhere, a chair overturned, and a teacup had spilled on somebody's forsaken needlepoint. At the heart of the chaos blazed a ginger-bearded man in pyjamas.

Father brandished his trophy: an unassuming paperbound book that I instantly recognized. "I tol' you," he declared somewhat raspily. "They stole ih." (Well, technically, *I* had said that, but this wasn't the moment to quibble.)

"Your sketchbook!" I seized Miss Judson and, pushing past Aunt Helena, waded through newspapers and cushions to Father's side. "How did you know?" I asked him, but before he could answer, Miss Judson snatched the evidence from his hand.

"Arthur Hardcastle, this is outrageous!" She shook the sketchbook at him, as Father struggled against the grip of the nurses. I had rarely seen her so angry—and I have seen her *plenty* angry indeed. My vow to stand by Father, no matter the consequences, began to strain under the circumstances.

"Theh in it togevver—the murher."

"What?" screeched Aunt Helena. "What did he say?"

"Mr. Hardcastle, please! None of that nonsense!" Dr. Greeley raised his voice for the first time. "Be nice to my nurses, I beg you. Matron, a wheelchair, if you please."

She dithered, clearly unwilling to miss the scene of

Father's Dramatic Downfall, but devotion to duty won. "Yes, Guv," she said, bustling off to retrieve it.

"Now, Mr. Hardcastle, what is the meaning of this?" Dr. Greeley's soft voice held a touch of humor. "Chasing murderers, are we? Well, you won't find one in here, I can assure you! You've scared these poor girls out of their wits, and when you're meant to be resting, my good man." He gave a chuckle that somehow sounded wise.

Nurse Ling clutched Father's arm for dear life. Miss Judson had gone very still, marshaling her reserves for an oncoming lecture. Aunt Helena said, "Did you say *murderers?*" And a vase on a delicate side table toppled to the rug with a painful thunk. Yet all I saw was the look on Father's face—a thwarted mixture of success and defiance. I recognized *that* expression far too well. My conscience squirmed. Father had dragged himself all this way on a quest to prove he hadn't imagined a crime, and I felt honor-bound to support him. Even if I wasn't convinced I *believed* him.

Before I could make good my vow, however, a nurse returned with the bath chair, putting an end to the scene. Nurses Pethwick and Ling—under the glaring oversight of Miss Judson—firmly impressed Father into the conveyance, holding him in place.

"Please see that our patient is returned to his bed—and that *he stays there.* Then send Matron Finch to me. Pethwick, Ling, please remain here." Dr. Greeley turned to Father. "I'm impressed, Mr. Hardcastle. Most of our patients don't require three women to restrain them." He gave Miss Judson and me appraising looks. "You two must have souls of extraordinary patience. You three," he amended, including Aunt Helena.

"Exceptional forbearance," I couldn't help mumbling. Miss Judson didn't look even mildly forbearing at the moment. Father hunched in the bath chair, sulking. Aunt Helena seized its handles and held Dr. Greeley in a deadly stare.

"When I return, Julius, I expect a *complete* explanation." And as only Aunt Helena could manage it, she whirled Father off with elegant hauteur.

In the Men's Ward, Matron Finch was waiting. She held a bundle of leather straps in her hands like a bride with a bouquet, glowing with sinister triumph.

Restraints? "You can't do this to him!" I turned to Miss Judson and Aunt Helena. "We can't let them do this! He was right about the sketchbook. What if he's right about the rest of it?"

"The rest of *what*?" Aunt Helena tried to ask.

But Miss Judson's forbearance had run out. "On the contrary," she said, "I think this is entirely warranted. It's high time you gave up this ridiculous notion and behaved like the respectable Englishman you're supposed to be. Miss Finch, please proceed."

Dear Reader, I shall spare you the details of the next several minutes, save to say that I had never before given sufficient consideration to the fact that Miss Judson had been born and spent her formative years in close proximity to a penal colony,* and had evidently picked up a few pointers regarding the management of the prisoners. When Father had been firmly strapped to the bed by his wrists and ankles, the manacles secured with impressive padlocks, Miss Judson turned to Matron Finch. "A moment alone with my employer, if you please."

Matron gave the restraints a final satisfied tug before departing. When the green doors had at last swung shut behind her, Miss Judson unleashed the full force of her fury upon Father. She planted herself at his bedside and spoke in her most level tones, voice fairly vibrating with anger. "I hardly know where to begin," she began. "This latest escapade is beyond the pale."†

Father made a sound, but Miss Judson cut him off more swiftly than any magistrate's ruling. "In addition to casting wild accusations against the staff of this facility, who have been more than patient with you, you are jeopardizing your health! Dr. Belden sent you here in good faith, Dr. Kinkaid put a great deal of time and

---

* French Guiana's notorious Île du Diable, where her parents were missionaries

† This seemingly nonsensical expression is most likely to crop up at moments when asking for a definition would be inadvisable, and refers to the area outside a palisade, or spiked fence—the trespass of which is apparently unforgivable. (I had to look it up once.)

skill into your treatment, and you are treating them and their efforts with the utmost disrespect."

I hid behind Aunt Helena, shriveling with cowardice. Even Aunt Helena remained silent, against every natural instinct she possessed. Father couldn't argue, either, but merely glared back, looking not the least bit penitent. He shook at his restraints.

"That's no more than you deserve," Miss Judson said. "Under the circumstances, I wonder if it wouldn't be best to bring you home. We'd have to hire a private nurse, of course, and I can't imagine the damage your behavior has done to our credibility as clients—"

"No!" The word burst from Father, leaving him cringing, eyes screwed shut against the pain.

Miss Judson paused in her measured tirade, one eyebrow minutely raised. "You wish to make a counterargument? I would advise you to choose your position very carefully. The court is not inclined to look upon your case with sympathy."

"Muhrl coul' stay." It took a moment to translate this into an utterance we could understand—which then elicited a strangled sound from Miss Judson. Or, no, that might have been me.

"If you think for a moment I am going to permit Myrtle to remain here overnight with you, given your recent behavior—"

"Actually," came a new voice to the debate, "as ideas go, that one's not half bad." We turned to see Dr.

Kinkaid ambling down the ward in his pristine white coat. "She couldn't possibly do any worse than our nurses."

"Don't tempt her," Miss Judson said.

"You do seem to have a positive effect on the patient, I've noticed. What do you say, Miss Hardcastle?"

"Why me? What have I done?"

"Well, I can hardly stay," Miss Judson pointed out. "That wouldn't be appropriate."

I could think of a few choice words about the idea of me staying, and *appropriate* was not among them. And when had Miss Judson taken such an abrupt volte-face? Was it possible Dr. Kinkaid's green eyes were having a questionable effect on her judgment, too?

"I would offer *my* services, as a representative of the Ladies Hospital Committee," Aunt Helena said grandly. "It certainly wouldn't be my first vigil at a patient's bedside. But alas, I am otherwise engaged." With significance, she elaborated: "I shall be attending Viscountess Snowcroft's lecture this evening."

Well, I thought wildly, *at least she can keep an eye on* somebody.

"Come, now, Hardcastle," Dr. Kinkaid said. "You strike me as a wain who doesn't shy away from adventure. Aren't you interested in learning what goes on in a hospital overnight?"

"We've heard what goes on here," I muttered.

"Well, I can't promise you another murder," he

admitted. "I've been here going on six months and haven't seen one myself yet. Your father's an uncommon lucky chap."

"Oh, stick around," Miss Judson said wearily. "We seem to attract them. Aunt, I'll explain everything on the way home."

In the end, Miss Judson, Father, and Aunt Helena all had their way. Before I could compose a defense that would allow me to escape my unwarranted sentence, Dr. Kinkaid made the arrangements, and a probationer brought a bundle of items hastily acquired from the Children's Ward: a nightdress washed to near-transparency, held together only by green embroidery; a tin of tooth powder and a toothbrush that *looked* new; and a white flannel dressing gown that would have fit Father. I clutched them to my chest as I watched Miss Judson and Aunt Helena depart, leaving me all alone in the cavernous hospital ward with Father and an army of now-hostile nurses.

"You'll be fine," Miss Judson said—but I heard the dire unspoken directive: *Keep your father out of mischief.*

I couldn't resist one parting comment. "He was right about the sketchbook."

She sighed and flipped absently through the precious book. "It scarcely matters anymo—" She cut off, hand frozen above the pages.

"What is it?"

Grimly, she shifted the book to face me. Beside a listless sketch of bodies strewn about a Crimean battlefield was the ragged edge of a torn-out page. Whoever had taken the sketchbook from Father's bed had also ripped out his notes about the murder.

11

IN FOR A POUND

The Medico-Legal Practitioner's duties will include not only work with the dead, but with the living. One of these groups is far more likely to provide reliable information to Investigators than the other.

–H. M. Hardcastle, *Foundations of Legal Medicine*

The reappearance of Miss Judson's sketchbook did not make me feel any better about staying in the hospital overnight with Father. Quite the contrary: it had propelled us into a realm of very real danger, and I was not at all sure I was up to the task of protecting Father by myself.

"Don't be ridiculous." Miss Judson glanced back at Father, who was now regarding his leather restraints with something like resignation—I hoped. "You need only protect him from himself. Keep him occupied, distracted. Read to him."

"Did you bring your textbook on the Crimea?" I asked sarcastically.

The hospital was surprisingly solicitous, given Father's behavior. Nurse Pethwick was assigned to Father and treated him like a stubborn nut she was bound and determined to crack. When she turned up for the night shift, along with Father's meal she brought me an enamel mug of watery cocoa and a crumbly biscuit.

"What's that flavor?" I asked. The sandy shortbread left behind a cloying aftertaste.

"Almond," she said, and I set it down abruptly. Deadly cyanide had a bit of almondy essence to it. "I'm sorry, Mr. Hardcastle, you're not to have solid food yet. But I brought you some chilled Bovril."

I looked away as she spooned the cold beef broth into Father's mouth. I was embarrassed, with Nurse Pethwick being so nice to us after Father had torn up their private parlor. I wanted to apologize, but I wasn't sure how, with him right here. So it went unsaid, even when she asked if she could bring us anything.

Father's face was red and shiny from being scrubbed, like a baby after a feeding. He looked mortified.

"A newspaper?" I suggested.

"*Tribune, Register,* or *Times*?"

I didn't wish to be greedy, but it was going to be a long night. "All three?"

Nurse Pethwick hesitated. "As long as you don't wear him out. He's recovering from surgery, you know."

I nodded vigorously, and Father made a gruff sound that the nurse and I both took for assent.

The very last thing Nurse Pethwick did before releasing Father to my custody was unhook his restraints, tucking the leather straps out of sight underneath the bed.

"Are you sure?" I asked.

"I won't tell Matron," she said with a friendly wink. "I trust ya."

"You shouldn't," I mumbled—with an anxious look at Father. On my own head be it, should he break the rules yet again. He gave us a look of wide-eyed innocence, earning a snort from Nurse Pethwick.

The London *Times* was two days out of date, but the *Upton Register* and the *Swinburne Tribune* were this morning's. Father was quiet—for the moment—so I settled back into the little trundle they'd provided for me (another hand-me-up from the Children's Ward), newspapers in my lap, notebook at the ready. Nurse Pethwick continued her evening rounds, doling out medications, tucking in the other patients, and lowering the lights. It was not quite dark—the nurses needed to see their patients as they walked through—but it was a far different place than the bright, sunlit Ward of daytime. Shadows blanketed the deep corners, and every odd piece of equipment took on an ominous and threatening aspect. Danger—not just invisible germs, but now unseen villains, too—could be lurking behind every curtain, beneath every bed. Even the potted aspidistra looked like a wild-haired fiend ready to pounce.

I could see why Father hadn't wanted to keep to his bed.

At least they'd mostly closed the windows so we could all sleep without freezing to death.

"Go 'head," Father mumbled. His voice was still weak, and I supposed I ought to be grateful that he couldn't scold me at the moment. Not that I'd done anything scoldable. I cleared my throat and ran through the main headlines, which were not terribly interesting. PARLIAMENT DEBATES LOCAL GOVERNMENT ACT and WORK TO BEGIN ON HIGH STREET DRAINS.*

I flipped through the entire *Tribune*. "There's no mention of your murder."

"Do'en't prove anythig."

Mrs. Dudley and SWOBS had taken out a full-page advert for Miss Snowcroft's latest appearances, **FEATURING CHARLEY THE DOG** and **HALF-PRICE MATINEES**. The editorial section was full of Swinburnian opinion on what should become of the Snowcroft fortune—everything from letting it revert to the Crown to building a home

---

* recent events involving the sewers having called attention to their poorly maintained condition

for retired draft horses.* What I *didn't* see, thank goodness, was any sign of the threatening letters Genie had
mentioned. Of course, they wouldn't print the most
malicious ones.

In ordinary circumstances, I would share my concerns with Father. I almost said something—until I
remembered the leather manacles Nurse Pethwick had
only just hidden away. There was no need to upset him
further.

Father made a sullen sound and glared across the
Ward.

I folded the newspaper briskly, as Miss Judson
would do. "We should cover the work you've been missing. Miss Judson will bring the papers that you need
to sign tomorrow, but I can give you a summary of the
correspondence that's arrived in your absence."

"Beh'er idea." Father glanced about the dark room,
and, seeing a distinct lack of nursely or doctorly oversight, flung back his blankets. *"Lessgo."*

"What are you doing?" I hissed, flinging them back
over his pyjama'd legs. "I promised to keep you in this
bed." I hovered a hand above the buzzer affixed to
his wall, which would emit an alarm that would bring
every nurse in the Private Ward running.

Father swallowed hard, started to say something,

---

* an idea I thought warranted deeper consideration. I would make sure
to mention it to Sally.

then thought better of it and caught up the notebook instead. A scribbly moment later, he showed me this:

2 HRS TILL NURSE BACK SEARCH NOW.

I snatched it back. "Search *no*! Father, we *promised*! Miss Judson will have our guts for garters." That expression was rather gruesome, if you stopped to think about it, but seemed entirely within the realm of punishments my governess would deem appropriate if she found out I'd failed in my singular task for the night.

"Oh'ly chazz," Father said. He coaxed the notebook from my hands again. *You're curious, too,* he wrote. *This is our chance to prove my theory.*

I crossed my arms and scowled at him. "What theory?" I said warily.

Raising his eyebrows playfully, he crooked his index finger at me. I sighed, closed my eyes briefly, mentally recited every Inappropriate Word I knew, in four languages (if ever they were *appropriate* words, now was the moment), and flung back my own blankets.

"Ferh," Father said, and I stopped to blink at him. *"What?"*

He gestured impatiently at the potted fern on the bedstand, which I hesitantly handed to him—and which he promptly turned over, depositing a handful of dirt and a shiny brass key into his upturned palm.

"Where did you get—" I tossed up my hands. "No! Don't tell me! I don't want to know." With a smug look, Father slipped the key into the pocket of his dressing gown, I grabbed my kit, and off we went.

At least we had slippers, Dear Reader, which made it infinitely more possible to sneak about the Royal Swinburne's shiny wooden floors.

"For the record, I am against this idea. And Miss Judson wouldn't approve, either."

Slinking through the shadows along the tiled wall, Father glanced back at me—and to my enormous alarm, his eyes were twinkling.

"You should be in bed."

He gave me a disappointed scowl and tiptoed onward. At night, the wide polished corridors of the Royal Swinburne were still impressive, still lit by (now dimmed) artificial lights, and still gleaming with new-ness. But, thank goodness, they were considerably less populated. The Unwelcome Desk sat abandoned at this late hour. This was where Father must have come to use the telephone—and probably also swiped the skeleton key that I did not want to know anything about.

"Just how many trips have you taken out and about at night since you've been here?" I felt like a naughty schoolboy sneaking about the dormitories after curfew.*

Father betrayed no such anxiety, speeding through the halls, soft and swift as Peony on a midnight mission to the kitchen. He led me round corners and past stairwells, tucking me out of sight as a porter whistled past, twirling his keys and looking for patients escaped from their beds, aided and abetted by their daughters.

After what seemed an eternity but must have been only a few deathly minutes, we paused outside the faintly luminous glass door to Dr. Kinkaid's laboratory.

"Here." Father's whisper was surprisingly robust, and I looked at him askance. Was this Unauthorized Excursion actually making him feel better? *I* had developed all sorts of alarming symptoms—cardiac palpitations, ghastly perspiration in unspeakable places, itchy palms, what felt like a rash on my tongue . . .

I pulled my thoughts back to the moment. "This is where you saw—" *Hang it all.* "The murder?"

Father nodded vigorously.

"We found the earring in there."

Father held out his hand for a closer look, and I retrieved the evidence from my kit. He pinched the

---

* This telling word comes down to us from Old French: *cuevrefeu,* or "cover fires," the hour at which medieval villagers were expected to douse their lights, lest they attract invaders or burn down the village. Lackadaisical modern attitudes toward curfews ignore the *very real dangers* of being out and about after hours, *Father.*

hoop of gold between his thumb and index finger and lifted it to the light filtering through the glass. But after studying it thoughtfully, he ultimately shrugged and relinquished it.

He gave the laboratory doorknob a hopeless rattle, at which point I reminded him that he had a key. Instead Father performed an exaggerated pantomime. He shook his head, he pointed down the hallway, he walked his two fingers across his palm, he held up his hands as if asking my permission.

I had more than half a mind to walk my own fingers back in the direction of his bed. Instead I nodded—and Father beamed, sneaking back out into the corridor.

I was afraid he was headed for the Nurses' Sitting Room again—one location sure to *not* be abandoned at this hour—but he had a much worse destination in mind. He led us directly next door, to an office whose brass nameplate I could just make out—and immediately wished I hadn't: JULIUS GREELEY, F.R.C.S.,* HOSPITAL GOVERNOR.

I halted, clapping a hand over my mouth to stifle my protest. It was far too late to back out now. Or sound the alarm. Or flee. (Un)fortunately, Father's purloined key worked, and an irrevocable moment later, we stood inside the center of business of everything that went on in the Royal Swinburne Hospital.

---

* Fellow of the Royal College of Surgeons, an even more exalted rank than *Member*. I'm not sure what they liked to be called.

It took a moment for my eyes to adjust to the dark, and for my heart to stop banging so loudly it would alert every porter and governor and murderer in the place. Dr. Greeley's office was furnished like a parlor, with a fireplace—still putting off some warmth—dark paneling, bookcases, and a thick rug. Heavy silk drapes were pulled tight against the windows to keep out the Healthful Fresh Air the hospital insisted on inflicting upon its staff and patients.

"Id migh've 'app'n'd 'ere." Father gestured toward the shrouded windows.

I dutifully tiptoed across the room to carefully shift aside the weighty silk. A distinct dusty odor arose as I did so, and I waved Father back so that the only speck of dust in the Royal Swinburne wouldn't find its way into his already irritated throat. I peeked round their edges, and the darkened Men's Ward peeked back at me, sleepy and dim across the cold night. "These haven't been opened in ages. The laboratory is more likely to be the crime scene."

"I 'gree." When I turned back, Father was doffing his dressing gown. I felt a spike of bafflement—was he feverish again? But he rolled it up and laid it along the foot of the closed office door. "So the ligh' woh' show," he said proudly.

"Oh." How many such tricks did Father have at the ready? I'd been wrong—this wasn't *my* Father at all. To avoid pondering that, I hastened to the desk and lit a lamp. It was small and old-fashioned, with a curved brass handle above the chimney, apparently meant for hanging. It didn't fit in with the stately furnishings, which made me wonder (entirely against my will, mind you) why it was here.

With a growl I didn't try to hide, I turned to study the room more closely as Father . . . did whatever we'd broken into a hospital governor's office to do. Somber nautical paintings hung between the windows and the bookcases. One frame displayed a letter from Her Majesty, on the occasion of the hospital's Royal Patronage, praising Dr. Greeley's humanitarian spirit. Another held a photograph of Aunt Helena shaking Dr. Greeley's hand—I gave a squeak. "He's *bald*!"

But Father's attention was elsewhere, so I continued my own search of the premises. Atop the long, low cabinets stood various Global Artifacts from tropical locales: a woven reed mask with a fearsome aspect, a drum with an animal-skin top—fur still attached—a handsome wooden parrot painted in gay colors. This was clearly the office of a sophisticated world traveler. But like the lamp, an old pocketknife mounted on a stand seemed out of place.

The implement—tool? or weapon?—was small and battered and ordinary, yet displayed with obvious care on the desk. I shifted the little lamp closer, and among the curlicues engraved on the folding ivory handle, I could just barely make out crude, age-stained letters gouged into the surface.

"*Cutty*," I read aloud.

"Mmph?"

"It's on this old knife," I said. "What's Dr. Greeley's first name, again?" It was Julius, I recalled from the nameplate on the door.

"Ni'name?" Father managed. "Ligh' Bohes or Dogh?" (I think that was meant to be *Bones or Doc.*) "He was shiv's surzh'ud."

"A ship's surgeon? How do you know that?" Piecing together the clues in the room, it was a logical conclusion. I traced the shape of the blade—flat on one side, smoothly curved on the other, and only a little longer than my fingers. A tiny thing, really. But no doubt up to its task.

Father found Governor Greeley's appointment calendar and spread it open. Disappointingly, *Commit murder in full view of windows while patient is watching* was not among the notations for 19 February. In fact, there was nothing for the evening at all, but he'd had a four o'clock appointment with an "A. P." Father pounced on this like Peony, flipping through the calendar, back and forth, searching for another notion regarding the mysterious A. P.

I turned to the letter tray. The outgoing box was empty, the incoming tray stacked with opened letters from cheerful donors: *Enclosed find £5 for the Children's Ward; My wife and I have remembered the Royal Swinburne in our Will; The Ladies Hospital Committee are pleased to have raised £500 for the Free Surgery Fund* (Aunt Helena again). The wastebasket contained only a handbill advertising one of Miss Snowcroft and Charley's lectures, ripped to pieces (we'd evidently identified the one person in England not obsessed with the mystery of the *Persephone*). Nothing sinister at all.

Father had better luck. "Muhrl!" He waved my attention to the appointment book, where several weeks ago, Dr. Greeley had met with one Mrs. Velma Dudley of the Seaman's Widows & Orphans Benevolent Society.

"SWOBS," I whispered. "That must be a coincidence."

"*Cou'* be," Father said. "Buh' I doud it."

I did swift calculations—that would have been just before Mrs. Dudley had first come to see us with Sally. It was too much to believe that Dr. Greeley's connection to Mrs. Dudley could have anything to do with Father's case—either case. But Father clearly didn't think so.

He ripped the page right out of the calendar. I gave a strangled yelp. "Father! We can't just take that. It's evidence!"

He nodded fervently. "Seizig it. Officeh of th' Courh'." He folded it neatly and tucked it into the breast pocket of his pyjama shirt.

"That won't do," I said, exasperated. "They're sure to find it on you. Give it to me."

Father hesitated, clearly unwilling to part with what must have felt like the first clue to grasp hold of.

"We'll look into it," I promised, holding out my hand. When he finally relinquished it, I shoved it into the recesses of my bag—out of Father's reach, at least.

That appeared to be the limit of the discoveries to be given up by Dr. Greeley's desk. We moved on, opening cabinets crammed to bursting with woolly waistcoats (one might even say *cardigans*), hot-water bottles, and a lifetime supply of tea—even a pair of oversized knitted mittens. Eccentric, but hardly incriminating.

"Aa-aa!" Father exclaimed. I glanced over to see him holding a wide leather book. "Fou' th' money!"

I couldn't help myself. "What money?"

Eyes bright, Father turned the book to me. It was an accounts ledger, pages full of tidy numerical notations. He carried it over to the desk, where he settled down in Dr. Greeley's leather chair. "Thzz coul' tay' while," he said.

"We don't *have* a while!"

"We've'n hour an' ten minnuzz," he said. "Se'll dowh'."

I dithered, but he gave me a very Fatherly look and pointed at the overstuffed armchair near the fireplace. "Sidh."

Grumbling, I obeyed. While Father worked, I pulled out my notebook, going over the list I had made last night, but there didn't seem to be anything to add, or to be gleaned from our Observations of Dr. Greeley's office. I grudgingly recorded the meetings with A. P. and Mrs. Dudley, then let my weary eyes rove round his masks and drums, mementos of a life at sea.

In the low light from the lone lamp, they looked even more intriguing. Names and images of all the most fascinating foreign lands in my encyclopædia swirled through my imagination: *the Galapagos Islands, New Guinea, the Antipodes, Madagascar* . . . Why would someone settle in Swinburne, of all places, having been to those other (warmer) lands? No wonder he needed so many jumpers.

The windows rattled behind their drapes, and I heard the haunting call of an owl. I pulled the collar of my borrowed dressing gown higher, tucked my feet beneath me, and leaned my head heavily against the chair, watching Father pore feverishly over the accounts ledger.

"Muhrl. Lessgo." Father was standing above me, folding a blanket that he'd evidently draped over me at some point. I jerked upright. I'd fallen asleep. I'd fallen *asleep* while I was supposed to be supervising Father! I lurched to my feet, heart banging.

"Easy," he said. "Ev'rythig's fine." His voice was getting stronger.

I studied him critically. His hair was sticking up everywhere, and he had *two* pencils behind his ears. But his color was high—warm and healthy—and his eyes were bright but not feverish. I hadn't seen him look this well in weeks.

"You found something," I hazarded. My grogginess fizzled away. "What? What did you find?"

Father grinned. "Look." He led me to the desk and the open ledger. "Mizzus Duh'ley. It was a donayshud—buh th'other way roudh."

I felt my brow scrunch, trying to translate that. "What?"

"*Greeley* donaded t' *SWOBS*. Twenny-figh pouh'z! An' loogh 'ere." According to Father's notes, there had been such a donation—twenty pounds, fifty—coming straight from the hospital's coffers, every few months for the past two years—to the tune of over five hundred pounds.

"That's very charitable," I said doubtfully. *One* such contribution would be generous—that many bordered on suspicious. It amounted to nearly Father's entire salary (not that I was supposed to know that). "So . . . Dr. Greeley strangled Mrs. Dudley to get out of being blackmailed by her?" That thought started slowly, but rushed headlong to the end in a torrent of relief. Finally, a case! Well, not *relief*, I supposed. Poor Mrs. Dudley! Poor Sally!

"Straggled Mizz Duh'ley?" Father scowled at me. "Whah're you talgig 'boud?"

"What are *you* talking about? The murder victim, with the earring—it could be Mrs. Dudley! Does—did—she have pierced ears?" I couldn't remember.

"Whah's th' earrig to do wiv adythig?" And just like that, Father dismissed the only physical evidence we had.

"Well, it either belongs to the victim or the murderer," I snapped. "And so far we haven't found any bald female doctors."

"Bahl female—?" Father pressed a hand against his forehead. "Muhrl, I've no idea whah you meadh."

"The widow who was murdered, of course. By the doctor. It's *your* murder—why are you looking at me like that?"

"Nod a womad," Father said, and I stopped, staring at him.

"What?"

"Th' vi'tim. It was a *man*. No' a woman."

I cast up my hands in exasperation. "We've been looking for a woman all this time!"

"Why? I nev' sai' adythig bou' women."

"You never said anything at all!" My voice had gone perilously shrill, and I forced myself to quiet down. "You've had Miss Judson and me running all over the hospital looking for dead bald widows. Why didn't you say something?"

"I hab my tozzils oud."

I made a wordless sound and shoved all my things back into my bag. "I should have listened to Miss Judson. You *are* delirious. There probably was no murder, and we've just vandalized an innocent hospital governor's office for no reason."

Father went very still. "Figh. If you doh' wanh t'hep me, I cah't mague you. Cub alog, izz time we got back. Don' dawdle."

He said this like being here was *my* idea! "Make sure you put the room back the way it was," I said crossly, "or Dr. Greeley will know you were in here."

By some miracle, we made it back to the Men's Ward with time to spare and (another miracle) no further discussion, and (wonders never cease) Father was tucked up innocently in bed when Nurse Pethwick came by for her late-night rounds.

"Aren't you looking better!" she said cheerily, fluffing Father's pillow, and then mine. "How about some more Bovril?" She'd come prepared with the ghastly mixture and spoon.

"How bouh some propeh tea, Zizzter?" Father said.

"You know you're not allowed hot liquids," she scolded.

"Our American neighbor drinks iced tea," I volunteered—to looks of horror from both Father and

Nurse Pethwick. (As if meat paste dissolved in tepid water was something to look forward to!)

"Well, no accounting for Americans, is there?" Nurse Pethwick moved on to taking Father's vitals, fumbling about her apron pockets. "Where's my watch? I had it here a minute ago. I swear, the way things go missing in this hospital . . ." Shaking her head, she fixed her gaze on the wall clock instead. "Your heart rate's up again, Mr. Hardcastle. You haven't been out of bed?"

"Juzz th' WC," he vowed, all innocence.

I studied my fingers and did not contribute to this conversation, but Father's jokey mood with the nurse put me even more on edge. As soon as Nurse Pethwick moved on again, Father returned to the case.

"Quig. Mague a list of thigs I neeh fro' th' office."

"Miss Judson won't like that. You'd better get to sleep. If you have a fever again in the morning—"

"Whah's goh ihto you?" he said. "A momeh' ago, you were keed to sohve this muhrer wiv me."

"You are not here to solve a murder! You're here to recover from tonsillectomy."

"I can do bofe," he said blithely—in a voice I didn't recognize (and yet was all too familiar). "Why shoulh you an' Mizz Judsod hab all th' fuh?"

"It's not *fun*! This is very serious, and you're treating it like a game!" Recalling Miss Judson's Observation from the night of the party, I went on before I could stop myself. "Just because you're envious of the cases we've solved—"

"*Ehvious?*" he croaked. "Yug lady, I was solvig muhrers before you coulh eve' *spell* hobicide!"

"Or *not* solving them," I muttered—not quite under my breath.

"Who's beig chil'ish now?" he returned.

"I don't know—maybe it's your *child*, which would make a nice change for once!" I flung myself back against my pillow and huffily crossed my arms.

"Ho now, what's this, then? You're waking the whole Ward with your row!" Nurse Pethwick stood above us, hands on her green-striped hips. "Young lady, you're meant to be helping your father rest."

I glared at her. "I told you to keep him restrained."

"Don't tempt me," she said. "I'll sedate you both if I have to. Last warning!"

After that, I turned my back on Father, rolled over in my not-creaky little trundle bed, and pulled the green blanket over my head. If Father went to sleep—or left his bed for another late-night adventure—I wasn't watching and I didn't care.

12

VISITING HOURS

There is no substitute for examining a body in situ at the scene of the crime. Vital evidence can be gleaned from Observations of the location and condition of the corpse . . .

–H. M. Hardcastle, *Foundations of Legal Medicine*

Dear Reader, it may surprise you to learn that a hospital ward is not conducive to a good night's rest. There are constant disturbances—from the other patients (coughing, moaning, whispering, snoring, and complaining about lost items), from the nurses on their rounds waking you up every hour on the hour to take your temperature or give you more Bovril, and from sulky parents glaring at you across the gap between your poky little uncomfortable beds. There is also a deplorable lack of feline company.

Thus neither Father nor I was in a particularly charitable mood when Nurse Pethwick returned for the final time on her morning rounds, turning off the lamps and flinging open all the windows. She noticed at once that something was amiss.

"Not still rowing, are we?" She regarded us with a critical eye. I cannot report on what she saw, for neither Father nor I would look at the other. "Miss Myrtle, you'd best run and get dressed while I give your father his breakfast. And a shave, I should think. Don't want you scruffy for the Tour."

Father made a pained noise, and Nurse Pethwick tut-tutted. "Overdid it, I see. Well, Dr. Kinkaid warned you that the third day is the worst."

"What tour?" I asked warily, untangling myself from the bedclothes.

"It's Inspection Day! The Ladies Committee is coming."

"Weren't they here yesterday?"

"That was just a reconnaissance mission. The real troops come today. And Sunday, of course, for the fair. Busy week here at the Royal!" She gave me an encouraging little swat on my rear, like I was a horse. "Off you pop. Your Miss Judson's already telephoned twice this morning."

I took my bundle of clothes to the public water closet to change. Nurse Pethwick was right—it was even busier than usual today. I dodged attendants bustling to and fro with breakfast trays, and passed a porter in shiny dress shoes and an ill-fitting uniform trying to accompany Dr. Kinkaid on an urgent rat-related mission to his laboratory. As I was returning to the Ward, I spotted Matron Finch circling the corridors like a hungry shark. I'm not proud of my next action, Dear Reader. I ducked back into the doorway of the WC to stay out of her path.

She never came past. After an age of tense waiting, I dared to peek out, expecting her to be lurking right outside, ready to strap me to a bed for malfeasance and pepper me with demerits. Surely she'd read on my face that I'd been Out of Bed After Dark—or worse. But she was still down the hall, holding the tail end of a length of bunting for a stocky, bearded porter on a ladder.

And she was *smiling* at him. I retract my previous statement, Dear Reader: somehow it made her look even less pleasant. "Very good, Mr. Bentley."

Mr. Bentley descended to the floor. "Thanks, mum. Matron . . . ?"

"Yes, Mr. Bentley?" Matron's invisible eyebrows lifted, and Mr. Bentley let whatever he was going to say next evaporate.

"Nothing, mum."

Matron stepped closer and put her stubby hand on his arm. "I hope you're not having second thoughts about our arrangement, Mr. Bentley."

"Ar-arrangement, mum?"

"To attend tonight's lecture, of course." She let out a twittering little laugh that fell flat. "What did you think I meant?"

"Oh, the lecture. Right. I'll fetch you at eight, then, aye?"

"Eight o'clock *precisely*. And it goes without saying that I don't care for gentlemen who go back on their word." With this, she patted his arm and continued her survey of her sovereign empire. Mr. Bentley abandoned the rest of his bunting and hastened off, leaving the ladder stranded in the corridor.

I extricated myself from my hiding place and shoved my borrowed night things down a huge laundry chute (a splendid innovation I should have liked at home—as would Cook, no doubt). I stood for a moment, frowning into its deep recesses. Had there been something ominous in Matron Finch's plans with her young man? No doubt *I* was imagining things now, too. At any rate, I felt distinctly sorry for anyone courting her.

"Miss! Don't hang about loitering. Your family's waitin'." Nurse Pethwick sailed by—I couldn't believe she still had so much energy after her long shift. "I'm off, then. I'll see your da' tonight."

"Thank you for looking after him." I meant that, although I might still have sounded a little cross, for she gave me a considering look before saying goodbye.

A surprise awaited me in the Men's Ward—a happy one, this time. "Cook!" She was seated by Father's bedside, along with Miss Judson, holding a wicker hamper on her lap.

She handed it off to me. "Breakfast. I can well imagine what passes for food round here."

I lifted the lid to reveal a lovely heap of freshly baked, beautifully iced, perfectly sticky Chelsea buns bursting with cinnamon and currants. I gave a sigh of bliss, breathing in the warm, yeasty aroma.

For his part, Father gave a tragic moan.

As I devoured my bun with ladylike efficiency, Miss Judson ("Don't mind if I do") regarded me and Father with her most appraising gaze. "Well," she said after delicately licking her fingertips, "report."

Father and I accidentally exchanged one hastily curtailed glance but said nothing.

"What's this?" Miss Judson studied us. "Do you mean to tell me you actually spent the night *resting*? Both of you? And here I expected to return to a wrapped-up case."

"Don't it just figure." Cook handed her a second bun. "You'll be doing all the work yourself, Ada."

Cook and Miss Judson shared a knowing, world-weary sigh that made me feel quite left out—and more than a little put out. It wasn't fair. This was all Father's fault, and (Chelsea buns aside) it seemed like I was being punished for it. I sighed. Audibly.

"Well, isn't this cozy?" Matron appeared from nowhere, wheeling an empty bath chair and looking like she'd just poisoned one of our buns and couldn't wait to find out who'd get the prize. "Since it's such a fine morning, it's high time Mr. Hardcastle got some Fresh Air."

"Isn't there enough coming in the windows?" I grumbled, not quite softly enough. I heard a noise like a cough from the hospital bed—which I ignored. Pointedly.

Miss Judson was on her feet in an instant. "Shall we?"

Any objections were summarily overruled, and moments later, the Hardcastles found ourselves in the courtyard—where a Highly Suspicious Figure perched upon a brick planter, primly washing her black ears like it was Perfectly Normal for her to be having a bath in a hospital garden. Black fur gleamed, soaking up the morning sunshine.

"You brought Peony?" I asked without thinking.

"She brought herself, as you know very well," Miss Judson said. Peony had the tram drivers wrapped around her little paws and regularly included herself in errands into town. Since Father was her favorite human on the planet, and had a ready lap draped in a fuzzy woolen blanket, she gave a luxurious stretch, kicked out one white-booted back foot, leaped neatly into the bath chair, turned a tight circle, and lay down, purring smugly.

"Don't let Matron see her," I warned. Peony yawned.

Miss Judson was all business. "As a Hardcastle

Plenum* has assembled, now would be the ideal time for the report on your findings." She folded her arms with expectation.

"Seconded." Cook folded her arms to match.

I looked at my shoes. Father nuzzled Peony.

"Nothing?" Miss Judson leaned in, peering at us both. "Tonsillitis isn't catching," she said critically. She turned to Cook. "Perhaps they misunderstood the task assigned to them."

Cook replied, "I'll wager you were clear enough."

"Assigned to us!" I exclaimed. "You told me to keep Father in bed!"

"And did you succeed?"

"Er—"

Miss Judson tapped her fingertips against her sleeve. "Exactly. Presumably you've therefore solved the Case of the . . . Midnight Murder?" She glanced at Cook.

"The Vanishing Victim?" the latter proposed, to a nod of approval from Miss Judson.

"Not exactly." I dug my toe into the cobblestones.

Peony answered for Father. *"No."* She sounded mournful. He hung his head guiltily.

Miss Judson's frosty pause to communicate the depths of her disappointment was interrupted by

* This woefully underused Latin word, literally the opposite of *vacuum*, refers to the complete assemblage of a company, all present and accounted for (unlike a *quorum*, which is the minimum number of people required for a task. Like bullying one's employer and his offspring).

162 }

footsteps and voices cutting through the crisp morning air.

"Good heavens, what's this! Patients in the courtyard, at this hour? You, there, Sister, fetch Matron at once." A woman with a walking stick stumped into the courtyard, joined by a much younger companion—and an entire gaggle of hangers-on of every description: nurses, porters, men in black suits who were either doctors or medical students or random strangers off the street, even a handful of small children trailing dressing-gown belts, rag dolls, and lost slippers.

"You brought Aunt Helena back, too?" I said, dismayed.

"Well, now I'm just insulted," she said.

"MuhMmmph Mmph-mmph Mmmmmpmph." That was Father, attempting to speak through a mouthful of Peony.

"The Ladies Hospital Committee!" I translated. "Nurse Pethwick told us they were coming."

"Did she mention they were bringing Miss Snowcroft?" Miss Judson said. "Poor Sally. But where's Mrs. Dudley?"

"Well, she's apparently not *dead*, if that's what you were thinking," I said.

"*Pardon?*" Miss Judson swung her eyes between me and Father. "Something is going on between you two," she said. "And I *will* figure it out, so you may as well confess."

"Where's Cook gone off to?" I asked—not just to weasel out of Miss Judson's interrogation.

"Oh, good heavens, can't we keep track of *anyone* in this family?" Miss Judson grasped the handles of the bath chair and set off across the courtyard in search of our errant housekeeper. Peony gripped Father's legs and hung on like a sailor, wind ruffling her fur.

The winding footpaths conspired to lead us straight toward Sally and Aunt Helena. Father turned about in the wheelchair, looking for avenues of escape, but Sally spotted us and gave a cheery wave. She was holding Charley—dressed in a knitted jumper—with the other arm. She untangled herself from the children and nurses and trotted over.

"Myrtle, you're here!" Sally smoothed her ruffled skirts, which hit just below the knee like a little girl's. Her whole outfit was oddly childish and old-fashioned, in fact—lacy and beribboned, her hair in ringlets under a bonnet-like hat. "But, Mr. Hardcastle—nobody told me you were ill. It isn't on account of me, I hope."

Father, still hiding behind Peony—who was regarding Charley with a suspicious flick of her tail—gave a weak smile and shook his head.

"What are you doing here?" I hadn't meant to be so rude. Apparently the night had not quite worn off yet.

"And how do you know our Miss Hardcastle?" Miss Judson indicated Aunt Helena, who appeared to be mustering the children into an army, brandishing her walking stick like a baton.

Sally glowed. "Isn't she wonderful? She came to my lecture last night and told me all about Hospital Sunday and the Ladies Committee, then offered to bring me to see everything for myself. You Hardcastles are all so marvelous."

I managed to hold my tongue, and Miss Judson cleverly diverted the conversation. "And Mrs. Dudley? We've never seen you without her company, Miss Snowcroft."

Now she looked embarrassed. "I . . . might not have told her. She's rather—" She took a deep breath and stroked Charley's brown-spotted ear.

"Overprotective?" Miss Judson suggested.

Loyalty prevailed. *"Busy.* She's very busy with SWOBS, you know. And you mustn't let me keep you, either! You all look like you're on an Urgent Mission." She said this with a wink and a nod, like something from a penny dreadful. What did she think we were doing?

Before Father could blurt anything out, I said, "We've lost our Cook." Next thing, he'd be recruiting Sally to the Investigation—and that poor girl had enough on her plate already.

"The woman in the splendid trousers? I think she went into one of those outbuildings." Sally signaled the direction with a subtle inclination of her head, pointing not being Viscountesslike. With thanks, we steered Father and Peony where she'd indicated. Father hunched in the bath chair, sulking.

"Thss is noh dihnified," he muttered.

"Not dignified," muttered Peony.

The sturdy brick structure's wide double doors were cracked open. Just outside, an iron sign reading LAUNDRY ROOM #2 politely stood guard, while a handwritten notice posted on the door apologized, OUT OF ORDER.

"Well," Miss Judson said, "that explains what became of Cook."

"Mmph," agreed Father, and she wheeled him through the doors. I followed on their heels.

The hospital laundry was curiously quiet. Well, of the clank of steam pipes and the clatter of wringers and washtubs and the splash of water, that is: laundry maids buzzed about in frustration, giving odd looks to a vast machine standing idle in the center of the room, and even odder looks to the unfamiliar woman currently inspecting their facilities for wrongdoing.

"Does it need more coal?" somebody asked.

"Mebbe the chimney's clogged."

The machine—I could just make out the label on its curved side:

HOWARD'S PATENTED STEAM DISINFECTOR

—looked like a train locomotive missing the wheels and driver's cab. A huge black drum sat in a curved brick base, with a great circular hatch like an oversized pressure cooker at one end. Queued alongside were great carts of folded white sheets, green blankets, and heaps and heaps of aprons.

"I'll fetch Maintenance," one maid said—but the burly woman beside her grabbed her arm with fingers like red sausages.

"You'll do no sooch thing. If'n we get *them* involved, you know what'll 'appen. 'Eaps o' paperwork—fill out this form an' that form and get it all signed by on 'igh, and in the meantime it'll take a fortnight for anyone a'tall to come oop an' 'ave a look at t'ings, and all the laundry piling up wiv nowhere to dry it—and then *you* can explain to Matron why the Private Ward has no clean sheets!"

Father, Miss Judson, Peony, and I went largely unnoticed amid the mechanical difficulties. Cook spotted us long enough for one brusque nod. "Now, then. Let's have a look at the patient. Move aside, girls, give us some room." The staff fell back with a mixture of awe and obedience as Cook sized up the situation.

"It won't fire up," one of the laundresses offered. "We can't tell what's stopping 'er up."

"Harrumph." Cook regarded the Disinfector with a sort of righteous skepticism, as if she could merely *stare* the equipment back into line. She walked about it, giving various parts of the machine pats or tugs or raps with her knuckles or spanner—and in one alarming instance, a good sound kick. I watched with growing respect and admiration. I'd never realized what a skilled Investigator Cook was!

I gradually worked out that a Steam Disinfector—when it was working, anyway—must be intended to send a powerful blast of steam through a cart of laundry wheeled inside, killing any germs left behind after washing. My eyes wandered from the machine to the building itself, with its high ceiling and network of steam pipes, along with the requisite huge windows set into the brick walls. At long last, Cook identified a potential source of the problem and addressed the machine's vast drum.

"Door's stuck," she huffed. She inserted the handle of her spanner into the door latch as a lever and began prying.

All at once, the metal hatch gave a furious squeal and popped open, spilling out a load of bedding onto the laundry room floor.

"Well," Cook said judiciously. "There's your problem." She poked at the linens, lifting the corner of one of the green blankets.

After a curious pause, one of the laundresses let out a powerful shriek.

Father burst to his feet with a cry of vindication. "Aha!"

A body had tumbled out with the laundry.

13

DIRTY LAUNDRY

> . . . just as vital evidence may be lost if the body
> has been moved to a secondary location from
> where the crime took place. Every effort must be
> made to locate the site of the murder and examine
> that scene in detail.

–H. M. Hardcastle, *Foundations of Legal Medicine*

After that, things moved swiftly. Father handed Peony to me, whereupon I promptly set her down on the bath chair, whereupon she promptly vanished, contaminating the crime scene with fur and crankiness. Father snapped his fingers imperiously—was that how he treated his clerks at work?—and everyone sprang to. Except nobody seemed to *know* what to do, exactly. Father's charades weren't much to go on.

Cook took charge. "All right," she said, clapping her hands at the army of shocked laundresses. "This is a Crime Scene, and it is now under the Jurisdiction of the Magistrate's Office. Miss Ada?" No one seemed to note that Miss Judson didn't technically work for the Magistrate's Office, at least directly.

"Quite," she said. "We shall need the police, a physician to examine the body, and . . . Governor Greeley, I should think." Father gave a superfluous grunt of approval, and Miss Judson deputized various laundresses and sent them on their way. "Cook, get someone to help you clear the area until the constables arrive. Now. What do we have here?"

As the onlookers reluctantly drained away, Miss Judson drew out her sketchbook and recorded the scene: the Steam Disinfector with its hatch flung wide, the tide of laundry pouring out, the body of the dead man. I approached the corpse with circumspection, carefully trying to determine what had happened before barging in and—

"Father!" I yelped. "Come back from there!"

Father had abandoned the bath chair and charged headlong for the man in the laundry, like he was greeting a long-lost friend. I tried to tug him back before he hurt himself—or the evidence—but he shook me off with a grunt.

Miss Judson glanced up from her sketch. "Really, Mr. Hardcastle, you ought to stay back. And sit down— you look quite pale."

"I do nod loog pale," he growled. "An' he's *my* muhrer viddim!"

Miss Judson and I exchanged a Look over the top of Father's bent head.

"Well, do you recognize him, then?" I said. "Who is it?"

Father couldn't answer that. The poor fellow was mostly still covered with tangled sheets, but the position he'd landed in exposed his head, at least. His most striking feature was that he was completely bald, and his head and face were very red, as if badly sunburned. He seemed older than Father, although that was difficult to tell for certain.

"Is he a doctor?" Doubt crept into my voice. Under the laundry, I could make out a shabby tweed jacket, a threadbare shirt-collar with the collar stay poking through. No white coat, if there ever had been one. "He looks more like a patient from the Charity Ward."

Before I could stop him, Father reached in—with his bare hands!—and tugged down the man's collar. "Father!" I wailed. "What are you doing?"

"Chegging for bruises," he said matter-of-factly. "Ligashure margs or"—he waved a hand—"Tardy spoz?"

"Tardieu spots," I said faintly.

"Ho—whazzis?" Father's raspy voice was full of disturbing eagerness as he looked up at Miss Judson. "Whah sor' of man has pierzed eahs?"

"At this point, a dead one," she said, kneeling beside him. They made a strange pair: she in her neat wool skirt and coat, smart felt hat perched on her dark coiled hair; he in his white pyjamas and flannel dressing gown, sitting together in a heap of laundry with a dead man like they were at a picnic. My stomach gave a curious flutter and I bit my lip.

"How'd he geh' so sunburd?" Father said. "Ih' February?"

"Scalded by the steam, perhaps?" Miss Judson suggested.

"Wouldn't his clothes be wet?" I said, but they weren't listening.

Father's disturbance of the victim's collar revealed something else. "Is tha' a bruise?" He peeled back the cloth to reveal a blurry blot of red, like Sally's birthmark. I think he would have whistled, if he could manage it. "A daddoo!"

Miss Judson bent closer to examine the evidence, her fingertips brushing Father's. Their gazes met, for far too long a moment.

I coughed. "The tattoo?" I prompted. Loudly.

Father winced. "A rose. I thig?" (It looked like a squashed plum to me, Dear Reader.)

"Earrings and a tattoo," Miss Judson mused, sketching away. "A sailor?"

"Ih Swihburh'?" Father frowned. Swinburne was about as far from the sea as you could get in England.

"In a hospital laundry Disinfector?" she returned. "But I see your point."

They went on in this vein for several minutes, making a thorough mess of the scene, surely scattering evidence everywhere. Although this was likely not the original crime scene, there might still be clues to be collected and it was best to disturb things as little as possible. Miss Judson knew better. Gradually I found myself creeping back, closer and closer to the bath chair, where Peony waited, looking insufferably smug.

Cook reappeared, huffing with satisfaction. "The constables will be here shortly, and your witnesses are organized and waiting. And Herself would like a word." She peered at the body with the look she'd given the Steam Disinfector—the sort of expression that made you think the fellow was lucky to be dead.

"That color ain't natural," she noted, with a cluck of her tongue, like she was checking an underdone roast. "You can get that from a coal stove. From the smoke."

"Mizz' Stazz'berry, you're a ge'ius," Father said. "Carboh' monogside, of course."

I crossed my arms. I would have concluded carbon monoxide poisoning. Eventually.

"Was that how he was killed, then?" Miss Judson raised her eyes to examine the vast cavity of the Disinfector. "He crawled into the machine and asphyxiated?"

"Grawled—or *puzhd*?" Father said.

Cook grunted noncommittally. I must say, Dear Reader, that she was handling her own first post-mortem exam with remarkable equanimity. "Think the heat would've killed him first," she said. "It's a good hiding place, though. Freezin' in here, until you start the water to boil."

She was right. The chilly laundry shed provided the perfect conditions to preserve a body. Which was our luck, I supposed—more than forty-eight hours had passed since Father witnessed the attack, and he'd been lying in here all that time.

"Suppose you could wheel 'im out in one of those carts," Cook continued. "Or down a laundry chute."

I looked up sharply—but held my tongue. If Father hadn't noticed the laundry chute right outside the WC, that wasn't my fault.

A gasp from the doorway broke up the party. Sally stood in the threshold with Charley, a hand to her throat. "I know that man," she whispered.

"What?" I don't know which of us said that, Dear Reader, but we turned to stare at her en masse. "How?" I demanded, just as Miss Judson asked, "Who is he?"

Sally shook her head. "No, I don't really *know* him—I mean, I've seen him. I think. At a lecture. A man—someone who looked a bit like that came up to me afterward. I thought he wanted an autograph, but he was raving something—I couldn't make any of it out. Mrs. Dudley sent him away, thank goodness."

Father got to his feet. "Whehr was thss legshure?"

He'd grown protective again, now that his client was in distress. "Ih Swihburh?"

Sally shook her head. "I can't remember. I meet so many people, and they're not . . . always friendly." Recalling what Genie had told us about the threatening letters the newspaper had received, I gave a shiver unrelated to the cold quarters, or the dead body at our feet. "That can't be the same man," she said doubtfully. "How could it?"

"Doh' let ih trouble you, Mizz Sowcroff." Father's voice was soothing. "Th' poor man's pro'lly jus' ad uhforshudate vagrad who made th' miztague of crawlig ih'side for warff."

What sort of nonsense was Father spinning for Sally? I noticed he hadn't dragged *her* off to a hospital governor's office in the middle of the night. All at once I felt a rush of something ugly and unfamiliar. I tried to quash it. None of this was Sally's fault.

"You doh' neeh to see this." Father tried to block Sally's view of the body. "Muhrl, why doh' you figh' Zally zomewhere ouh of th' cold?"

Maybe she'd like a tour of the morgue.

I caught Sally by the frilly, childish arm and pulled her—more firmly than she deserved, I'm afraid—away from the crime scene. Charley gave one soundless yip at my effrontery toward his mistress, then licked my wrist, ashamed of his rudeness. Sally kept glancing backward, craning her neck at the dead man. "Who could he be?" she asked.

I tried to remind myself that Sally was (probably) a Viscountess, and more importantly, Father's client—and with Father indisposed, she was my responsibility.

"Please don't concern yourself, Miss Snowcroft." I summoned my most professional tones. "I'm sorry you were subjected to such a distressing sight." I meant the words, yet somehow they felt false and faintly traitorous. More gently, I led Sally to the nearby brick planter to sit, well out of view of the laundry shed. "Would you like me to hold Charley?"

It was nothing at all like holding Peony, who snuggles firmly into your shoulder and grips with needlelike claws. Charley wouldn't stop *wriggling*, and his fur was spiky and strange poking out from his jumper. And his tiny darting tongue went absolutely everywhere.

In a moment, Sally was laughing at me. "You can put him down," she said. "He won't leave me." (Yet another difference between the species, Dear Reader.)

As Charley curled atop Sally's feet, I settled beside her, torn between interrogating her about the dead man and protecting her, like Father would do. Her freckled face was pinched, and she tugged one long sandy curl.

"I'm about to say something terribly selfish," she warned me, "but will your father still be able to help me, now that he has to work on a murder, too?"

Selfish wasn't exactly the word that came to mind.

Still expertly channeling Father, I choked out, "Murder? Oh, no—like he said, surely it's just a terrible accident."

Sally's expression was as scornful as Peony at her best. "I saw the bruise on the back of his head. Someone killed that poor man."

Now I was torn between interrogating her, protecting her, and dashing back to get a better look at the dead sailor's skull. I managed a very Hardcastlian "Er" before recovering my professionalism. "You mustn't worry," I said firmly. "The police will take over here, and your case is being *very* well looked after. Father's finest people are working on it night and day." Father's finest people being, naturally, Miss Judson, Mr. Blakeney, Peony, and me. (I kept that bit to myself—my efforts to inspire confidence in my client would fall rather flat if she learned the identity of her crack legal team.) "He's very close to proving your identity."

"That won't really help, though, will it? I still won't know what happened to me—how Charley and I wound up in Australia with the Cookes, or what became of everyone else aboard the *Persephone*. We'll still be an unsolved mystery." Sally opened her square locket, sadly peering at the silent figures within. "Sometimes I wish I'd just stayed in Melbourne. I wouldn't have come at all, but Mrs. Dudley . . ." She flicked tears from her eyes. "I'm afraid she told your father the truth. There wasn't anything left when Father—Mr. Cooke—died. I couldn't pay the fees for school, and I couldn't run the shop. So I took the settlement from the SWOBS Benefits Club and came here. It just about covered the fare."

A benefits club was a sort of inexpensive insurance policy. Popular among tradesmen, they were sometimes called friendly societies (as in the Friendly Society of Seamen or Woolworkers or Orphaned Viscountesses). Families joined together and paid in a few pence each week, then received back a settlement if the member died or was injured and unable to work. This clicked something in my brain. "Your father had insurance with SWOBS? I thought you said he wasn't a sailor."

Her eyes lit up. "But he must have been, to join the fund and receive the benefits! Why didn't I think of that?" This was the first spark of excitement I'd seen from her, and she clasped my hands eagerly.

"We'll look into it," I promised her, excited to have something to go on now as well.

Sally gave herself a shake that Charley would have appreciated. "Oh, I'm just horrid!" she exclaimed. "Going on about my nonsense when your father's in hospital and that man is dead." She bit her lip so fiercely I thought she'd draw blood. Charley lifted an eyebrow in concern.

"It's not nonsense," I couldn't help saying. "Your case is important."

She gave a brave sniff. "Maybe I can help, some-how. With this, I mean." She waved a hand toward the laundry shed. Admittedly, my experience with Viscountesses was rather limited, but Sally seemed to be more interested in murder Investigations than was commonly advertised. Of course, I reflected, she was new to Viscountessdom, too.

The treacherous part of me that knew what Father would say threatened to intervene, but I pushed it down firmly. "Try to remember where you might have seen that man before."

She nodded uncertainly. "I really don't think it was him. But I'll try."

I never got to find out where Sally might have encountered the dead man, for in the next moment, our tender scene fell absolutely to pieces. Aunt Helena loomed up before us like a threatening storm in her purple-and-grey morning suit.

"Helena Myrtle, how *could* you!" She fairly yanked me to my feet, and Sally bounded to hers in solidarity. Charley bounced around like a tiny whirlwind, yapping frantically. "Your ladyship, I'm dreadfully sorry. My niece should have more sense than to subject you to something so unseemly. Honestly, Helena Myrtle, you're as bad as your father."

"Oh, but she didn't. They didn't—" Sally tried to say, to no avail. Aunt Helena had taken her firmly in hand and was herding her away from the laundry like a sheepdog collecting a wayward lamb.

They didn't get far before running headlong into

the rest of the Ladies Hospital Committee, who were not overjoyed to have their visit inconvenienced by a murder, let alone discover that their prize acquisition—the Right Honorable Ethel, Viscountess Snowcroft—had been usurped by Aunt Helena and her morbid great-niece.

One of them was particularly unhappy. Caroline Munjal took one look at me standing beside—well, a bit behind—Sally, and her face crumpled with betrayal. "Myrtle!" she cried. "You came here with Ethel— without *me*?"

14

MALPRACTICE

Innovative scientists are experimenting with "optography," attempting to capture images within the retinæ of the dead, much like a photograph. It may one day prove possible to reproduce the very last sights seen by murder victims.

-H. M. Hardcastle, *Foundations of Legal Medicine*

Dear Reader, some days in the life of an Aspiring Investigator are fated to be more challenging than others. Looking after one's father in hospital, identifying murder victims, comforting overset clients, dodging angry aunts, and soothing sulky friends is enough to try the most Exceptionally Forbearing soul.

Aunt Helena and the Ladies Committee took Sally off our hands, although frankly I think she'd have been safer with us. Then Miss Judson, Cook, Peony, and I were summarily excluded from the Investigation proper by the arrival of the constables. Father, of course, held court over the scene, forgetting he was still dressed in hospital pyjamas. The policemen politely pretended to forget as well.

Detective Constable Carstairs had brought three other men, including two junior members of the constabulary that I recognized. D.C. Carstairs had recently been promoted (solving three murders in a fortnight does wonders for one's career), and I knew him well. Although I must say he didn't seem especially pleased to see me again.

Miss Judson and I bade farewell to Cook and Peony (who was perfectly happy to be returned to the basket that had borne the Chelsea buns) and withdrew to a sunny corner of the courtyard.

"Now what?" I demanded.

"Now we wait," Miss Judson said with annoying composure. "With hope they'll identify the body quickly, the killer will step forward, and this whole unpleasant episode will be wrapped up by the end of the day."

"You must be feverish," I said. "What about Father? He's not safe here—not only is he making a spectacle of himself, what if the murderer comes after him next? We must bring him home."

She sighed and straightened her hat. "As much as it pains me to admit, I am not a qualified nurse. Do you know how to care for someone recovering from tonsillectomy?"

I hadn't read the clinical manual, but I imagined

it involved more rest and less breaking and entering. Miss Judson continued, "Furthermore, I can state with scientific certainty that there is approximately zero chance that your father would consent to leave the hospital now."

"Based on what?" I scoffed, and she eyed me evenly.

"Would *you* leave?"

"Point taken." I slumped down onto one of the planters, the cold bricks chilling my backside through my skirts and petticoats. I dug out my notebook. "We'd better get to work, then."

"Beginning with what you and your father uncovered last night."

"Are you sure you wouldn't rather *he* tell you?"

She glanced across the courtyard, to where Father was once more engaged in pantomime, acting something out for the bemused constables. It appeared to be a gorilla riding a unicycle. "No. Proceed."

I explained our errand to Governor Greeley's office, including his curious artifacts, and Father's discovery of the donations to SWOBS. "Although that doesn't seem particularly suspicious anymore, since the victim turned out to be male."

"Your father didn't recognize him." She flipped her sketchbook to the drawing of the victim. "We should pass this picture around the staff and patients and see if anyone else does."

"We found his earring in Dr. Kinkaid's laboratory,"

I reminded her. "He should be considered a suspect. He's been acting strangely since we met him."

"He might say the same about us."

I ignored that. "Father told us the killer was a doctor. Remember? *White coat.*"

"He also said *bald* and *choked.* So far he's only been thirty percent correct. All our original arguments for doubting his testimony still stand: he was under the influence of anæsthesia and morphine and witnessed the attack from some considerable distance. At night. Perhaps now he'll be able to give us a more cogent account, but until then, what else do we have?"

I returned to my notes. "Nurse Ling knows something. And Matron, too, probably—you saw the way she demoted her, just for talking to us. But are they suspects or witnesses?"

"Miss Ling will require a subtle approach. We don't want to get her in even more trouble."

"Why don't we just tell the constables?" Let them handle a murder for once while the Hardcastles focused on Hardcastle problems. Like tonsillitis and the Snowcroft inheritance.

"I said *subtle.*" She was looking at D.C. Carstairs, whose questions appeared to have reduced one of the laundry maids to tears. "What do we know about the victim? Besides being a sailor, that is?"

"A down-on-his-luck sailor. Did you see how shabby his clothes were?" As I said that, a keen light dawned in Miss Judson's eye—and I think I had the very same revelation.

"Well, how fortunate that we know someone who has devoted her life to helping sailors who are down on their luck. Perhaps Mrs. Dudley might recognize him."

I drew a circle in the dirt of the planter, then another, and joined them with a single bar. "We also know how he died. Carbon monoxide poisoning makes the skin look red." It was a fascinating, if diabolical, toxin: it fooled the body into thinking it was oxygen, crowding out oxygen in the bloodstream, until the victim simply ceased to breathe. It often struck people sleeping in rooms with poor gas fittings or leaky stoves. The deep red flush suggested that he'd suffered significant exposure before he died.

"But how was he exposed to it? Perhaps he did crawl inside the Steam Disinfector for warmth, as your father said."

"Father saw someone being choked. That means an attack—a *crime*—occurred inside this hospital. What are the odds of some unrelated person just happening to die in the laundry on the same night?" I tossed up my hands, such a calculation beyond me. "This is Father's body, and the killer hid him in that machine."

"Mmm. But who was it?"

I stood up. The constables were dispersing—and I wanted to get back to the original crime scene before Father led them there. "I told you. Dr. Kinkaid. Or

Matron. Maybe they were working together." It would have taken two people to move the body, if one of them was tiny Matron Finch.

"How do you suppose they even poisoned a man with carbon monoxide? Not to mention, why?"

"We won't know why until we learn who," I said. "But *how* is something we can figure out."

A few moments later found us rapping on Dr. Kinkaid's laboratory door once more. The porter with the ill-fitting coat and shiny shoes was in the hallway, and ducked away swiftly at our approach.

Dr. Kinkaid was working at one of the microscope stations, studying something on a Petri plate through a magnifying headset, which he wrestled from his head when we stepped inside. "Now what?" he said crossly—which made Miss Judson turn her sunniest smile on him.

"We thought we'd warn you to expect a visit any moment from the police."

"Are you *still* on about the phantom murder? I thought we'd settled that."

"Didn't you hear about the dead man in the laundry? My father was right." Those words filled me with a warm rush of satisfaction.

Dr. Kinkaid slammed a drawer shut, but he seemed more inconvenienced than concerned. "Well, who was the poor devil?"

"We thought you might know." Miss Judson held

out the sketch she'd made, complete with pierced ears and squashed-plum tattoo.

Dr. Kinkaid offered up the surefire admission of any suspect who'd known the victim very well indeed: "Never saw the man before in my life."

I pounced on this as concrete proof. "Where were you Monday night between the hours of three p.m. and one a.m.?"

"Ah, my alibi. I figured we'd get to this eventually."

"Alibi?" I echoed.

He misunderstood me. "Latin for *elsewhere*. I assumed you'd know that."

"I *do* know it. Why did you *say* it?"

Dr. Kinkaid yawned. "Customarily when presented with a murder*ee*, one expects there to be a corresponding murder*er*. You asked where I was when—presumably—the crime occurred. And presumably expect me to give you some story that can be verified by unimpeachable witnesses. Perhaps a bishop or a member of the royal family."

"Your sarcasm is contributing little to this discussion," Miss Judson remarked. I agreed—and what's more, his defensive attitude made him look even more suspicious. I thought back to the newspaper article about the Fenian bombers. Perhaps the dashing but disdainful Dr. Kinkaid had a dark past he wished to conceal. True, killing someone with dynamite was quite different to poisoning them with carbon monoxide—but they both took some knowledge of chemistry. Which Dr. Kinkaid clearly possessed.

"Do you have an alibi or not?" I pressed.

Dr. Kinkaid rose to wash out the Petri plate. "As it happens, I do not. *Nor* do I have a motive. I'm a doctor, not a murderer."

"But it happened here, in your laboratory," I pointed out. "Where we found the victim's earring."

Dr. Kinkaid focused on his washing-up. "What was the cause of death in this so-called murder? If you recall, we saw no signs of a struggle, not a single drop of blood, not even a beaker out of place."

"He was poisoned with carbon monoxide." I described the victim's physical condition.

He betrayed his interest by whistling. He set the plate in the sink and turned our way. "That's almost brilliant. But how would you do it? It could probably be administered during surgery, I suppose, but it's not like we keep tanks of the stuff . . ." His voice trailed off.

"What?"

He swore under his breath. "That explains it. Hardcastle! Describe the condition of this room when you opened it yesterday morning. Quick now."

"Dark," I said automatically.

"And?" he prompted.

I thought back. "Cold. You thought the heat was broken."

Dr. Kinkaid was nodding. "I even had Maintenance

up to check the radiators. But they never checked *these*." He clapped a hand against one of the brass fixtures mounted in the long workbenches: a delicate pipe extending upward from a circular base, with a wooden handle for adjustments. The Bunsen burner.* The *gas* Bunsen burner. I gasped—I couldn't help it. The very idea made me suck in my breath, as if I, too, could not get enough oxygen.

Dr. Kinkaid wiggled the handle, and we heard the telltale hiss of gas. It worked exactly like a light fixture. If you turned on the gas but did not light the flame, it would flood the room with poisonous fumes.

"Is your laboratory open twenty-four hours a day?" Miss Judson asked.

"Certainly not. I have valuable experiments and equipment in here." He paused, realizing that his security was not nearly as strong as he'd thought—or that he'd just incriminated himself.

"Someone had to know that opening one of the valves would prove deadly," I said. "Carbon monoxide gas doesn't kill instantly. The victim would have to have been incapacitated long enough for the poison to take effect." Which accounted for the bruise Sally had spotted.

---

* One of the many useful innovations of busy German chemist Robert Bunsen, who has also discovered two elements, had a mineral named for him, explored Icelandic volcanoes, and survived arsenic poisoning (probably not all at the same time).

Miss Judson was regarding the Bunsen burner grimly. "That's premeditation."

"Wait, wait." Dr. Kinkaid's scowl had deepened. "Let's go back. Your father said he saw *what*, exactly?"

"A bald man choked by someone in a white coat," I said flatly.

Dr. Kinkaid's hand instinctively patted down his own lapels. "Ah. Did anyone happen to mention *why* I might want to kill a total stranger, at random, for the he—heck of it?"

Inadvertently, my gaze darted to the poor Norway rats, some of whom were already sulking because they'd missed breakfast. (Dear Reader, if you've ever had a pet, that expression is unmistakable.)

Dr. Kinkaid let out a laugh. "Aha, a fiendish experiment! You fancy me a Jekyll and Hyde character, do you?" He rubbed his hands together, adopting a hunched and menacing posture.

"Now that you bring it up . . . ," Miss Judson said.

Shaking his coat back into place, he said, "May I ask who your other suspects might be? Or am I the lucky winner?"

"Who else has access to the laboratory? Matron Finch?"

Dr. Kinkaid recoiled with distaste. "She has keys to every room in the hospital, I'm afraid. I've never seen her in here, though, thank goodness."

I glanced at Miss Judson. "She would know how the Bunsen burners work."

"So would anyone who works in a hospital," Dr. Kinkaid countered. "Or anyone who's ever operated a gaslight—which is everyone."

"But *not* everyone would know how to kill someone with it," Miss Judson said, voice dark.

15

STATEMENT
AGAINST INTEREST

The human skeleton contains a meticulous record of a person's life. Many details of a subject's identity—not merely age, height, and ethnicity, but also occupation, diet, economic class, and health conditions—can be determined from skeletal remains. Our life story is literally written in our bones.

-H. M. Hardcastle, *Foundations of Legal Medicine*

The police did come to Dr. Kinkaid's laboratory after that, and he welcomed them much more magnanimously, showing them the burners and where we'd found the earring as if pointing out Destinations of Note on a holiday tour. But Father was no longer among them, which sent a spike of alarm through me.

"Relax," Miss Judson said. "Nothing could have happened to him between the courtyard and the Men's

Ward." Ominous tension hung in the air after that remark—and a moment later we dashed off down the shiny corridor to Father's Ward.

We swung through the green doors just in time to see a familiar nurse tucking him back into bed. "You'll sleep well tonight," she predicted, "after all that excitement and fresh air!" I recognized her now; we'd met her with Probationer Ling the morning Father was admitted.

Father looked weary but victorious, like after winning a tough case. "Father, you were right!" I cried, seizing him by the arm. A hug didn't seem quite appropriate, but the moment should be marked somehow. Father gave me a warm nod and squeezed back.

"Nurse Keene, did you hear about the man found in the laundry?" Miss Judson slipped the question in as naturally as asking about the weather.

She did not look up immediately, just kept arranging Father's blankets. "Zizter?" Father's voice was gentle. "D'you know soh'thig?"

She dipped down below his bed, as if to check the chamber pot. "Careful," she murmured. "There are little birds everywhere."

Little birds—*finches*? Matron's spies! I stiffened and clutched at Father all the harder, but Miss Judson calmly doffed her coat and draped it on the back of the hard bedside chair as if nothing at all was amiss. She seated herself, and Father patted the edge of the bed for me to follow suit. I wasn't sure what was up, but I could tell Miss Judson had a plan.

"Well," she said in her schoolroom voice—the one that reverberates from walls and ceilings and reaches even the farthest corners of a room. Or a cricket pitch. "It's a good thing the police are involved now. You must be so relieved, Mr. Hardcastle." She nudged me with her knee, sending my heart leaping into my throat—but I recovered in time to follow her cue.

"Especially since you can't remember what happened," I said, earning a look of bewilderment from Father.

"Buh I saw ev'rythig—"

"Yes, it's really too bad it was *too dark to make out any details.*" Miss Judson's eyes bored into Father's. "And you can't identify the culprit."

He finally understood. "No, I cadt," he muttered—which was no more than the truth. "An' this is nod helpig."

"Dr. Kinkaid said you probably won't remember anything else," I added. He'd said nothing of the kind, of course, but all things considered I felt nary a twinge of remorse giving false testimony against a murder suspect. Two beds down, another nurse had paused in the act of re-sleeving a pillow, face eagerly turned our way. "But we'll pass around the sketch and see if anyone knows who the vi—the poor man is, or how he happened to fall asleep in the laundry."

Father's scowl returned, and Miss Judson rose grace-
fully and bent as if to kiss him on the cheek. He pulled
away, startled, but she murmured something in his ear
that I couldn't make out. "Good night, then. We'll see
you tomorrow, sir."

She grasped me by the hand (she was going to dislo-
cate my shoulder at this rate) and hauled me from the
Ward, personally saying goodbye to every nurse and
patient we passed. But I Observed that she had left her
coat behind, still hanging on the back of Father's chair.

We lingered outside in the courtyard, making a
show of admiring the stunted shrubbery. Porters were
taking down the welcome banner, this month's visit
from the Ladies Hospital Committee having proved
a disappointment, and the police had cordoned off
the laundry room. I wondered where they'd taken the
body—off to Dr. Munjal's Police Morgue, or down to
Mr. Davis here at the hospital?

After a few minutes, we heard the hush of rubber
soles on the cobblestones. We spun round, expecting to see Father's new nurse. Instead, a breathless
Probationer Ling hastened toward us, carrying Miss
Judson's ulster.

"You ought to be more careful," she said softly.
"Things have a way of disappearing round here."

My heart leaped with sudden understanding. "*You*
took the sketchbook!"

"I'm sorry about that—I didn't want Matron to find

it. I didn't know what else to do." Nurse Ling fumbled in her pocket and withdrew a couple folded pieces of paper, the very pages that had been ripped from Miss Judson's book.

"How kind of you." Miss Judson hooked her arm into Nurse Ling's, the better to hurry her to an unobtrusive corner. But Miss Ling took us in a different direction.

"Behind the stables. There's a blind spot where the porters go to smoke." She managed a slight smile. "And some of the nurses."

The stables were adjacent to the old Anatomy Building and morgue, and Nurse Ling led us to a narrow alley between the two buildings. It proved to be warm and private, but not especially welcoming. The brick yard was full of refuse, stubs of cigarillos and matches, and smelled strongly of horse and manure. And other odors that were best not examined too closely.

"I really shouldn't be talking to you," she began, glancing round the brick corner for lurking finches. A pigeon perched in the eaves possessed a particularly suspicious attitude, and I shooed it away.

"How dare Matron threaten to sack you!" I burst out. "We can't let her get away with this!" If Nurse Ling lost her post at the Royal Swinburne, it could mean the end of her medical career. If she was fired without character references, it could mean she'd never work again.

"The Charity Ward's not so bad. And you oughtn't make a fuss over me."

Miss Judson's eyes were full of righteous fire. "I'm afraid 'not making a fuss' isn't something we're particularly good at."

Nurse Ling kicked at a matchstick, smile twitching. "I noticed that."

"We know you saw something," I said. "Or else Matron wouldn't have threatened you."

Her gaze went everywhere but to our faces. "Gossip's against the Royal's Code of Conduct," she finally said.

"Well, you've already been demoted for it," I pointed out. "It's not like you can do any more harm by telling us."

"I'm not sure that logic holds up," Miss Judson said. "But carry on, Miss Ling. Whatever you know could be important."

"Did you see something the night of the murder? At Dr. Kinkaid's laboratory, maybe?"

"Dr. Kinkaid?" Her voice was sharp with surprise, and she shook her head. "No, not then."

"Then *when*?"

Miss Judson put a forestalling hand on my arm. "You could always tell the police if you're more comfortable." That comment was calculated to guarantee that Miss Ling would *not* find offering a witness statement to the constables the preferable alternative.

She hesitated, then said in a determined rush, "The

morning your father was admitted, I was changing the sheets in the Men's Ward—it's part of our duties, as probationers, you know, the linen shifts. And when I came down here with the dirties, I saw Dr. Kinkaid out back near the laundries, arguing with someone." She glanced about, too well aware that we were not as concealed as we might have liked. "A man. Not from the hospital. I didn't know him."

I sucked in my breath. "Was it this man?" I waved to Miss Judson to show her the drawing. Nurse Ling studied it for a moment, but shook her head.

"He had a hat on. I'm sorry."

"It's quite all right. Please go on. Did you happen to hear what they were arguing about?"

"I couldn't understand them. They were speaking French or something."

Miss Judson looked thoughtful. "Gaelic?"

"Maybe." This idea seemed to intrigue Nurse Ling. "I've heard him—the surgeon, that is—singing sometimes. The tunes sound Irish, but I can't make out the words."

I sank against the warm brick, trying to make sense of her account, images of Fenian bombers bounding about my brain (not that I exactly knew what one looked like). Dr. Kinkaid had argued with an unknown Irish man near the laundry where the body was found. But that had happened hours before Father had seen the struggle in the corridor, so it was unlikely that he was the victim. Unless he'd come back later.

"Did you stay to the end of the quarrel?" I asked.

"I had the *laundry*." Her grin broke free. "I marched it right between them. The Code of Conduct applies to doctors too, doesn't it? Sent him packing, I don't mind saying."

Miss Judson hid her smile. "Quite right. Did you relate this to Matron Finch?"

"Course not," she said. "But I told the other girls so they could have an eye out, should the man come back. I did think he and Dr. Kinkaid seemed very familiar."

I asked the question I'd been avoiding. "Was Dr. Kinkaid angry?"

Nurse Ling's eyes flashed. "Spitting, I'd say. Looked like to wring the bloke's neck, if I hadn't interrupted them."

ༀ

As Miss Judson and I wended our way through the outbuildings to finally take leave of the Royal Swinburne for the day (for two days, in my case), we spotted Sally attempting to disentangle herself from a crowd of adoring children. Aunt Helena and the rest of the Ladies Committee, including Caroline, were nowhere in sight. Sally was pressing Charley's paw to an inkpad and stamping every surface offered to her, including a couple of casts. Charley was remarkably tolerant of this.

"The poor thing must be exhausted," Miss Judson said. "Let's go rescue them."

"They survived a shipwreck," I grumbled. "I think they can manage some sick children."

Sally's face brightened at our approach, and she finally signed the last "pawtograph," for a little girl whose face was bandaged and her arm in a sling. She clutched it to her chest like a treasure and toddled off, only to be scooped up in a huge embrace by Dr. Kinkaid, appearing from nowhere and *not*, I noted, in the custody of the police. Evidently they'd found his story more convincing.

"Polly," he said sternly, green eyes twinkling, "how is your arm?"

Her mouth was not visible due to the bandages, but her eyes shone, and she let Dr. Kinkaid examine the injured limb. "Very nice," he said. "You'll be home playing with your brothers in no time. And there'll be no more running into the street, aye?" He swung her into the air, then deposited her as gently as a feather onto the cobbles. All the while she gazed at him in adoration. A waiting nurse shepherded little Polly back with the other children, as Dr. Kinkaid watched with affection.

"That poor wain had her arm crushed in a carriage accident," he told us. "We were able to save it. There'll be some scarring, but she has her right arm." He seemed to marvel at his own success.

"Are you the doctor who's going to lead up the Free Surgery?" Sally sounded eager. "The Ladies Committee can't stop talking about the handsome, noble Irish surgeon."

Dr. Kinkaid—usually so self-assured—turned distinctly pink.

Miss Judson stepped in. "Miss Snowcroft, may I introduce Dr. Russell Kinkaid, Mr. Hardcastle's surgeon? Doctor, this is the Right Honorable Lady Snowcroft."

Dr. Kinkaid had to recognize her name, too, but gave no sign of it. "How do you do, your ladyship?"

"*Sally*," came her automatic reply, as she attempted to find a hand to shake with. She slipped the inkpad into her reticule, and Dr. Kinkaid gallantly produced a hankie, which she used to wipe Charley's paw. She was not completely successful; there were several smudges on her flouncy skirt. He pointed this out, and she laughed it off. "This is nothing. You should see what I can do to a pair of hockey bloomers!"

"You play field hockey?" Dr. Kinkaid sounded bemused.

Her smile clouded over. "Sally Cooke played hockey," she said. "Ethel Snowcroft probably doesn't."

"Boll—rubbish," said Dr. Kinkaid. "I have it on good authority a Viscountess can do whatever she likes."

"Tell Mrs. Dudley," she said. "Oh, dear. We've a lecture tonight, and I'll be late now. Myrtle and Miss

Judson, will you walk me out?" She took my arm and headed toward the gates.

"Where's my aunt?" I asked.

"You do seem to have a knack for slipping away from your chaperones," Miss Judson Observed.

Sally didn't answer directly. "Did you know that when you're a noblewoman, people will do almost anything you ask? It's really quite breathtaking."

"Er," I said, not sure I wanted to know what request Sally had made of Aunt Helena that was being miraculously granted. Before we could request clarification on the matter, Sally leaned closer to whisper in my ear.

"Myrtle—that man over there. I think he's following me."

I jerked to a stop, heart banging. Sally tugged me forward again. "Don't look," she said. "I mean, look, but don't *look* like you're looking. You see him?"

I chanced a peek over Charley's head, past Sally's fluffy hair and bonnet strings, and recognized the skinny porter with the polished shoes moving among the outbuildings. I could see why she was suspicious, though: hunched in his oversized jacket, he moved in a way best described as *slinking.* "It's all right," I said. "He works for the hospital."

Sally was walking faster now, squeezing Charley hard enough that he fidgeted. "I don't think so. See his shoes? They *squeak.* The staff here all have soft soles."

Miss Judson took up Sally's other side. "You're right," she said softly. "Well spotted."

I tried to keep pace with them. "I've seen him several times with Dr. Kinkaid. What should we do? We can't leave Sally— What if—?" I stopped, helpless, unwilling to say what Sally was probably already thinking: *What if it's the murderer? What if he's come back? What if he means to harm Sally?* And that led to worse thoughts, like, *What if he'd come back for Father?* I froze in my tracks, utterly unable to decide.

I have never been happier to greet an oncoming storm, Dear Reader. At that moment, a great purple cloud blew up to us, thunderclapping her way along with her walking stick. "Oh, your ladyship!" Aunt Helena waved a paper packet. "I'm afraid I couldn't find any pear drops, my lady, but I do have horehound, humbugs, and a jelly baby."

Sally clasped her hands together. "Aren't you a wonder, Miss Hardcastle! But my throat is quite better now."

Aunt Helena eyed us skeptically, as if Miss Judson and I had deliberately done something to make her errand irrelevant. I gazed longingly at the sweets; I rather like humbugs and I hadn't eaten anything since Cook's Chelsea buns this morning, which felt like an eternity ago. But Aunt Helena snatched them back. "These are for the Viscountess."

"Aunt Helena," Miss Judson volunteered, "we were just walking Miss Snowcroft to the tram."

Aunt Helena looked horrified. "You can't possibly take that filthy public transportation. I'll fetch us a cab. Come along, your ladyship."

And with that, Aunt Helena swept Sally off once more, thundering in her ear. Sally shot us a look of gratitude, and unless I am very much mistaken, I think Charley was laughing.

I was less reassured, but Miss Judson summed up the situation nicely. "Don't be silly. What better bodyguard could a Young Lady of Quality have than Aunt Helena?"

16

Balance of Probabilities

Close study of a wound can reveal the most minute details of murder: the type and size of the
weapon used, whether the assailant was right-
or left-handed, if the victim struggled or fought
back, even the time or location of the crime. This
evidence speaks as plainly as any eyewitness.

–H. M. Hardcastle, *Foundations of Legal Medicine*

Of course, getting Sally safely off the Royal Swinburne
grounds hardly solved the problem of the lurking
porter. I glanced around the courtyard, but he was
nowhere to be seen. "Where did he go? What if he's
after Father?"

Miss Judson tried to hide her own concern, but I
Observed the faintest crinkling of her brow. That
clinched things. I turned on my heel and set off across
the courtyard, in the direction Squeaky Shoes had

gone, I thought. We should have been able to track him by his footfalls, but the noises of a hospital settling in for the evening were surprisingly distracting.

Our path took us behind the outbuildings again, then looped back to the main gates. "There he is!" I tugged Miss Judson onward. Squeaky Shoes loitered in the brick archway, chatting with a nurse in a black mantle, his hand on her arm. I didn't recognize her at first, but as we drew surreptitiously closer, I spotted red curly hair. "That's Pethwick coming back on duty." I let out a sigh. "It looks like all he's guilty of is violating the Code of Conduct."

"Not much of a violation," Miss Judson noted, as Squeaky Shoes gave Nurse Pethwick a businesslike nod and headed away from the hospital—in exactly the opposite direction Sally and Aunt Helena had gone. "Well, that's a relief," she added, in a firm voice that *demanded* we feel relieved, whether we wanted to or not.

⁊

We did not have a chance to discuss the murder on the tram ride home, as it was far too crowded with commuters. But that hardly kept me from speculating about it. Who was the victim? What was a sailor doing skulking about the Royal Swinburne Hospital after hours? Someone at the hospital obviously knew him— but who? Dr. Kinkaid? Matron and her "little birds"? What about that dodgy porter? The trouble was, they all had access to the entire crime scene, not to mention the knowledge to commit the murder and cover it up—means and opportunity—but what was their motive? And why hide the victim in the laundry, instead of slipping him quietly into the morgue, no one the wiser?

I bit my fingers, fretting. As much as I longed to get home at last, I didn't like leaving Father alone. We might have put the killer off his trail for now, but that didn't mean he wouldn't change his mind and come after him later.

The tram clanged to a stop on High Street, and a familiar and very welcome personage climbed aboard, surprised to find us. "Stephen, Miss J.! Just the people I was coming to see." Mr. Blakeney, our favorite legal clerk, squeezed in beside us, annoying a lady whose frilly skirts were taking up more than her share of the seats. He carried a crisp file folder, which he handed off to me. "For your father," he said. When I started to peek inside, he put a hand atop mine. "Himself's eyes only, I'm afraid. It's not about the Snowcroft Affair."

Himself? That's what Father's staff called him. Before I could question him further, however, Mr. Blakeney added, "I do have good news on the Snowcroft front, though."

"We could use some," Miss Judson said, but this made Mr. Blakeney falter.

"Or bad news," he said. "Well, let's just go with *news.*"

"Perhaps you might tell us, and let us decide," Miss Judson said mildly.

"Right. Well, the probate court has set a date to hear Miss Snowcroft's case."

"That is good news!" I said. "She'll be so relieved."

"Reserve your judgment till you hear the rest." Mr. Blakeney rarely looked somber, so I commenced my reservations—and I had many. "It seems the Privy Council have taken an interest in the case, and somebody there is pulling strings to have the courts make a final decision. If we can't prove Sally's identity, conclusively, the property will revert to the Crown. She could lose everything."

I glared at him. That was the very opposite of good news! "Can they do that?" I demanded. "It's a civil case. How can the government interfere like that?"

He grimaced. "Well, it's technically Her Majesty's land, remember? My guess is it's the railway—they don't want the case tied up in probate court for years, so someone nudged someone, who called in a favor or two, and here we are."

I chewed on my cheek. Her Majesty's advisors—the Privy Council—included the Board of Trade, which oversaw the railways (and also apparently failed to properly Investigate shipwrecks). It would be just like them to meddle in something like this. Fuming, I kicked at the bottom of my seat.

"Which reminds me: where *are* we?" said Mr.

Blakeney. "Any further progress on tracing Sally's background?"

I glanced at Miss Judson, who sighed faintly. "We've been somewhat preoccupied with another matter, I'm afraid." She declined to elaborate on the Other Matter, so I followed suit.

"What about Genie's source?" I asked. "If she could get him to come forward . . ." I trailed off. Her source might just as easily have proof Sally *wasn't* Ethel Snowcroft.

But Mr. Blakeney shook his head. "Haven't heard anything. Although"—he snapped his fingers—"almost forgot. She gave me this. I've not read it, so I am not responsible for its contents." He passed me another envelope and raised his hands in a gesture of abdication. I peeled it open—one never knew what might be in a note from Genie Shelley!—and we three squeezed together to read it, right there on the tram.

Myrtle & Miss J.: Do you know how to reach Velma Dudley? I'd like to do a human-interest piece on her organization. I tried the SWOBS headquarters in Liverpool, with no luck. Did you know that building we pictured is really a bank? (My editor is Not Pleased.) I did find the Shipwrecked Mariners Royal Benevolent Society in Surrey, but they don't know her. Encl. is my card, if you'd be so kind to pass it on to her whenever you see her next. ~VTY, G. S.

"I shall leave it to your discretion whether or not to sic my sister on this poor woman." It was apparent that Mr. Blakeney had never met Mrs. Dudley.

"Or vice versa," Miss Judson murmured.

"There's a Lecture I'd pay money to see," I put in. "Genie and Mrs. Dudley going head-to-head!"

Miss Judson put the note in her reticule, Genie's card tucked safely within. "As it happens, we have some business to discuss with Mrs. Dudley," she said. "Perhaps we'll pay a call on SWOBS tomorrow after checking on your father."

"That's in Upton?" Mr. Blakeney put in. "Mind if I tag along? I'm supposed to drop off some filings for Magistrate Fox."

I pounced on this. "Can we?" I asked Miss Judson. Someone, somewhere must have answers for us.

"Well, then," Miss Judson said, "an Outing it shall be." No one pointed out that Outings typically involved things like picnics and kites and ice cream sodas, not attempting to identify murder victims.

⁓

Back at home that evening I got straight to work on Sally's case. The courts weren't leaving Father—meaning me—much time to come up with absolute proof of Sally's claim, and Father was in no condition to handle this latest development, not on top of everything else. I wasn't sure what I could accomplish by myself on a Thursday night, but I could hardly abandon Sally simply because Father was Indisposed.

I let myself into Father's study and lit a lamp. For a moment I stood on tiptoe, burning match in hand. If I never lit the flame, this room would fill up with toxic gas, rendering me first unconscious, and then dead.

I touched the match to the jet before I got carried away with morbid thoughts and inadvertently asphyxiated myself. The lamp sprang to life—safe, golden, glowing life. How had Father's victim been overcome by gas from the Bunsen burners? It was obvious he hadn't strolled into the laboratory on his own and flicked them open. Plus someone *hid* his body afterward, which all but guaranteed malice aforethought.

"Ouch!" The match burned down and singed my fingers. I hurriedly stomped out the stub, rubbing at the smudge of soot on the rug, reasonably certain Cook could get that out. (It hardly compared to the splatters of ink Father got everywhere. We'd been trying to convert him to a modern fountain pen for ages, but he claimed to like the smell of India ink.)

"*No.*" Peony trotted in and sniffed the guilty mark with accusation. What she said next sounded suspiciously like *mens rea*.

"Other cats say *meow*, you know."

"*No.*"

"French cats say *miaou*. Roman cats said *miau*. Even Greek cats say νιάου!"

"*Non.*"

"You won't tell on me," I hazarded—although she is not *completely* trustworthy. She is, however, susceptible to bribery. "Shall we get to work?" Peony loves Father's desk even more than I do,* so she hopped aloft, brushing her whiskers along the blotter and the letter trays and the typewriter and the inkwell—which I rescued before her affections grew too passionate, and I had a serious stain to explain to Cook.

For a moment I merely sat in Father's chair, breathing in the officy air and trying to put murderous thoughts aside. The file from Mr. Blakeney stared back at me. What could possibly be within? It was not my business, I told myself firmly, despite a nagging feeling that Father—and Mr. Blakeney!—were keeping something from me.

With some determination, I returned my focus to Sally's case. If Father were here, what would his next move be? (It would probably involve coffee, which would have been very little help to me.) Mr. Blakeney had taken most of the relevant correspondence, but perhaps he'd missed something—something so dispositive it couldn't possibly be disputed by the Courts, no matter how many people were pulling strings.

* I offer as evidence the fact that I have never once eaten anything I've found there.

"No."

For once I agreed with her. Trying not to be discouraged, I flipped through the unopened letters. One fat envelope stood out, expensive paper with an Upton postmark I recognized, sealed rather elaborately with wax, with another, even smaller envelope within. This one was faded and yellowed, its foreign stamp unrecognizable. I turned to the Magistrate's letter:

Dear Arthur,

Or Miss Myrtle, as I suspect you've taken on the job of Law Clerk,

Forgive an old man for indulging in some sleuthing of his own. All this talk of the Persephone has stirred up old memories, and I found myself stirring up some of my late wife's mementos. And lo! She had a letter from her niece Audrina, which I now forward to you. If nothing else, Sally will enjoy reading the news of her parents, and of herself.

Yours affectionately,

Magnus Fox, J.P.

I shook the old letter onto the desk, looking at the envelope in awe. It had been sent from Portugal, close to the beginning of the *Persephone*'s journey. How strange that something as huge and solid as a whole ship—and all the people aboard her—could vanish without a trace, and yet this ephemeral little scrap of someone's thoughts should survive to land on my father's desk after all this time.

19 MAY, '84

Dear Aunt Jane,

This is our last port of call before we set sail for the Antipodes! Doesn't that sound much more exotic than "Melbourne"? How dull and English that is! Despite your teasing, I have become quite at home on my little ship, and you should see how the men baby Ethel. One of them has given her a puppy, a little terrier with a spotted ear. Andrew tried to refuse (of course), but she has named him Charley after his benefactor, and with the whole crew against him, even the stern Captain Snowcroft cannot stand firm. Truly, there would be a mutiny if that child's every whim were not indulged! She shall become quite the little tyrant by the time we make land.

It is a good thing they are so fond of Ethel, for I fear they do not care too much for her father. There is tension with the men, but none will tell me the source or cause, for I am merely the captain's wife. But I have heard murmurs about the funds Andrew has brought aboard for the railway. The end of this journey cannot come soon enough.

Remember me, cast adrift on the high seas, only a little dog for company, deserted by husband and child both! I remain,

Your loving niece,

~Aud

Poor Audrina! She'd been so happy, looking forward to a grand adventure, doting over her little girl. And yet her thread of anxiety had proved all too accurate. Poor Ethel. Poor everyone. I traced the faded script on the envelope, wondering why Magistrate Fox had sent this letter to Father instead of giving it directly to Sally. Was it possible even he still had his doubts?

"Mmmrrrrrb." Peony threaded her way across the desk, to settle herself in the least convenient place: right atop Audrina's letter. She rolled to her side, seizing my hand with her paws and teeth as I attempted to withdraw it.

"Whose side are you on? Don't you want to prove that Sally is an heiress? And Charley?" I added, teasingly.

She answered by attempting to disembowel my ulna.*

* Do not believe that cats have no imagination, Dear Reader. My forearm was plainly a stand-in for a wildebeest or crocodile that she had brought down on the savannah.

Oddly enough, though, she'd given me an idea. If I could not solve this through legal means, I would approach it scientifically. Which meant I was in entirely the wrong room. I collected the stack of everything Mr. Blakeney had left—all the records we had from the *Persephone*, the photograph of the Snowcrofts, and the notes on inheritance law Miss Judson and I had prepared—and barged uninvited into Miss Judson's room. She was not there. I am embarrassed to admit, Dear Reader, where I barged upon her uninvited next, but it was already too late by the time I had thought better of it.

"Myrtle!" Miss Judson let out a steamy yelp and grabbed a towel as she sank lower into the bathtub. I spun round, cheeks burning, staring at the damp wallpaper, trying to convince myself I'd seen nothing mortifying.

"I'm sorry!" I cried. Uttering horrified apologies, I made to slip back out the door.

"Wait. Come back. You must have something you wanted."

"It can wait," I mumbled. I had had occasional glimpses of Miss Judson's fascinating adult underthings—her corsets and garters and chemisettes—which seemed so alien and mysterious. I'd seen the ones of Mum's that were packed away. I may even have tried one on, once or twice, when no one was looking.

(They were more complicated than you would expect.) Miss Judson had promised to one day induct me into their secret rituals, though she'd been infuriatingly vague about when, exactly, that might be. But seeing her in complete *déshabillée* in her bath—that was—

Well, Dear Reader, it was beyond the pale.

"I'm decent," she said. "You can turn around."

I did, slowly, eyes squeezed shut.

I heard a stifled snort, and cracked one open. Only her head—covered in a lacy cap—was visible above the white curved rim of the tub and a layer of soapy water.

"You happily climb about crime scenes and murder victims—and morgues!—but the sight of a fellow Young Lady of Quality in the bath is unbearable? Heaven help you at boarding school."

"Never mind," I mumbled.

"What did you want? My water's getting cold."

But my burst of enthusiasm had dissipated with the steam from the bath. "I just thought we could go through the Snowcroft file again." I halfheartedly showed her my stack. "Maybe we missed something the last time. Times." Even I had to admit, a nice bubble bath sounded more appealing than that.

Miss Judson cut through my mortification with one crisp nod. "Let me get dressed. I'll meet you in the schoolroom, and we can discuss it properly."

A warmth unrelated to the steamy bathroom or my

bone-deep embarrassment spread through me. "I'll ask Cook for cocoa." I slipped out the bathroom door just as Peony slipped inside.

"No! Out, you! Scat! Kindly stop biting my toes—you are not a lioness, and I am not a gazelle."

⤠

Ten minutes later, wrapped modestly in her dressing gown, Miss Judson reappeared in the schoolroom. I had toted in all the original documents pertaining to the *Persephone*, along with one of Mum's medical textbooks and an old copy of *Archives de l'Anthropologie Criminelle*, a forensic science journal. Just for good measure, I also brought every note I'd managed to take during the hectic Investigation at the hospital, although it was impossible for the two cases to be related—unless Father was now attracting murders as well, a thought that did not bear close examination.

"He's always attracted murders. He's the Prosecuting Solicitor," Miss Judson pointed out.

"That is not comforting." As if I'd forgotten that Father was all alone in that shady hospital, surrounded by Suspicious Characters and *all* of our suspects! "What do you think was in that file Mr. Blakeney had?" That was meant to merely sound curious, but some of my concern seeped in. "Is he Investigating without us?"

Miss Judson did her best not to betray any curiosity of her own. "I'm sure he knows better than that," she said. "Back to the matter at hand, *s'il te plaît*."

With a (small) grumble, I explained my idea about looking at the evidence from a new angle. "We haven't been able to prove Sally's identity with wills or birth certificates or documentation."

"Right . . . ?" There was a note of impatience in her voice. I decided to consider it encouragement.

"But the dead man gave me an idea. What if we can prove it through some other means?"

"I must point out that we have not yet been successful employing *any* means to identify said decedent."

"But we know a lot more about Sally! Here." I started handing her things, which she hastened to tack to the blackboard. "We can build a *scientific* case for her identity." I refused to let Miss Judson's skepticism dampen my spirit.

"Intriguing. State your case." She took her accustomed place by the blackboard, studying my exhibits.

"First, her locket. There are *lots* of clues there. Like the maker's mark. That should be traceable. The jeweler might recall selling it to Sally's parents."

"I hate to remind you, my sketch of the locket—*and* its trademark—was published in the *Tribune*, and failed to produce any leads." She indicated the very drawing, now pinned to the blackboard.

"But the locket didn't come from Swinburne," I said. "So that doesn't mean anything. Genie can distribute it to other newspapers around the country. Somebody is bound to recognize it."

"We thought someone would be bound to recognize Sally, too."

Gritting my teeth, I pressed on. "There's more: the curl of hair." It was theoretically possible to match the sample from Sally's locket to the hair from Sally's head. I could do it here with Mum's microscope, but I suspected the probate court judges might prefer the evidence come from the laboratory of someone, well, *older.* "Dr. Munjal could do the comparison." I was sure Caroline would have no trouble persuading her father to participate. We'd once spent a fascinating afternoon comparing our hair—her sleek black strands and my rather mousy* ones—to Peony's and Miss Pigeon's (the Munjals' placid carriage horse), using the doctor's fine equipment.

Miss Judson looked cautiously impressed. "Although Sally might have easily substituted a lock of her own hair in the locket."

I glared at her. Anyone would think she didn't want to prove Sally was Ethel Snowcroft.

"Too bad your father's victim is bald," she said. "We could test him, too. Anything else?"

I hesitated before answering. My next idea was on even shakier evidentiary ground. "Bertillon measurements." I opened the criminology journal to an article

* not *literally* mousy, although I'd been unable to procure a sample from *M. musculus* for comparison

detailing the technique. "If we could compare Sally's measurements to those of her parents, we might convince a judge"—assuming we could find a scientifically minded one to hear Sally's case, which was by no means certain—"that she's their daughter."

Miss Judson's fingers tapped her elbow. "How do you propose we acquire the physical measurements of two people lost at sea ten years ago?"

I produced my next exhibit. "From their photograph. Mr. Snowcroft is looking straight on, so that's a bit harder, but we can probably estimate his height from that pillar thing next to him. Mrs. Snowcroft is in three-quarter profile, so we can measure her ears and everything, too."

Miss Judson closed the journal and smoothed the cover. "That's expecting rather a lot. Measurements from an old photograph won't be strictly accurate, and Sally might still be growing."

"But they'll be *compelling*," I argued. "Father only needs to come up with a Balance of Probabilities, remember? It just needs to be more likely than not that Sally is Ethel. And we have that: her birthmark, her resemblance to her parents—especially when scientifically supported by the evidence we've collected—the chronometer, the locket. It adds up."

"It adds up for *us*," she said gently, "because we know Sally, and we want to support her."

"It worked for the Tichborne Claimant," I said. They'd disproved his claims once and for all on the strength of a tattoo.

"It worked *against* him, you mean. And don't forget, that courtroom was packed with people who knew Roger Tichborne, including his mother."

"Well, we don't exactly have Sally's mother, do we?" I snapped. Why was she being so, so—*Socratic*? I took a great, unprofessional sniff. "This is the best I could do. Don't you want to help her?"

"Of course I do." Miss Judson put her arm around my shoulders. "And you've made an excellent effort. I just think we mustn't get our hopes up."

"Sally's hopes, you mean," I muttered, pulling away to wipe my nose, lest I give up and toss all my exhibits in the rubbish bin.

17

GOOD WORKS

A fractured hyoid bone, a small, horseshoe-shaped
bone in the throat, presents us with irrefutable
proof of strangulation: it is exceedingly rare for
this bone to be broken in any other manner except
forcible and violent assault by choking.

–H. M. Hardcastle, *Foundations of Legal Medicine*

Even after Miss Judson's counterarguments all but
whittled away my entire case, I refused to let her doubts
squelch my enthusiasm—or, to be strictly accurate, my
stubborn unwillingness to abandon the effort despite
all reasonable opposition. Miss Judson and I had pres-
sured Father into taking Sally's case, after all. I felt
responsible for her—and for him.

To properly draw up my clear and persuasive
argument, I returned to Father's study. To my disappointment, even Peony forsook me, preferring the
certainty of Cook's bed to my spurious medico-legal
efforts.

"Fine," I called after her. "See if I care." I tugged on the desk drawer, but it, too, was unmoved by my pleas. Locked? Father never locked his desk. He barely remembered to lock the *doors*. Fortunately, I knew where he kept the key (~~under the inkwell~~), and soon had that anomaly sorted. The drawer sprang open, and a handful of papers sprang out.

Brrrb? Even without Peony, I heard her questioning voice in my head as I riffled through the items. They didn't seem the sorts of things someone would need to lock away: a railway timetable, two catalogues from jewelers, and several brochures for boarding schools, including Boswell, Miss Judson's beloved *alma mater.* I peered more closely at the catalogues—perhaps Father had had the same notion as I, and had already begun the research. But I saw no lockets similar to Sally's. Still, I might as well include them as supporting documentation for my argument.

As I worked, however, something about that assortment of adverts nagged at me. Why would Father be looking into boarding schools for Sally? Surely that was Mrs. Dudley's role, or Magistrate Fox's. I bit the end of my pen, momentarily distracted from microscopic hair analysis and anthropometry, and flipped through one, noting its Academic Discipline and Rigorous Moral Standards. The nagging grew naggier. Had Father locked these things away so *I* wouldn't find them? I'd seen him tuck something out of view, after all, and he'd been angry when he learned I'd been working in here. My eyes drifted once again to the file Mr. Blakeney had delivered, and my fingers practically burned with the need to untwine its red string and examine its contents.

What could be so important that Father would share it with Mr. Blakeney—but not with us? With *me*? Surely it wouldn't do any harm just to peek . . .

"No." Peony returned just in time. Saving me from myself, perhaps, she leaped neatly onto the desk and planted herself—an unshiftable paperweight—squarely atop Father's secret file. I gave up.

It felt like nobody was on my side.

ഏ

The next morning, I could not quite conceal my lingering disappointment in Miss Judson. And Peony. And Mr. Blakeney. And Father. And the whole of the British Legal System. Miss Judson knew better than to mention it, however, so we were a silent twosome that arrived at the Royal Swinburne. I had my carefully prepared notes and supporting evidence, including Audrina's letter (with only minor feline toothmarks), but it was immediately obvious that we weren't the only ones who'd been hard at work last night. Father was sitting up in bed, his own tweed jacket pulled on over his Royal Swinburne pyjamas, rosy-cheeked and beaming as he chatted—well, communicated—amiably with none other than Mr. Davis from the hospital morgue.

A sea of paperwork swamped his bed, and he scribbled vigorously on a notepad. Who'd smuggled that in for him?

Against all reason, I felt my own interest flare back to life. "Did the post-mortem report come in already?" Momentarily setting aside my quarrels, I scurried down the Ward, ignoring glares from the nurses and patients. "Has the victim been identified?"

For once Father didn't scowl at my eagerness, but held a hand toward Mr. Davis, inviting him to answer.

"I'm afraid not, Miss. But—that is, I was just telling your—er, Mr. Hardcastle about some irregularities that cropped up in my records."

Father seemed very pleased with this news, so I pounced. "What sort of irregularities?"

"A porter showed up after hours, asking for admittance paperwork. But new admissions must be signed off by a doctor. He didn't have the necessary authorizations."

"Someone wanted to bring an unauthorized body to the morgue? When was this?"

"Around midnight on Monday. The overnight clerk didn't make note of who the porter was, though, and as far as I know he never came back. With anyone, I mean."

That was just about the time Father had witnessed the murder. "That explains why they hid the body in the laundry," I said. This meant that the killer came from inside the hospital, and wasn't some random person off the street. And I knew exactly who the mysterious porter must have been. "Squeaky Shoes!"

Without giving Father a chance to scowl, I explained about the skinny porter we'd all seen lurking about—the one Sally thought was following her. (Father *did* scowl then.)

"He doesn't ring any bells." Mr. Davis scratched his disorderly hair. "But I can ask around. Anything else I can do for you, miss—er, sir?"

Father pantomimed a gracious dismissal, and Mr. Davis actually bowed as he departed. Father seemed to think that no more than his due (Peony must be rubbing off on him). Now he reached an arm out and drew me in for a squeeze. It was not quite an apology—or maybe it was. He smelled strange, alien soap and laundry powder and a peculiar sweet, medicinal air. But he was *acting* like Father, and that was what mattered. I squeezed back, hard.

"That's more like it," a new voice chimed in. Cheery Nurse Pethwick appeared, arms laden with fresh bedding. "Haven't they found out who that poor man was, then?" She clucked her tongue.

"You hadn't seen him before?" I inquired, saving Father the effort of trying to question her.

"Don't know all the porters yet, I'm afraid." Nurse Pethwick swapped Father's pillow out for a fresh one. "I've only just started this week. Met with the Guv

Monday afternoon, and he put me straight to work. You're my first patient."

We both stared at her in astonishment. "You don't seem new," I said skeptically, and she stifled her clap of laughter.

"I'll take that as a compliment. I must say, t'weren't nearly this many constables at my last post. The Guv would like them all gone by Hospital Sunday—" She nodded to the poster emblazoned on the wall and added in an artificially stilted voice, "So I'm to *respectfully suggest you 'urry things along*."

In all the excitement, I'd forgotten about the upcoming charity event. "We'll do our best," I assured her—although how we were supposed to solve the anonymous man's murder *and* prove Sally's identity in two days was beyond me. At least Hospital Sunday wasn't one of my responsibilities, too.

As Nurse Pethwick efficiently took care of Father's needs, she prattled on happily about the Snowcroft lecture she'd attended the night before. I seized on this. "Did you see anyone suspicious there? Anyone following Sall—Miss Snowcroft?"

"Not 'ardly. That Dudley woman's like a bulldog, the way she guards her ladyship. Reminds me a bit o' Matron and Governor Greeley, if you know what I mean."

After a long moment during which she failed to elaborate on this peculiar statement, we nudged her. "Oh, don't tell me *you* 'aven't noticed, the lot of you Nosey Parkers! But you watch, next time they're together. I think she's sweet on 'im."

"Th' Dragoh Lady?" Father's eyes were wide with disbelief.

"You *never* heard me call her any such thing." Nurse Pethwick thoughtfully creased the pillow slip she was folding. "Course, most of the staff 'ere are devoted to Governor Greeley. They'd do almost anything for 'im. And no wonder. But Matron Finch is something else entirely. Now, you didn't hear this from me, mind—" She bent closer to Father, fussing with his bedding, speaking low. "But there's something fishy about her—how she left her last post, I mean."

"Like what?" I said.

"Couldn't say. Rumors, mostly. Some kind of scandal at her last hospital. Neatly covered up, of course, and the Guv hired her anyway."

Maybe she murdered a patient.

"So naturally, she's even fonder of the man than most of them. Us. But I saw her—Matron, I mean—hangin' round Himself's office when I had my interview. If I didn't know better, I'd almost say she was spyin' on him."

Another detail caught my notice. Matron's spying and possibly murderous past could wait. "Monday afternoon? Was that around four o'clock?"

"That's right," she said, with some surprise.

Father gave her a sharp look (which she might easily have misinterpreted as a scowl). "Sizteh, wha' ih your gibbeh neigh?"

At her puzzled expression, I translated. "What's your first name?" My heart had sunk—was Father thinking what I was? Another clue that led nowhere?

"Why, Mr. 'ardcastle, don't *you* go gettin' sweet on *me!*" Nurse Pethwick gave him a friendly swat with the pillowcase. "It's Annie."

Father and I both said it: "*A. P.*" The notation from Dr. Greeley's calendar. We sighed.

Nurse Pethwick fixed Father in a stern gaze, hands on her hips. "You *will* make sure that little girl gets what's due her, won't you?"

During our conversation, Father and I had somehow failed to Observe that a member of our party was missing. Now we seemed to realize it at the same time. Just as I was getting ready to present my scientific case for Sally's Snowcroftness, the green Ward doors swung inward, and we heard two familiar, yet incongruous, sounds: a *tappity-tap* like a telegraph and the *thunk-thunk* of a walking stick driven into the floorboards. We looked up together to see Miss Judson strolling along beside Aunt Helena.

"Wheh hab *you* beed?" Father asked.

"Investigating," Miss Judson said smugly. "Matron might have her Little Birds, but *we* have the Ladies Hospital Committee."

"My Ladies have unfettered access to the Royal Swinburne." Aunt Helena sniffed proudly.

"Perfect for exploring untouched areas of the hospital," Miss Judson agreed.

"I don't especially *want* to touch them," I muttered.

"Nohse'se," Father said grandly. "Thzz pehfeh. Puh' my gihls to worg, Auht."

"Arthur, for heaven's sake, don't attempt to speak unless you can do so coherently. You sound like a clogged drainpipe."

There was a muffled sound from Miss Judson, whose gloved hand politely covered her mouth. She turned to me, checking her watch. "Have you presented your work for review? I've promised Aunt Helena we would attend the Hospital Sunday meeting. Sally will be there," she added with a little smile. "I've borrowed some calipers and a chart from Nurse Keene so you can take her measurements."

One did not squeeze Miss Judson, certainly not in public, but I met her gaze with gratitude.

"Whah's this?" Father inquired, and I started to explain, but Miss Judson intervened.

"Myrtle has done some extraordinary work in preparation for the upcoming hearing. It's all in her report." With a crisp nod, she signaled me to hand everything to Father. "She'll expect your reply"—her expectant gaze passed to Aunt Helena—"no later than lunchtime. Very good." She turned me round and steered me, much more gently than habitual, from the Ward, Aunt Helena chugging behind like a stately tugboat. "You know, this will make an excellent science lesson. I honestly can't think why we haven't done this before."

"What changed your mind?" I asked her, out in the hallway.

She stopped and gave a vague smile. "I spoke to Sally," she admitted. "I'm afraid I might have got her hopes up."

⁓

I didn't have a chance to take Sally's Bertillon measurements that morning after all. Something came up.

At first I was so surprised that Miss Judson had supported my idea that I scarcely registered the fact that she had recruited us into one of Aunt Helena's Causes—in one fell swoop adding Hospital Sunday to my ever-growing list of obligations. If twelve-year-old Investigators had social calendars, mine would have collapsed under its own weight.

We accompanied Aunt Helena to a room in the administrative wing that had been seconded for the Ladies Committee's Good Works. Sally was there, helping Nanette Munjal wind yarn, Charley asleep in her frilly lap. She half-lifted one of her wool-wrapped hands in a little wave. The room was crammed with Ladies of Quality assembled to do whatever a Hospital Committee does. One woman bent covetously over a cashbox, counting and tallying. Others addressed envelopes with their ideal penmanship. More sorted pamphlets into neat stacks, while a final group, under the supervision of Mrs. Munjal, knitted away vigorously.

"Well, Aunt," said Miss Judson, "put us to work."

The cashbox lady looked up hungrily. "We need someone to sort the tombola prizes." But Aunt Helena seemed to think this below us.

"Judson, your needlework is adequate, I believe. See if you can't salvage Mrs. Wainthropp's embroidery. That woman simply *refuses* to wear her spectacles. Where is Caroline?" Caroline looked up from her stack of pamphlets. "Miss Munjal, take Helena Myrtle to the Charity Ward and distribute our Literature to the patients."

There was a mysterious, meaningful glint in Aunt Helena's eye as she said this, so I stifled my protest. Not that I longed to spend the day in this stuffy room winding wool or sorting tombola prizes, mind you (although it was probably the only warm spot in the hospital).

But Caroline seemed happy to make her escape, and Sally watched us eagerly. "Miss Hardcastle?" she piped up, in her sweet, accented voice that made the entire room stop and listen rapturously. "May I join them? I should like to see the fruits of all your good works."

Aunt Helena glared at me and Caroline severely for some moments before answering. "Very well. I suppose my niece can't get you into too much mischief down there." There was absolutely no mistaking that warning: I'd just had Viscountess's Bodyguard added to my duties.

Caroline hooked her arm into Sally's, chattering as she led us out and down to the Charity Ward. "Those patients know *everything* that goes on here," she said. "And they'll adore you, your ladyship."

The Charity Ward was not difficult to find; we merely had to follow the queue lined up at the gates. The admitting porter (not Squeaky Shoes) immediately recognized that we did not belong among the patients and swiftly ushered us within. Probationer Ling stood guard with a clipboard, checking each patient's ticket against her subscription rolls. The Charity Ward was for the "Deserving Poor"—working people who couldn't afford private care like Father was getting. Employers and prosperous benefactors took out subscriptions to the hospital, allowing them to sponsor patients, and the rolls were strictly monitored for abuse or fraud. What became of the *Un*deserving Poor was not explained.

Nurse Ling paused to say hello. "Didn't think I'd see you down here!" Far away from Matron, she seemed happier and more relaxed. She bobbed a quick curtsy. "Your ladyship."

"*Sally.*" She showed her the pamphlets we'd brought.

"Between you an' me, milady," Probationer Ling said, "I reckon they'd rather read the latest *Illustrated Police News.*"

"We have that!" Caroline put in. "Charley's on the front page. Is Mr. Collins still here?" she asked. "You'll love him. He knows everything about everyone."

The Charity Ward went out of its way to be as different as possible from the spotless modernity of the Private Ward. The floors were stripped bare from constant scrubbing, and the whitewashed walls lacked the sparkling tiles and cheery green trim. Dimly flickering oil lamps swung from the low ceiling, not a single tiny fern adorned the patients' meager bedstands. They even had to wear their own pyjamas. A stately photograph of Governor Greeley in an ostentatious gold frame graced the entranceway. "That was a gift from the matron," Caroline said.

Sally's appearance caused an immediate sensation. A ripple of hushed whispers sped through the Ward, and soon all faces were turned our way. Sally hoisted Charley to one shoulder and waved his paw at her fans, simultaneously fishing in her reticule for her inkpad. I could see our errand to deliver Improving Literature had turned into an autograph session.

Caroline led us first to the bed of an older man with bandaged legs. A woman sat beside him, all Sunday-best in a ruffly cape and a hat with bright velvet flowers. "Mr. Collins, I've brought my friends, Miss Hardcastle and Lady Ethel."

"Colin Collins, at your service!" He had a broad grin and twinkling grey eyes. "And this is the missus,

Colleen!" They both laughed at what must have been an old joke. "Coll, look—it's the Heiress! Scoot, you, and let the girls set."

We protested, but Mrs. Collins insisted. She had barely vacated the seat before Mr. Collins patted the chair eagerly. "Now, then. Give me the buzz."

"Well, Mr. Collins," Caroline returned, pushing me into the chair, "why don't you tell us?"

He eyed Sally shrewdly. "I dunno, now. Might scare the little miss."

"You can't scare me." She gave a toss of her sandy curls and grinned.

Mr. Collins wheezed with laughter. Glancing sidelong at Sally, I had the unsettling feeling that she was telling the truth. "Do you know anything about the—er, the unfortunate man in the laundry?" I finished weakly.

"She means the murdered bloke," Sally clarified cheerfully. I sank lower in my seat. I was certain this wasn't what Aunt Helena had had in mind.

"Might know a thing or two," he said. "Might, indeed. You got one of them autographs for me, Duchess?"

Sally let out a laugh. "That's *Viscountess*, and here you go." She handed over one of the pamphlets, upon which she'd scrawled, *To Mr. C.: Love, Sally.* "Fair's fair. Your turn. What've you got?" Sally seemed more comfortable with Mr. Collins than I'd ever seen her. Heiress or not, at heart she was still a shopkeeper's girl and hockey player who brought her dog everywhere she went.

"A lot more than those daft constables." He hoisted himself up to sitting and leaned in conspiratorially. "For instance, 'ave they identified the dead chap yet?"

I fidgeted, feeling like the interrogation had turned round on us. "Not that I know of."

"Ha! I knew it. Look 'ere. Betcha you didn't know he was a patient right 'ere in this very Ward."

"That's more like it," Sally said. "We're on to something now, Myrtle." Caroline nodded in satisfied agreement.

"He was *here?*" I echoed. "In the Charity Ward? Why didn't anyone say so?"

"I don't mean when he were kilt. It were a few weeks ago. I been in a full month." Mr. Collins seemed to think this was an accomplishment. "He was in for a few nights—pneumonia—but if you ask me, they oughter have sent him to the asylum. Half barmy he was. Half starved, too. Dunno why anybody'd bother to kill the poor blighter." He shook his head sadly. "Drunk 'imself halfway to the grave already."

Sally leaned closer. "What else? Did he say anything about himself?"

"Never spoke to the man," he confessed. "But you ask Missus Hendricks in Bed Twelve. They seemed close. Heard 'em whisperin' together, more'n one night." He grinned and showed his autograph to his waiting wife, and we shuffled across the Ward to question our next witness.

Bed Twelve was occupied by a woman with sunken cheeks and weary eyes, who accepted Aunt Helena's pamphlet with a trembling hand. "God bless you," she whispered. Sally gently placed Charley alongside her in the bed, and he lay still as her frail fingers touched his bristly fur. I couldn't bring myself to ask her about the murder, but she surprised us. "You want to know about Mr. Jonah."

I started. "Mr. Jonah—you know his name?"

She started to nod—or shake her head—but was overcome with coughing. Caroline gave her a sip of water from her cup (chipped china, obviously brought from home). "I ain't catching," she reassured us. "Tumor in me chest."

I sucked in my breath. "My mum had cancer," I said without meaning to. She read the rest of that story in my face, apparently, for she squeezed my hand. Sally gave me a sympathetic pat.

"Brave girl," Mrs. Hendricks said. "I hope my Molly's as brave as you."

I nodded, not sure what to say. Still petting Charley, she continued her account of Mr. Jonah. "He weren't here when I were brung in, but I woke in the night, an' he were kneeling at my bedside, praying."

"That was kind of him," Sally said.

"Thought he were an angel, at first. But he seemed

troubled. The drink, you know. After that we prayed together every day." Her fingers were wrapped around a scrap of brightly colored cloth, and she released her grip, revealing a crumpled hankie. "He give me this when he left. Said he wouldn't be needing it anymore."

"What did he mean?" whispered Caroline, but Sally and I were transfixed by the handkerchief. Only it wasn't a handkerchief. It was a scrap of something else—white silk with a painted emblem that made my heart bang, faster and faster.

"It's a flag," Sally breathed, helping me smooth the wrinkled fabric. "What is that, a rose?"

It looked like a squashed plum to me. But now that I saw it again, it was perfectly clear—and I had seen this very thing before. So had Sally. Abruptly I was on my feet. I tugged the flag from Sally. "I have to go," I said. "Mrs. Hendricks, may I borrow this? I will make sure you get it back."

She squeezed my hand. "Keep it, if it will help him rest."

"Myrtle, what is it?" Sally's features were taut with bewilderment. I could only offer her a single word.

"Pomegranate," I said, fleeing the Charity Ward, aged signal flag from the brigantine *Persephone* clutched in my hand.

18
FALSE FLAGS

Although a human body can reveal much about its death, it cannot tell us the state of mind of its killer.

–H. M. Hardcastle, *Foundations of Legal Medicine*

Abandoning all decorum, I raced back up to the Private Ward, banged through the swinging doors, and thundered down to Father's bed. "Where's Miss Judson?" I gasped.

Father caught me by the arms. "Steathy," he said. "Tague a deeb bref."

I couldn't. All I could do was wave Mr. Jonah's hankie in his face, words tumbling out about where it had come from. Father took the scrap from my hands and spread it across his blanketed lap. It was torn and stained, barely recognizable as the snappy pennant it once had been. "This came froh' *Perseph'ne*?"

"You remember—there's a flag *just like this* on Magistrate Fox's model."

Father was nodding. He'd gone pale again, but put a hand on my shoulder. "Sih," he commanded. "Breave. Calm dowh."

I obeyed, although I desperately wanted to pace. My sprint to Father's bedside had done nothing to cool my feverish thoughts. "It's a pomegranate," I said, "like his tattoo"—though Father surely recognized it. He was the one who'd read me the Greek myth of Persephone in the Underworld, and the six fateful pomegranate seeds she'd eaten. "How did he get this? Who was he?"

Father's fingers touched his own neck, as if he could somehow conjure the answers from the tattooed man's ghost. "Zhailor," he said, unhelpfully. "Buh froh Mizh Sowcroff's shiff? Quig—did you brig th' ma'ifest?"

Frantically, I dug through my satchel—then overturned the whole thing on Father's bed, spilling out notes, sweet wrappers, used hankies, and my evidence kit. Father frowned at the skull of a mouse that tumbled out with everything else. "That's Peony's," I mumbled, stuffing it back inside. I didn't have the official manifest, of course, but I'd made my own list of the *Persephone*'s passengers and crew. I'd long since memorized every name on this list, and there was no Mr. Jonah on it. But finding pomegranates on the person of Father's dead man was far too much coincidence.

"He's not there," I said as Father pored over the list. "But he had to be on that ship. Right?"

He nodded absently, and I did my best (which was not quite good enough) to stay silent. "How did he end up *here*? At your hospital? *Murdered?*"

He shook his head absently, and it was all I could do not to yank the page from his hands. Instead, I shuffled through my other notes, trying to see the connection. Any connection. Who was Mr. Jonah? Seizing Mrs. Snowcroft's letter again—tearing a fragile corner in the process—I scoured her buoyant text for clues. And there, at last, I found one, although not the one I sought.

"*One of them has given her a puppy,*" I read aloud. "Ethel named him Charley, after the crew member who gave him to her. Can I see the manifest?" Sally's father, whom she knew as Edwin Cooke, wasn't listed either, and I knew that. But there was— "*There!*" I jabbed a finger into the page. "Nicholas *Charles*, navigator."

Father regarded me with wide eyes, Mr. Jonah temporarily forgotten. "*Thad's* how he had th' gradobether."

It took me a moment to decipher this. "That's how he got . . . yes! The chronometer!" We said the next thing together: "Then why did he have (hab) *Sally*?"

"Gidnabbed?"

"Kidnapped! Father! That's awful." But it would explain why they never came forward, why Cooke-stroke-Charles simply took little Ethel and didn't return her to the Snowcrofts. Although not really. "But why? Why not ask for ransom? Why *keep* her?"

Father's jaw was set. "Tha' man hid th' truth from Ethel fo' her whole life. Wha' seecrud is so bad you chage your names, flee to Auzhdralia, an' hide out for th' rezzt of your days?" He was frowning at the paper, but his thoughts seemed far away.

Around us, the noises of the busy hospital ward faded away, and for a moment there was just Father and me, working on the case together. His pale fingers lay smoothly on the papers in his lap, and I Observed something with a painful jolt. Father wasn't wearing his wedding ring.

All at once, thoughts spinning, I recalled the file from Mr. Blakeney that Father hadn't wanted me to see—Mr. Blakeney, who'd worked for a firm specializing in wills and estates—the hastily locked drawers, the grim look on Dr. Belden's face, and the boarding school brochures. My banging heart settled in my stomach like a hunk of lead. What else could those clues mean—what awful secret was Father keeping from me? I searched his pale face, willing my conclusions to be wrong. Surely Dr. Belden—or Dr. Kinkaid, or Nurse Pethwick, or *somebody!*—would have told me. Unless Father had sworn them all to silence, too.

"Maybe he was trying to protect her," I ventured softly, looking at my own hands.

Father squeezed my hand with an understanding

that sent a chill through me. "Maybe. Maybe so." He shook out the pomegranate flag again. "Now. I would ligue to know *ezzagly* who thih Mr. Jonah was, an' wha' he was doig at this hothpiddal in the mithle of th' nigh'."

☙

The need to identify the dead sailor had taken on new urgency, and the instant Miss Judson reappeared and was filled in on our deductions, Father dispatched us to Upton to call upon Mrs. Dudley. Now that we knew more, I ought to have felt better about leaving Father alone. It was one thing to kill an anonymous patient from the Charity Ward. Horrible as that was, such a victim might go unidentified and unmissed for ages. Malice against a high-ranking member of the Magistrate's Office would be harder to explain away.

But in the back of my mind still rattled Mr. Davis's ominous statements about just how easy it was to disguise a murder at a hospital.

We were a grim and determined party exiting the Private Ward, but before we made good our escape, we ran into further complications. Rounding the corner toward the stairwell, we heard angry footsteps approaching, accompanied by angry voices.

"Matron Finch!" The lilt to Dr. Kinkaid's voice had become a growl.

Matron Finch, gliding along the corridor, paused.

Her wide hem swung like a bell. "I'm very busy, Mr. Kinkaid."

I tugged Miss Judson into a recessed doorway to Observe. Was this a falling-out between co-conspirators? I felt Miss Judson's tension through her sleeve. But it soon became apparent they had other matters in mind than murder.

"Where is Nurse Ling? She's supposed to attend on my surgery this afternoon."

Matron Finch turned and smiled. Well, she probably thought it was a smile. "*Probationer* Ling has been reassigned to the Charity Ward. You have Nurse Pethwick to attend for you now."

"Pethwick can't tell the difference between a suture needle and a bone saw!" (I suppressed my yelp of indignation on Nurse Pethwick's behalf.) "This is unacceptable. I demand you return Nurse Ling to me at once."

"I have complete discretion about staffing in the wards. You know that."

Dr. Kinkaid's face was turning dangerously red. "Dr. Greeley will straighten this out."

She put a pleasant hand on his arm. "Governor Greeley trusts my judgment. I doubt anything will come of bothering him about this trivial matter."

He shook her off, stalking toward the office wing. "We'll see about this."

"Oh, Dr. Kinkaid?" Matron Finch called sweetly.

"I'll give you some friendly advice, since you're new here. It's hard to keep a secret at the Royal."

Dr. Kinkaid slowly wheeled back. "What the devil are you getting at?"

She folded her tiny hands at her plump waist, looking more than ever like Queen Victoria. "Oh, just that word travels fast in a place like this."

In a heartbeat, he was at her side once more, towering over her. "Indeed it does, Miss Flora Finch of Blackpool." He looked down on her for a long, heavy moment. She barely reacted—hardly more than a flicker of her gaze down the hallway—but it seemed to satisfy Dr. Kinkaid. "I think we understand each other."

Matron brushed at an invisible speck on her apron. "If you find Miss Pethwick unsatisfactory, I suppose I could recommend a replacement."

He stood straighter, and in his normal, musical voice replied, "I'll expect Nurse Ling in Operating Theater Number Eight at two o'clock." He strode down the hallway, whistling "The Wearing o' the Green" as Miss Finch stood and simmered where he'd left her.

"What was that about?" I exclaimed when we were alone in the corridor once more. The hidden undercurrent of their conversation left behind a chill I could not shake off.

Miss Judson was gazing intently at Matron's path, as if she'd left an oozing trail like a snail's. "It seems more than one person at the Royal Swinburne is awfully keen to keep their secrets."

⌀

We went straight from the Royal Swinburne and collected Mr. Blakeney at the tram stand. Miss Judson was her typical composed self, but—secrets or not—I was relieved to have Mr. Blakeney along. Not that I expected anything to happen that Miss Judson and I couldn't handle. It's just that Mr. Blakeney was a useful ally. We'd relied on him more than once in our Investigations for his brains, resourcefulness, and courage. And Peony liked him, which was the best character reference anyone could get.

We disembarked at Upton Railway Station, whereupon Miss Judson strode briskly across the platform to the waiting cabs, to procure a carriage bound for "The Seaman's Widows and Orphans Benevolent Society, Shorecross Street."

The coachman leaned down. "Eh? I know Shorecross, miss, but not this Orphan's Whatsit."

"The Seaman's Widows and Orphans Benevolent Society," Miss Judson repeated smoothly. "SWOBS?"

"Oh, aye," the cabbie said slowly. "I know th' place. But it's not for the likes o' you."

"That's why I'm here," Mr. Blakeney said, but the coachman remained unconvinced.

"Suit yourselves," he replied, adding under his breath, "it's your fun'ral."

I had been to Upton often, of course, and it is not a town with much Picturesque Beauty to recommend it. But as we rode farther from the station, the dirty streets grew dirtier, the dinge dingier, and the run-down buildings more run down. Mr. Blakeney watched out the window in growing dismay.

"I say, does this seem right to you?" he inquired, as a woman in a tattered satin opera cloak and a straw boater dodged the cab, toting what for all appearances was a kidnapped child—or a stolen side of mutton—under her arm. She made a Rude Gesture at the cabbie and shouted something unprintable.

Miss Judson's grip on her brolly tightened, but "Hmm" was all she said.

The cab pulled up alongside a string of shabby shop-fronts with cracked windows and men loitering about. "'Ere you are then, Shorecross Street."

As we alit, we instinctively huddled closer together, like a flock of cold pigeons. We were certainly not blending into our surroundings like the Baker Street Irregulars.* Mr. Blakeney's smart new suit was far too smart and much too new for the neighborhood, which apparently went in more for muddy tweed and garish waistcoats. A band of boys knelt in the street, playing a

---

* the enterprising London street urchins† who work as operatives for Sherlock Holmes

† *urchin* coming from the Old French word for "hedgehog," although how it came to apply to homeless children is less clear

game involving dice and knives, and giving us looks of unwelcoming curiosity.

Miss Judson glared at the cabbie. "What is this?" she demanded.

"Swabs. Like you said." He gestured to the sign on the tavern behind us—a faded, swinging piece of wood depicting a sailor mopping a deck. Letters stenciled above the door read **Swabs** and I saw Mr. Blakeney's hope crack a little more.

I frowned. "What's going on?"

But Miss Judson said, "Ah, I see." (I didn't see at all, Dear Reader.) "Please wait for us here," she told the cabbie.

"Nothin' doin'," he said, holding out his hand for payment. Miss Judson considered withholding it—but finally relented, giving him only the exact amount and no tip. Her judgmental expression was all the gratuity he could expect.

"Miss J.," Mr. Blakeney said, "are you sure about this? I don't think this is really the place for Stephen."

"Don't be silly," I said stoutly. "I've been in public houses before." Which didn't come out at all like I'd meant.

Miss Judson's face was set. "I'd like an explanation." She hauled open the door, which gave a painful groan. A waft of yeasty, sweaty, sad-smelling air greeted us, along with smutty coal-smoke from the choking fire. It was not nearly as nice as my previous tavern expedition. That establishment had been a working-class pub where fishermen gathered at the end of a long day for a pint, a pie, and conversation. This seemed to be a place where down-on-their-luck folk went to crawl away from the world. I clung closer to Miss Judson.

Coming across the sticky wooden floor was a buxom woman in an old dress and stained apron, dark hair pinned up and a great deal of powder on her pale face.

"Mrs. Dudley!" I exclaimed.

The woman lifted her eyes to mine, spotted Miss Judson, and lost her grip on her pitcher, which dropped to the hard floorboards and shattered. If possible, Mrs. Dudley's face had gone whiter than ever.

Miss Judson crouched to help her pick up the broken glass (the pitcher had thankfully been empty), and I joined them. Mr. Blakeney guarded our flank.

After most of the mess had been cleared, Mrs. Dudley looked at us squarely. "I suppose you'll be wanting a word."

"I think that would be best," Miss Judson replied.

Mrs. Dudley left the shards on the bar, then gave a sideways nod toward the back of the building. "Come up to mine, then. Your friend can stay here, if it's all the same to you. Can't have gentleman callers, you understand. Sends the wrong message."

The wrong message? I stared about the space, trying to figure out which of the mixed messages Mrs. Dudley had already sent we were supposed to believe.

"Mr. Blakeney will be coming with us. If it's all the same to you."

Mrs. Dudley knew Miss Judson well enough by now to realize that that tone brooked no objections. She just shrugged and led the way upstairs to a small flat—one bed-sitting room with a gas jet and basin for a kitchen. Hooks behind the door held a tired ivory overcoat and a familiar purple taffeta gown.

Mrs. Dudley paused to push a handful of cracker crumbs through the bars of an undersized cage holding a sleepy parrot who shifted restlessly at our arrival. We found places to sit—Mr. Blakeney took the windowsill, I claimed a hassock, Miss Judson perched neatly on the edge of the room's single chair (sprung; the faded upholstery had given up the ghost).

Mrs. Dudley lowered herself heavily to the edge of the bed. "Well," she said, just as heavily, "what would you like to know first?"

I had a million questions, but they'd all fizzled up in my confusion.

"Your real name would be a good start," suggested Miss Judson.

"Velma Dudley, just as you know me." She jerked her thumb toward a framed photograph on the wall behind her. It, too, was cracked and shabby, but it showed a plump young bride and her once-dashing husband, who wore a smart black uniform with braid on the sleeves.

"That's my Roge. The late Cap'n Roger Dudley, lost at sea. I been a widow eight years now, surviving on nothing but me own wits."

"Didn't SWOBS help you?" I asked—then realized we were probably sitting in their headquarters right now. "Oh," I said, feeling my cheeks redden. But why should *I* be embarrassed? "You *lied* to us."

Mrs. Dudley's temper flared. "Not in so many words, I never did. Everything I said was strictly true. There *is* a Swabs, an' it keeps me afloat, it does—and there's no crime in dressing above your station."

"But why?" I demanded. "What's it all about?"

"I know I'm confused," Mr. Blakeney said cheerfully. His long legs were practically up to his ears, thanks to his awkward seat on the windowsill. "How about a round of tea while we hear the lady's tale? Mrs. Dudley, do you mind?" He rose and set about rummaging in her minuscule kitchen, as she offered directions for the kettle and the tea. He was uncommonly gallant given the circumstances.

"I haven't broken any laws," Mrs. Dudley said, voice starchy with virtue.

"You hired a solicitor under false pretenses," Miss Judson pointed out.

This raised Mrs. Dudley's hackles. "No, I did not," she said, pointing her finger at my governess. "I hired him to prove that Sally's Ethel Snowcroft, an' I *never* pretended otherwise!"

"But why do it at all?" I said, trying to work this out. "Are you just, what, a confidence artist?"

She made a sound like a huffing steamship. "Andrew Snowcroft owned my Roger's ship," she said. "He were always talkin' big—grand plans for this an' that. Convinced Roge to invest in some mad venture, a vessel carrying passengers to the Antipodes, emigrants to Australia and New Zealand, and sail her, too. When she ran aground on a reef, Snowcroft blamed Roger and refused to pay him for the whole of the journey. Roger couldn't get a decent berth after that and went down in a coffin ship five years later. An' the Snowcrofts got richer and richer, thanks to me an' Roger's investment. So aye, I do think I deserve just a little bit o' the Legacy. But Sally Cooke—she's the real thing. I'm sure of it."

Mrs. Dudley adjusted her patched skirts. "And I have no intention of telling *any* o' that to poor Sally. She were already made an orphan when the *Persephone* were lost, she don't need to know her da' were a crook and a cheat to boot. But she *does* deserve every penny that's coming to her. And wot's the 'arm in me getting what's due me as well? I ask you."

I chewed on my fingers, feeling doubtful. None of this tallied with what Sally had told us, about the SWOBS Benefits Club and how Mrs. Dudley had reached out to Sally when Mr. Cooke died. But it *did* accord with Genie's claim that Captain Snowcroft had been a dishonorable businessman.

{ 253

Mr. Blakeney returned with the tea, which I was afraid to drink. "It's possible that Captain Snowcroft didn't have a legal obligation to pay your husband anything," he said gently.

Mrs. Dudley waved this away. "Not a legal one, maybe—but a Christian one, a human one! His negligence sent us to the brink o' the gutter—and Roger's death did the rest. I've survived on this rundown gin joint since he died. Somebody owes me."

"So you're going after Ethel Snowcroft's inheritance." Miss Judson was skeptical.

"She's a good girl. She'll do her duty to a widow."

I looked around the space. "Does she know? About Swabs, I mean?"

Mrs. Dudley sniffed and sat up straight, much more the woman I recognized. "Ethel Snowcroft comes from breeding and refinement, for all her colonial upbringing. I could hardly bring a Viscountess *here*, could I?"

"But what about all the people who've donated to her fund? You conned them into thinking they were contributing to a worthy cause."

Mrs. Dudley glared at me. "None taken, I'm sure."

"Be that as it may," Miss Judson said, producing her sketchbook. "None of this is why we've come, Mrs. Dudley. We're actually here in a professional capacity— although perhaps your connections to the seafaring community are not as strong as purported?"

Here she flushed even more deeply. "I were born in

Liverpool an' lived in Falmouth fifteen year," she said. "Still know ev'ry wharf and harbormaster by sight. What d'you want?"

Miss Judson held out her sketch. "Do you know this man? Granted, it's not a strong likeness—"

Mrs. Dudley took the paper and scowled at it. "Can't be," she muttered.

"Can't be *who*?" I demanded.

"Why, it looks like Albert Pittman, mate on the *Persephone*!"

19

Three Men
in a Boat

The number of bones in the human body is commonly totaled as 206, but in fact this number varies by individual. Children, for instance, typically possess some 300 separate bones, several of which fuse together during growth. This useful fact allows the examiner to estimate a subject's age—presuming he counts accurately.

–H. M. Hardcastle, *Foundations of Legal Medicine*

I was dumbfounded. "You knew the crew of the *Persephone*? How? Do you know what happened? Why haven't you said anything?"

"Slow down, Stephen. Let the woman answer at least one question."

Mrs. Dudley twisted her apron strings while she stared at Miss Judson's sketch. She reached out as if to touch the dead man's face, but snatched her hand back before making contact. "Bert Pittman, as I live and breathe," she said. "I'd heard he was back, but I didn't believe it."

I could hardly believe it, either. Even after reviewing the evidence with Father, it was hard to credit. Another *Persephone* survivor? What else didn't we know about that shipwreck?

"But this is brilliant," Mrs. Dudley said. "Bert can come forrard, confirm Ethel's true identity! He knows her. He'll remember her." She shoved the sketchbook back at Miss Judson in triumph.

"Probably not," Mr. Blakeney said.

Mrs. Dudley's gaze grew sharp. "What's he mean? What's happened?"

Miss Judson put a hand on my arm before I could answer. "We're not sure. Do you know how to find him? It's important."

I sat back heavily—or I would have. The shabby hassock didn't have anything to sit back against. If someone had wanted to stop Mr. Pittman from testifying on Ethel Snowcroft's behalf . . .

Mrs. Dudley shifted uncomfortably. "He don't know me," she said at last. "He'd have no reason to darken my doorstep, unless he just 'appened in one day for a pint. But there's a boardin'house takes in old soldiers an' sailors. Mrs. 'udson's, down the way. North end of Shorecross."

❧

The boardinghouse that Mrs. Dudley directed us to was readily found, and proved to be part of a minor empire.

"Aye, that's Pittman," a surly landlady confirmed when presented with Miss Judson's sketch. She pointed to a building across the lane. "Second floor, third on the left. Rent's due. Six shillings." She surveyed us and our clean and prosperous clothing, and held out a hand. "I can let you look for 'alf."

I was about to make an objection about tenancy laws, when Miss Judson opened her reticule and handed the woman the coins. "And a little extra to keep quiet." Miss Judson can appear formidable when need be.

The boardinghouse was little more than empty window frames tenuously held together by crumbling bricks. "I can see why he'd want some of Ethel Snowcroft's fortune," Mr. Blakeney Observed. "Careful," he added, picking his way across the rubbish-choked yard. "I think that water pump has cholera."

Miss Judson found an exterior stair and struck upward without a second thought. Mr. Blakeney had second thoughts, and I left him with them as I followed Miss Judson. His restraint was wise; it was unlikely the stairs could've held all our weight.

We reached a landing whose door yielded to Miss Judson's touch, swinging inward with a creak like a scream. At the sound, Mr. Blakeney scrambled up the steps like a squirrel, causing them to rattle alarmingly. He leaped to the landing as if expecting the entire affair to come collapsing down in his wake.

"Third on the left." I squinted into the dim, musty hallway. "There."

Mr. Pittman's room was likewise unlocked—or so shoddily locked that the latch shook free with only a little jiggling of the worm-eaten door. Mr. Blakeney let out a long whistle, stepping inside to let us follow.

Calling the room "furnished" was being generous. (Calling it a *room* was kind enough.) It barely offered a sorry excuse for a bed, one broken chair, and a wobbly deal washstand. The chipped basin had probably cost extra. A deep, curtainless windowsill held a row of empty brown bottles and a battered cigar box beside a neatly rolled shirt and socks: the worldly goods of Mr. Albert Pittman. Despite the spartan* surroundings, however, it was plain that Mr. Pittman had had a lot on his mind.

Or, rather, one thing on his mind.

The walls were papered with handbills and newspaper articles about Ethel Snowcroft. Little Charley had his own corner—dozens of his pictures cut out and pinned to the soot-stained walls. He seemed to

---

* named for the ancient Greek warriors who preferred to surround themselves with no luxuries of any kind. They'd not have got on with Aunt Helena at all.

have saved every article Genie—or anyone else—had ever written on the *Persephone*. The picture of the fake SWOBS headquarters had a circle drawn round it.

"This explains why he looked so familiar to Sally," I said. "He must have been to her lecture. Lectures." All of them, by the looks of things. Ticket stubs stamped with Charley's paw were tucked into the mirror frame.

"He certainly was keen to forget something, though." Mr. Blakeney hefted one of the empty bottles. It had a sour smell reminiscent of Mrs. Dudley's bar.

"Perhaps there's something here that explains what he was doing at the hospital." Miss Judson handed me the cigar box. "Either time."

Upon the lid, Mr. Pittman had inscribed his name: *A. Pittman*, the first tangible connection between his suspected identity and this room, these belongings. Inside was a jumble of oddments—the sorts of things someone *would* keep in a cigar box: a key to some long-lost lock, a reel of darning cotton, matchboxes and foreign coins, a wad of bright green felt.

"Aha!" Miss Judson seized on this last item. "I recognize this pen-wiper!" She uncrumpled the bundle to reveal an assemblage of felt petals, *RSH* embroidered upon the outermost leaf. "I just spent three hours stitching these silly things for the Hospital Committee. They give them to the Charity Ward patients upon discharge, in addition to—"

"Improving Literature?" I held up the pamphlet about Temperance and Modesty that I'd inflicted on poor Mrs. Hendricks.

"Well, we can now place Mr. Pittman in the Charity Ward at some point, as your witness told you. Unfortunately, it doesn't prove he was ever in Dr. Kinkaid's laboratory."

"He doesn't give out tickets, I suppose?" said Mr. Blakeney blandly.

"What?" Miss Judson and I both whirled about, to where Mr. Blakeney was performing a systematic dissection of the papers plastered to Mr. Pittman's dingy walls. He carefully peeled out a slip of paper with one ragged edge, an embossed seal, and a scrawl of unreadable handwriting.

"And *that*," said Miss Judson, "would be a Visitor's Ticket for the Royal Swinburne Hospital."

"What's the date? Does it say who he was visiting? It might be the killer!"

"That, alas, is not recorded."

I kicked at the floorboards. We'd never find out now.

"Chin up, Stephen," Mr. Blakeney said. "Maybe he had another hiding place."

Miss Judson and I slowly turned to look at him.

"Er—what?"

"I believe this is your area of expertise," Miss Judson said.

"Oh, right." Mr. Blakeney spurred to action, striding across the space in two cramped steps. He stooped down to examine the baseboards, peered above the cornice, turned over the chair to reveal its empty backside, shifted aside the small smoked mirror on the wall, and then, at last, reluctantly lifted up the mattress. Something scurried out, and Mr. Blakeney dropped it with a bang.

"Well, that was productive."

At the window, Mr. Pittman's socks, tidily darned and rolled up so neatly waiting for his return, seemed terribly sad. I picked them up—and they crunched. My heart rebounded as I unrolled them.

"Coo-ey, Stephen!" Inside were two crisp five-pound notes—surely far more than he'd need for an entire *year*'s rent.

"If he had this kind of money, why was he living here?" I asked. Of course, we might very well be looking at Mr. Pittman's entire life savings, but still. People with banknotes kept them in *banks*, or in safes or money clips, not rolled up in their only spare socks.

Miss Judson's frown intensified, and she searched the rest of his clothes, but found nothing else. "We appear to have checked everywhere, and that money is definitely incongruous."

"What about the heating grate?" I crouched beside it. "Look, the screws are loose."

"I'll say," muttered Mr. Blakeney.

They untwisted easily with my bare fingers. I handed all three (one was missing) to Miss Judson, lest they roll away and be lost. The ornate iron grille pulled free with no resistance, as if it was opened regularly. I said a quick prayer against spiders then thrust my hand into the cavity, feeling about the space. Finding nothing affixed to the walls, I reached all the way in, and found, at the far side of the opening, a ledge. And upon the ledge . . .

I retrieved not money, but a bundle of paper bound in butcher's twine, neat and fresh as though it had just been tucked away. I tugged off the twine, revealing a letter in blotchy, uneven handwriting. It was pages and pages long, and my hands trembled with anticipation as I unfolded them and found the start.

> To Whom It May Concern,
> What follows is the true & compleat Accounting of the Terrible Events which befell the passengers & crew of the brig PERSEPHONE on her final journey under command of Capt. Andrew Snowcroft in 1884. I was second mate. My name is Albert Pittman, and if you are reading these pages, I am surely dead. Or imprisoned—which is only the Lord's justice.

"'Terrible Events' sounds promising," said Mr. Blakeney.

> It is believed that PERSEPHONE
> sank in foul weather with all hands.
> But five survived to take to the
> lifeboat: Capt. Snowcroft, our ship's
> Surgeon whom we called Cutty—

"Cutty!" I breathed—the name on Dr. Greeley's little knife!

> —and the Navigator, Mr. Charles.
> Myself and the little girl, Ethel, along
> with her puppy, made up the last
> of the survivors. We were nineteen
> Days upon an open boat with little
> Provisions, having lost our Supplies in
> the Wreck. Capt. Snowcroft salvaged
> his chest of Money, bound for a
> bank in the Colonies, despite pleas to
> abandon it and save the water butt
> instead.
> Our captain became despondent,
> having lost his Ship and his Wife,
> and so Dr. Cutty assumed an air of
> authority among the men. The little

girl was very ill, and clung to Mr. Charles like he was her father. He would let no one speak against her— even when she came close to death and some would have her put overboard to lighten the burden on the rest.

At first we attempted to collect rainwater from the constant storms, but most was Contaminated by seawater and could not be drunk. On the fourth day we captured a Turtle, and this sustained us a few days longer.

As we grew weaker and more desperate, we became a sorry and quarrelsome lot. Our tongues and Feet were Swollen and turn'd black, our skin Blistered from the sun and salt, and with no prospect of rescue the mood aboard our little Vessel was very dark. A sort of madness descended. None of us trusted the others. Mr. Charles claimed the captain was hoarding food. The captain succumbed to paranoia, convinced we were all plotting against him, that we had sunk PERSEPHONE deliberately and turned his daughter against him. Dr. Cutty tried his best to keep order. I sat by. _I sat by._ I was too weak to intervene.

By the fifteenth day we were in a very Bad state. We sighted a Ship on the horizon, and—believing we were spared at last—Cutty sent up a signal flag we had salvaged from PERSEPHONE. But in his madness, Captain Snowcroft made to pull it down. Who can say what possessed him? Two desperate men, crazed with thirst and hunger—you would not think them able to do each other more harm, but Dr. Cutty and the Captain struggled over that flag. The little babe began to cry—a piteous whimper of "Papa! Papa!" When Mr. Charles tried to comfort her, her father in his rage did tear the little dog from her arms—and in the next moments I truly cannot say what transpired, but that Cutty had his knife in hand, and Captain Snowcroft went overboard. Weakened by privation, he could not get back into

*the longboat. And none aboard had
the strength to pull him in.*

There was a break in the pages, a spot where something had spilled on the paper, turning the ink to blurry pools.

"Is that the end?" Mr. Blakeney's voice was hopeful. I shook my head. Much as I wanted to, I could not stop now. Part was a ghastly curiosity, but the greater share, I hope, was my feeling that if Mr. Pittman had had the courage to put these words to the page, then I could do him the justice of reading his full account. I took a hard swallow and continued.

*Did we kill him? Did he fall, or
was he pushed? All I can say is we
did not save him, and what name
to give that crime but murder? But
we were one less in the boat, one less
mouth to try to feed, one less mad
wretch bringing us closer to our
doom.*

*Afterward, in the Captain's
sleeping-place, we discovered two tins
of turnips and a shriveled orange.
Why had he not shared them, even
with his dying daughter? What sort of*

man lets his own child starve to save himself?

What sort of men let their captain drown, to save themselves?

At last, on the Nineteenth day of our Ordeal, we were by unfathomable Providence delivered from our trials by the arrival of the ship GLORIA MUNDI. Her skipper, ~~⬛⬛⬛⬛~~, at great risk of his own Vessel, undertook to rescue us.

The words—the name of the rescuing captain—were there, but Mr. Pittman had gone back to blot them out most thoroughly, after they were written.

Mr. Pittman—or someone else.

The crew of the GLORIA MUNDI were very Accommodating and Sympathetic to our Plight, though Dr. Cutty urged us to hold our peace about what had occurred. It was agreed that little Ethel must be spared. She had become a little pet to us, we three wretched souls.

But I could not forget so easily. On GLORIA MUNDI I fell very Ill and, believing I was on my Deathbed, asked to make my Confession. There being no Chaplain aboard, the Captain's wife, Mrs. ⬛⬛⬛, consented to hear it. Why God saw fit to Spare me I cannot fathom. I no longer know what is real or merely my tormented memories, but even now when I close my eyes, I see the Captain in the water, blood on the knife, and hear the child crying for her father.

Captain ⬛⬛⬛ and his wife were Persuaded not to tell our tale, by means of some sum of the Cash salvaged from PERSEPHONE's coffers. The rest—Captain Snowcroft's blood money—we divided among ourselves.

I did not learn at first what became of the others, save that Mr. Charles refused to be parted from the child. Later I discovered that he had Settled in Australia and was raising her as his own. What she may recall of her Ordeal is unknown. I hope it is nothing.

But Circumstances have lately Arisen that Compel me to come

forward with my Dreadful Tale, even
in this cowardly manner. I swear upon
whatever remains of my soul, it is the
truth. I must go now to confront my
Past, to do the right thing at last,
come of it what may.

    Signed, 15 February, 1894 Albert H.
Pittman, Upton.

I wanted to drop the pages, fling them away from me—as if doing so could somehow erase what I'd just read from my mind. "Poor Sally!"

Miss Judson's face was creased with consternation—but Mr. Blakeney had gone thoughtful. "What's the name of that rescue ship again?" he asked.

"The *Gloria Mundi*. Why?"

"I don't know—it's familiar somehow." He shook his head. "Must be in the records somewhere. Mine or Genie's."

"You cannot breathe a *word* of this to her!" I turned on him, inexplicably fierce. "Not one word! Do you understand?"

His face creased with concern. "Of course not, Stephen. Cross my heart and hope to—d——n." That vow ended in a curse, uttered with nameless feelings we all understood.

Miss Judson swiftly took the pages from my hand,

folded them neatly, retied the twine, and placed them in my satchel. The banknotes she slipped into her own reticule (minus the socks). They wouldn't last long in a place like this. "This is not our secret to share—or to keep," she said firmly. "But it may be the best evidence we have, both of Sally's true identity and of what led to Mr. Pittman's murder."

"Dr. Cutty," I said to Miss Judson. "It had to be him."

"Wait—" Mr. Blakeney looked from Miss Judson to me. "Are you saying that this Cutty fellow mentioned in the letter—the *Persephone*'s surgeon—you know who that is?"

20

DON'T FORGET YOUR OLD SHIPMATE

The physical signs of extreme malnutrition–
starvation–are evident in every tissue of the
body. Even the brain does not escape and, indeed,
nervous symptoms are among the first to be
Observed.

–H. M. Hardcastle, *Foundations of Legal Medicine*

We were all silent on the way back, both the long, dark, bitter walk to the railway station (there were no cabs, but we were not accosted; our looks of benumbed horror now helped us fit in to the neighborhood) and most of the ride home. I sat on the hard third-class seat beside Miss Judson, feeling the *snicker-snack* of the rails beneath our feet, the gentle rocking of the carriage. We were as far away as imaginable from a lifeboat adrift on the Indian Ocean, but instead of a damp English winter night, all I saw out the train window was a merciless sky of burning sun and endless empty water. It was a miracle any of them had survived.

No, not a miracle. That was exactly the wrong word for what I'd just read—and yet. Despite the horrors described by Mr. Pittman, I could not help feeling his own sense of awe at their deliverance. I didn't know what to make of any of it. My companions evidently felt the same way.

Finally Mr. Blakeney broke the unbearable silence. "What d'you mean to do, then, Stephen, Miss J.?"

Miss Judson turned a tense, answerless face to me— as if I might know what to tell him. I could only shrug.

"I reckon Miss Snowcroft deserves to know the truth," he said. "She did say she wants to know everything."

I whirled on him—again. "She doesn't want to know *that*!" I sounded like Peony at her hissiest. I sank back into the seat. "No one wants to know that."

"We won't be able to keep this a secret forever, though." Miss Judson's voice was low. We were alone in the carriage, and there was no chance of anyone uttering so much as a syllable that might give away our topic of conversation, but this subject called for hush and solemnity, like a funeral. "We'll have to report it to the authorities."

I knew Miss Judson wasn't abandoning her previous

position. She had recognized the terrible weight of the matter, and we were all now working through who needed to be told what, and when, and in what order.

Mr. Blakeney looked even more uncomfortable at the thought of turning the letter over to the police. "Your Dr. Cutty—whoever he is—could be charged with the captain's death."

"That hardly matters anymore," I said glumly. "Since he *also* killed Mr. Pittman."

"There is that, I suppose," Mr. Blakeney said. After another pause, he said, "Look, I hate to keep harping on this, but it does put a spanner in the works. It could end up bearing on the Snowcroft Legacy."

In my shock, I hadn't even realized what else that letter meant. Mr. Pittman's confession proved—as much as anything could—that the *Persephone*'s navigator, Nicholas Charles, had taken Ethel Snowcroft, and her puppy, to Australia and started over with new identities. "It's hearsay, though. Albert Pittman can't testify anymore, and we can't prove that the letter is authentic. Even if we wanted this made public."

Mr. Blakeney nodded slowly. "But was he the only potential witness? What about this Cutty fellow? He's not going to be keen to testify on her behalf, not if he's gone and murdered someone to keep *him* from coming forward." Mr. Blakeney held up his hands in confusion. "As if this case weren't already complicated enough."

"I doubt Miss Snowcroft's identity was the motive,"

Miss Judson said. "It's far more probable Mr. Pittman was killed to protect this very secret. Which was *also,* I'll point out, something Sally's father never meant her to find out, bringing us right back around to what we do with this information."

"We need corroboration," I said. "We can't just take Mr. Pittman's word for it."

"I don't know, Stephen, I'm inclined to believe the poor chap. It's not the sort of thing you'd just invent for the attention." He shuddered.

I understood what he meant, but not everyone would believe Mr. Pittman's version of events. "It will be a dead man's word against the killer's." Especially if that killer were a distinguished humanitarian and beloved public figure like Dr. Greeley. I took a deep breath and prepared to retract a statement I'd made just moments ago. "We have to learn more about this ship that rescued them. The captain knew what happened to them. What they did. Can you see what you can find out? Ask Genie if you have to—but don't tell her *why* you want to know!"

We hadn't had the greatest luck with Mr. Blakeney keeping secrets from his sister, but the last time she'd forced a confidence from him, she'd nearly brought down disaster upon herself—so perhaps she would be less enthusiastic about prying the truth from him again.

We could hope.

～

That night we sat in the schoolroom, Mr. Pittman's letter between us on the workbench. Even Peony stayed away from the pages and their tempting, bitable corners, as if she, too, could feel the tainted secrets with her clever whiskers. The day's discoveries had successfully kept at bay my fears about the secret Father was keeping from me—from us—but in the quiet safety of the schoolroom, I felt them lurking about the perimeter, waiting to pounce.

"So," Miss Judson said, rousing me from dark thoughts into even darker ones, "Dr. Cutty?"

I explained again about the knife in Dr. Greeley's office, with *Cutty* engraved upon its handle, and his past as a ship's surgeon. Miss Judson held Peony on her lap, stroking her thoughtfully.

"It's hard enough to imagine Dr. Greeley killing a shipmate ten years ago at the height of a catastrophe to save four other lives—five," she amended, to include little Charley, who had become an unwitting co-conspirator in the deed. "But murdering another one now, in cold blood, in the heart of his very own hospital?"

She unfolded her legs and set Peony on the counter. "Furthermore, there's no Cutty *or* Greeley on the *Persephone*'s manifest. How does he enter the picture? Did he change his name, too?"

"Not necessarily. Ships change crews all the time, don't they?" I'd heard that, surely. "Maybe he came aboard later—when they stopped in Portugal, for instance."

"Just a quick trip ashore for a puppy and a doctor?" She sighed. "I'm sure he never regretted that decision."

An abrupt thought hit my hollow stomach like a blow. "He came to see Dr. Greeley that night. The A. P. in the calendar—it wasn't Annie Pethwick. It was *Albert Pittman*. That money we found—what if he was blackmailing Dr. Greeley? Dr. Greeley has the big unveiling of his plans for the Free Surgery coming up. Pittman showing up now would ruin everything. Greeley had to get rid of him!"

I was back to the first theory I'd had that made any sense—and this time I had both money and a murder victim to back it up.

"No." Peony's reaction was one of distaste, not skepticism.

"I don't like that idea," Miss Judson affirmed.

I sighed and kicked the rungs of my stool. I didn't like it much, either—and it was the very best one we had.

∽

We didn't get a chance to fill Father in the next morning. He'd passed a bad night and was running a fever; in too much pain to speak; and had finally settled into a fitful, morphine-induced sleep. Nurse Pethwick met us at the doors to the Men's Ward to deliver this report, and the news that we were not to be admitted this morning.

"I am sorry," she said, holding the swinging doors shut behind her. "But it's not my call." She glanced up and down the corridor, then added in a low voice, "There's a big to-do today—the Guv has a meeting with the Trustees, and between you and me, he's counting on the patients being well behaved. Matron's orders: *Keep them quiet.*" Matron stood just inside, like a lacy green bulldog, guarding her domain.

"I suppose a murder *would* look bad to the precious Trustees," I said crossly.

"And we would hate to jeopardize the Free Surgery," Miss Judson said firmly. I knew she was right, but even so.

"What do we do?" I said to Miss Judson as we turned away. "Do you believe her? What if they've"—I gulped—"got to him? Or—" Or something worse had happened, and he was sicker than anyone was saying?

"Don't get carried away," Miss Judson said. "He probably *is* feverish and exhausted. How much rest has he had in the past few days? The man was already run down when he was admitted, and he's refused to follow the nurses' instructions—" Her voice reached a strained pitch, and she halted, taking a measured breath. "It's no wonder this has happened."

I had to pull myself together, for Miss Judson's sake. "You're right. He just needs rest. But *we* need to do something. Dr. Greeley's going to go into that meeting and charm all those Trustees, no one the wiser that he's really—"

"*Shh.*" Miss Judson shushed me, as a skinny porter squeaked by in his noisy shoes, doing his worst to disappear into the nonexistent shadows. We watched him skulk down the corridor, hunched in his black uniform like he was hiding something.

"What is that man up to?" I said. "He's totally out of place here, and yet he's *everywhere*. I want to know where he's going."

Miss Judson watched him, too. "Dr. Greeley can wait. Let's find out."

As loud as our own footfalls were, Squeaky Shoes did not seem to notice he was being followed. He passed the reception desk (which had added a second jar to collect donations for Sally, the first full to overflowing) and continued round the corner to the administrative wing.

"Just as I thought," I whispered to Miss Judson, as Squeaky Shoes slipped into Dr. Kinkaid's laboratory. "Those two are up to something."

"Well, he *is* a porter," she pointed out. "His job is to follow the instructions of the doctors here."

"Is he, though?" I countered. "Why hasn't Matron written him up for his shoes, then? Or made him get a proper uniform? No, he reminds me of somebody— and it's not the hospital porters." I just couldn't place it, though. "We haven't seen him do any real hospital work, either. All he does is hang about Dr. Kinkaid."

"One might say the same thing about us," she noted. "Maybe he's a fan of surgeons. Maybe he likes rats."

"Maybe he tampered with the Bunsen burners."

"So he's Dr. Kinkaid's accomplice now?" An uncharacteristic tension had crept into Miss Judson's voice.

"What's your theory, then?" I snapped.

She pressed a hand to the bridge of her nose. "Oh, I don't know," she sighed. "Mr. Blakeney was correct—the closer we come to a solution, the more complicated this case gets. And without your father to consult . . ." She trailed off hopelessly.

It was clear I would have to be the one to carry on, so I took a deep breath and made a bold decision. "Father or not, we're running out of time. We need to confront Dr. Greeley. We can be delicate," I added hastily, at Miss Judson's expression of alarm. "Or, well—*you* can."

The Look Miss Judson bestowed upon me next made me glad we had not yet mastered Telepathic Communication. I suspected she was tarnishing my name in three languages. Finally, all she said was, "We'd best make it quick. Here he comes."

Dear Reader, I should very much have liked the opportunity to consult with my client (Father) before proceeding with my Investigation and the interrogation of my chief suspect. Questioning a suspect typically didn't unsettle me, but this was an unusually sensitive matter. I hadn't decided where I stood on the first homicide—Captain Snowcroft sounded like a beast, and his death probably *had* saved Sally and the others. But there was no justification for killing Albert Pittman. Self-defense did not cover protecting hospitals. I gave a Miss Judson–like tug on my bodice and smoothed my unsmoothable hair. There was no telling how this conversation might go.

Dr. Greeley stepped out from his office, cradling folders in the crook of one arm. "Ladies?" He gave us a small smile. "Is everything all right? No more problems with Mr. Hardcastle, I hope?"

Miss Judson said, "In fact, we're here about the other matter." The weight she gave those words made it impossible to mistake which Other Matter she was referring to. "We've come on behalf of the Magistrate's Office."

"By proxy," I clarified. We didn't technically have any authority to question a suspect, but with Father indisposed, circumstances justified our deputizing ourselves. I was sure Father would understand. Mostly sure.

Dr. Greeley carefully locked his office door, double-checking that it was secure before tucking the key inside his waistcoat pocket, which he smoothed neat. He clearly didn't realize how useless *that* precaution was. "Well, I'm afraid I don't have time to talk at the moment. I'm giving a presentation to the Trustees about the Free Surgery." He gazed fondly at the grand drawing of the prospective new wing that took up most of the opposite wall, another splendidly modern building that fairly sparkled with the promise of brilliant medical advances. "This will be the culmination of all I've tried to do here at the Royal Swinburne. You're welcome to attend, if you're interested. As my guests." He straightened one corner of the frame with fastidious fingers.

Miss Judson politely declined. "This can't wait, sir. We believe we've identified the murder victim. One Albert Pittman?"

Dr. Greeley did not react to the name. "Well, that's good news, surely? Or not, I suppose. The poor man. Have his family been notified?"

"We're speaking to his acquaintances now." Miss Judson let that statement hang in the air for a very long moment. "Dr. Cutty."

Dr. Greeley's kindly face turned ashen, but he set his jaw and continued his walk down the corridor. I could hold my tongue no longer. "It *was* you, wasn't it? You were on the *Persephone*—the ship's surgeon."

Dr. Greeley wheeled on me, temper flashing in his benign features, quickly stifled. "The *Persephone* was lost with all hands," he said gruffly. "*All hands.* It was a terrible tragedy. But it has nothing at all to do with me."

"It has everything to do with you." I realized something even as the words escaped me. "You commissioned a study on starvation!"

With effort, he recovered his calm, fatherly demeanor. "Thousands of poverty-stricken Britons are afflicted with malnutrition. It's the role of medicine to relieve suffering." His voice broke, just the slightest bit.

"From what we understand, that's what you did," Miss Judson said. "You saved lives."

"You understand nothing! There is nothing to be said. It has nothing to do with me."

"Albert Pittman came to see you, didn't he?" I pressed. "Was he blackmailing you?"

And that's when I caught a glimmer of the man who could slay his captain and throw him overboard to save his crewmates. Dr. Greeley stood cool and unflinching, gazing at me levelly. "Young lady, I have a meeting to attend. I expect to hear nothing from either of you on this matter again. If I do, you shall be hearing from *my* solicitor. Good day."

With that gushing confession, Dr. Julius Greeley took his stack of paperwork into the Trustees' Assembly Rooms and clicked the door shut with finality. "Well," I sighed, glowering at the stately oaken door, "we broke him."

Miss Judson uttered a highly undignified snort.

21
ALBATROSS STEW

In addition to external examination of a subject, the astute Medico-Legal Investigator will also search for any foreign objects within the body, particularly in the airways and digestive tract. A surprising number of injuries occur when seemingly innocuous items are ingested or inhaled.

–H. M. Hardcastle, *Foundations of Legal Medicine*

"Now what?" I'd thought Dr. Greeley might crumble with guilt at the very mention of the events aboard the *Persephone*. He was a harder man than I'd anticipated, for all his outward kindness—which meant it would be even harder to prove his involvement with Mr. Pittman's death. Anyone who could cover his tracks so well for ten years would not be an easy man to pin a murder—two murders—on.

Miss Judson frowned into the distance in consideration. Finally, she made up her mind. "I have another idea," she announced. "Come along."

I will follow Miss Judson anywhere, Dear Reader, but I hesitated. "Where?" I had not forgotten how her most recent Outing had turned out.

"Matron's office. She knows everything that goes on in this hospital, with an especial interest in the illustrious Julius Greeley. If anyone can shed light on his activities, she can."

If I'd thought Dr. Greeley a formidable suspect to approach, that was nothing in comparison to how I felt about facing down Matron Finch. I gave my most forbearing sigh and followed.

Miss Judson rapped soundly on the door, but there was no answer.

"Good," I said. "We'll come back later."

My accomplice caught me by the collar and forestalled my escape. "*Au contraire.* Our timing is ideal." After a glance up and down the empty corridor, she reached into her dark braids, coiled neatly into their perfect knot, and twisted free a long, dangerous-looking hairpin without disturbing a single springy curl. Bending to the doorknob, she inserted the pin into the keyhole.

I had to bite my tongue to keep from exclaiming. Miss Judson paused, hand stilled.

"Never speak of this," she said severely.

A moment later, the tumblers tumbled free, and the door clicked open.

Dear Reader, perhaps *you* can explain what it was

with my parent and governess and breaking-and-entering at the Royal Swinburne Hospital. Had they been given noxious gas when I wasn't looking, too?

"Technically," Miss Judson said cheerfully, pushing me inside, "it's just entering."

"Technically it's a *crime*." Matron's leather restraints sprang to mind—not to mention the rumors about how she'd lost her last post. Or the fact that she was still high on my list of Suspects Likely to Kill Off Hospital Visitors. This wasn't like Dr. Greeley's office in the dead of night; there were people swarming all over the hospital at midday, and Matron (and her murderous impulses, spies, co-conspirators, and hench-porters) could return at any moment.

"Panic is not beneficial in this situation."

"Really?" I snapped. "What *would* be beneficial? Calling Security?"

She shooed me along with her hands. "Search something. Go see if she has incriminating letters in her desk, *cartes de visite* from Blackpool, or evidence of suspicious activity."

"A canister of carbon monoxide?"

Miss Judson was no longer listening. She'd paused before a large display case mounted beside the door, showing an assortment of small objects—not dissimilar to the items in Mr. Pittman's cigar box, incidentally (except for the five-pound notes—although there was sixpence, a couple of ha'pennies, and at least one huge silver coin I didn't recognize). Against my will, I too found myself drawn to the peculiar piece of . . . art?

Miss Judson's hand was at her mouth, her eyes wide. When I read the brass plate affixed to the stately gilded frame, I stood likewise.

> FOREIGN OBJECTS SWALLOWED BY &
> RETRIEVED FROM PATIENTS

I recoiled. There were needles, buttons, a pair of dice, a bullet . . . "It ought to say Objects *Fed* to Patients," I grumbled. "Where's the Bovril tin?" Miss Judson didn't answer, so I moved on to Matron's desk.

Matron's chambers were the twin to Governor Greeley's, but furnished in lighter, softer tones. There was lace everywhere: spare lappets stacked neatly upon a tall narrow chest, dresser scarves across desk and mantelpiece, soft billowing curtains on the open windows, and doilies on every other surface.

"Horseshoe nails? A wedding ring—how does someone swallow a *seahorse*?" Wonder filled Miss Judson's voice. "Where do you even get a seahorse?"

"Miss! She'll be back any moment! There's probably a case in the other room of all the patients *Matron* has eaten!"

"Yes. Quite." Miss Judson coughed and joined me on the hunt. Although frankly it looked like she was just snooping: trailing her fingers through Matron's belongings for curiosity's sake alone. "Do you suppose she was born with one of these lappets?"

I ignored this. Miss Judson knew as well as I did that the lappet was the badge of office of hospital Matron, the long lacy tails commanding so much awe and respect. I made a systematic perusal of Matron's desk. Her precious keys and notebook were on her person, of course—but there was a journal in the top drawer. With a spike of hope, I flipped through it, but instead of confessing her innermost thoughts to the page, she'd only committed a list of the offenses perpetrated by her patients and nurses.

"She wrote Nurse Ling up five times last month!"

Now Miss Judson frowned. "She could lose her post at that rate. What does it say she's done?"

"Tardiness, slovenliness . . . *sauce*—?" Scrunching my nose in bafflement, I looked to Miss Judson for clarification.

She suppressed a smile. "Backtalk. Now who's being literal?"

"Those aren't exactly felonies," I said, but Miss Judson took the book from me.

"You've never been to boarding school. I'll wager there are also demerits for uneven apron ties or—*voilà*." She held the book out to show me where Nurse Keene had received a black mark (literally: a great inky X, gleefully drawn beside her name) for letting the Nurses' Sitting Room fire die down.

The doctors hadn't escaped Matron's rebuke, either. "Here's a notation about Dr. Kinkaid. *Have spkn to Gov. Gr. re: Mr. KINKAID's qualifications & the allotment of my own Sitting Room for his use. Why has he taken on that Fenian terrorist? I will make him see sense.*"

I lifted my eyes from an assortment of tatting shuttles (probably not swallowed) to meet Miss Judson's gaze. "Terrorist?" I echoed. Had Matron Finch learned the truth about Dr. Kinkaid's secrets and threatened to exploit them? "She must have seen the same article we did."

Miss Judson's brow furrowed as she leafed through a few more pages.

"Is there anything about Mr. Pittman?" I asked.

"Not that I saw." She sighed. "Nor does she happen to confess any misdeeds from her days in Blackpool, or wherever she came from."

"Blackpool! They have seahorses in Blackpool."

"Do they?"

"Well, they don't grow wild in Swinburne." I marched back to the display case and yanked on its glass door—half expecting the whole thing to come crashing off the wall.

To our surprise, it swung open instead, granting access to the Cabinet of Curiosities within. We regarded one another for a guilty moment, then set to work. Miss Judson plucked out the spiny little seahorse, evidently forgetting that it had once been *inside* a patient. Beside a small celluloid fountain pen, a sparkle of gold caught my eye, and I withdrew the wedding ring. I wasn't sure why I was drawn to that ordinary object, in lieu of the stranger items, until I held it in my hand and gasped.

"This is Father's ring!"

"What? No. Surely not."

I was shaking now—with confusion or outrage or some emotion yet to be named. Father *hadn't* taken it off himself! I held it to the light so she could see where the gold had rubbed thin from wear, the engraved initials within. "She's stealing from the patients!" I leaped to an even more horrifying conclusion. "She's going to kill him."

"Stealing, yes," Miss Judson said slowly. She, too, had found an item that did not seem to belong among the ingested paraphernalia: a second hoop of gold, nearly as familiar as the first.

"Mr. Pittman's other earring?"

Miss Judson closed her fist around her treasure, expression grim. "Something very odd is happening here, and I mean to get to the bottom of it."

She got her chance sooner than we expected. Before we could tidy up after ourselves or make ourselves scarce—indeed, while we were still standing there, display case open, holding Father's wedding ring and an undigested seahorse—the door to Matron's private sanctuary swung open, and a small furious figure caught us red-handed. *Hippocampus*-handed.

"Just exactly what do you think you're doing in here?"

"What are you doing?" I flung back. "This is my father's wedding ring!" I waved it in Matron's face.

Miss Judson tsked. "My word. Not exactly practicing the Nightingale* ideals of purity and sacrifice, are we, Miss Finch? Could you perhaps have lost your post in Blackpool because of theft?" She fanned the pages of the diary with her thumb. "Looks like someone deserves a demerit."

Matron Finch lunged at Miss Judson and snatched back—of all things—the seahorse. She tucked it carefully into its niche in the display cabinet and shut the door. "You have no right to come in here and go through my personal things!"

Miss Judson's cool eyes flicked toward me, then back to Matron. "I feel like there's a saying that applies here—something about pots and kettles."

Matron's face turned scarlet, and went on turning redder and redder until even her white lappet took on a faintly pink glow. "I should call the porters and have you thrown out—you *and* Mr. Hardcastle!"

Honestly, I half wished she would, and we could all

* Florence Nightingale, famed nurse of—you guessed it, Dear Reader— the Crimean War

go home and be done with this hospital and the case—but we had a duty to Mr. Pittman. And to Father. "Not until you explain yourself. We ought to summon the police."

That threat had more of an effect than I could have imagined. "You horrid people," Matron gulped. "Nothing at all has gone right since you started coming round. You have no respect for me at all!" Her beady eyes filled, and great round tears spilled down her cheeks.

I stared at her in disbelief. Was she really crying?

"I'm afraid we *don't* countenance theft and murder, no," Miss Judson said.

Matron didn't stop crying, but she gaped at my governess. "Murder? I never killed anyone!"

Miss Judson uncurled her fingers to reveal the hoop of gold.

Matron took a step backward. "Now you wait a minute! He was dead when I found him. I swear it."

"I knew it! *You* hid the body in the laundry room. You got that porter to help, didn't you? Did you use the laundry chute? And Nurse Ling—she witnessed everything. That's why you've been threatening her!"

Dear Reader, it's possible that I occasionally, in my enthusiasm, let my tongue run away with me.

Matron pulled herself up to her maximum height, until we were nearly eye-to-eye. "As if I would put that filthy corpse in the laundry chute! Children today."

Miss Judson intervened calmly. "Perhaps you'd care to start at the beginning. You claim to have merely . . . come upon the deceased body of Mr. Pittman. Where?"

"Pittman, was that his name? Knew that bunk about 'Mr. Jonah' was a lot of cock-and-bull." Her back stiffened at the memory. "Coming round here, bothering the Guv."

"And you can't have anybody bother your precious Governor Greeley, can you?" I said, somewhat nastier than I'd intended. "Not when he'd hired you on, despite the scandal in Blackpool. You *owe* him." I was guessing now, Dear Reader, making wild stabs in the dark—but they seemed to strike home.

Matron gave a dignified sniffle. "Julius Greeley is a *great* man. *You* wouldn't understand—sullying our ward, bringing in all kinds of criminal elements."

Miss Judson's eyes shifted pointedly to the case of Matron's collection. "As you were saying? How did you 'find' Mr. Pittman's body?"

Matron studied her blocky red fingers. "I came round late that night," she said. "Monday. I knew that the Guv—that Dr. Greeley had a meeting what he was upset about. I wanted to be sure he was all right after."

"A meeting with Mr. Pittman?"

"I don't know. That wasn't in his calendar. But when I came to check on him, his office was locked. Dr. Kinkaid's laboratory, though—the lights were on, but no one was inside. I went in to switch them off—wasting the hospital's money like that—and that's when I found the—when I found Mr. Pittman."

"Hmm." Miss Judson's brown fingers tapped skeptically against her elbow. "Go on."

"Well, I saw he was in distress, didn't I, and I thought to revive him, if I could—but it was too late. Then I heard the sound of the gas burners."

"Burners?" I said. "All of them?"

She nodded, too eager. "I covered my mouth and nose with my apron, opened the windows, and shut the valves. Then I left to get Mr. Bentley—the night porter on duty on this floor. He helped me with the rest. And that little snoop Ling saw the whole thing."

"You tried to take the body to the morgue," I said, and she nodded even more vigorously. Her steady stream of tears had not abated, but she was at least coherent.

"But that oaf Bentley couldn't get the proper paperwork. We had to hide him instead."

Her story was plausible, barely. One thing—well, *at least* one thing—still didn't make sense. "*Why?*" I said. "Why didn't you just send for the police? Why go to such lengths to cover up the murder?"

"Oh, I think we know the answer to that question," Miss Judson said. "Matron Finch knows who the real killer was."

Matron gave one last great sniff. "Julius Greeley is a great man," she said again. But what she said next surprised us both. "And I'm not about to stand by and let that Irishman who calls himself a surgeon ruin him or this hospital."

Dear Reader, that statement left us momentarily speechless. Fortunately, Matron Finch did not require our questions; she was clearly delighted to have an audience for her grievances at last. "I knew he was a bad sort from the moment he first set foot on the grounds. And he proved me right, too, didn't he? All those Irishmen skulking around, meetings at odd hours, deliveries to his laboratory that he has no call to order. I ask you," she said with a self-righteous huff, "what does *he* need with a shipment of nitroglycerin? He's a surgeon, not a heart specialist."

The word sank in slowly, and Miss Judson and I turned to stare at one another. Nitroglycerin. The key ingredient in dynamite.

22

DEAD RECKONING

The Medico-Legal Investigator often becomes the
bearer of bad news.

–H. M. Hardcastle, *Foundations of Legal Medicine*

Miss Judson issued her sternest warning to Matron
Finch, and we left her to snivel over her ill-gotten booty
(I took Father's ring for safekeeping). I argued with
Miss Judson all the way back to the Men's Ward.

"Why *can't* we go to the police?" I demanded—
quietly, so the army of porters setting up for Hospital
Sunday wouldn't overhear. "We know who killed
Pittman *and* we know that Dr. Kinkaid is plotting to
build another bomb!"

She seized my arm, propelling me into the stairwell.
"We do not know any such thing," she said severely.
"Well, we have a good idea about that first one. But
all we have is the word of that—megalomaniacal klep-
tomaniac, against the reputation of a distinguished

surgeon." She took a breath. "Yes, admittedly, a shipment of nitroglycerin does raise questions. However, we have no actual evidence that our Dr. Kinkaid is in any way related to a bombing in Manchester ten years ago, let alone that he means to attack his place of employment. And I'm certainly not going to be the one to start pointing fingers, not while your father is still at their mercy."

"That's why we should tell the police! Let *them* point fingers. Wait—" Something else occurred to me, and I flung up my hands in frustration. "Matron said *Bentley* helped her hide the body. Then it wasn't Squeaky Shoes. Which means we still don't know what *he's* doing lurking about!"

On that note, the stairwell door whispered open. "Hardcastles? You down there?" Nurse Pethwick trotted down the stairs. "'E's up and asking for you."

My heart leaped. Or plummeted. I frankly couldn't tell anymore. "Is he all right?"

"Cranky, I'd say," was Nurse Pethwick's considered medical opinion. "But stronger. His fever's broke. Come along."

Back in the Men's Ward, Father was sitting up and alert, and looking more than ever like a sulky little boy. He crossed his arms and glowered at everyone.

"Now, Mr. Hardcastle, none o' that," Nurse Pethwick scolded. "Haven't these two been running all over and back for you? Be nice, then. Or shall I bring you more

Bovril? Ten minutes, no more," she told us sternly. "Dr. Kinkaid's orders."

"Weh?" Father whispered once we were alone, holding out his hand impatiently.

"Well, what?" I said. So much had happened since yesterday afternoon, I hardly knew where to begin.

"Dih—" Father dissolved in a wince, waving his hand impatiently. He fumbled through the sea of papers on his bed for a notebook, in which he scribbled impatiently: *DID YOU ID'FY DEAD MAN?!!!* (Personally, I felt this was an excess of exclamation points.)

"Did you know Matron Finch stole your wedding ring?" I returned. "Or that Fenians are plotting to bomb Hospital Sunday? Or that Dr. Greeley—"

Miss Judson stepped in. "Rather a lot has come to light in the past twenty-four hours. Perhaps we should begin with Mr. Pittman's letter?"

Father frowned impatiently, mouthing, *"Pittman? Who is Pitt—"* His expression changed as he recognized the name of the *Persephone*'s second mate. He grabbed for my satchel, scarcely letting me dig the evidence out and surrender it.

He read hurriedly, flipping from page to page in Mr. Pittman's long confession. It was like watching an eager child devour a bedtime story—*Robinson Crusoe* or *The Pirate*. His fevered eyes glittered and he sat up straighter, gripping the edges of the paper. When he reached the end, he stared at the page for a long, breathless moment, then blinked and rubbed his face, like he was waking up from a strange dream.

I knew how he felt, and yet I nearly expired from suspense, waiting for his verdict. Miss Judson efficiently filled him in on the details not included in Mr. Pittman's confession: the truth behind SWOBS, the condition of Mr. Pittman's room, his obsession with Sally. Finally, I could bear it no longer. "What should we *do*?"

But Father hadn't made up his mind. Which I suppose was reasonable; he'd only just learned what we'd had the whole day to digest. Even so, it was an agonizing age before he finally took up his pen once more. He wrote a rapid page whose contents he did not disclose, then penned a second—this one much shorter. He ripped it right from the notebook and handed it to me. *1) Give encl. to Fox*, it read, and *2) Send me Carstairs*. Then, gesturing for me to return the paper, he inserted a sheepish addendum: *3) My ring?*

Miss Judson regarded our orders in silence for a long moment, folding the note for Magistrate Fox neatly into her reticule. "We understand, sir," she said, but I wondered if it was enough. Would the police come simply because Father called for them? Would they arrest Governor Greeley? What about Dr. Kinkaid and the dynamite? But Father didn't know those answers any more than I did, so with some effort, I held my tongue.

"Wuh moh thig." Speaking with slow, painful effort, Father drew me closer. Heart stuttering, I let him. "I wanh you t'stay hobe t'morrow."

I pulled back. Stay home? "What? No!"

"Too daygerous."

"Exactly! You need me. What if something—" But I couldn't put voice to that thought. What if *what*? I only gripped him hard. We'd found his wedding ring, proving it, at least, wasn't part of some Great Dark Secret—but what about the rest of it? Father *was* hiding something from me, and if it had to do with the case— "No. *No*." I wished Peony was here. *She* would convince him.

I looked to Miss Judson in appeal, but her face was set. "I'm of a mind with your father on this," she said solemnly. Wait—was *she* in on the secret now, too? "Things are getting serious."

"And the *murder* wasn't serious? I can't believe this. Sally is counting on us! If it's too dangerous for me, why isn't it too dangerous for *her*?"

Father held my hand, and he held my gaze. "I'm not her father. Thss's fidal, Muhrl."

I closed my eyes. I knew that tone of voice, raspy and odd as it was. He meant it.

∽

We returned to Magistrate Fox's house that very evening. It was another impossibly long train ride to Upton, made even worse by the sullen silence between me and Miss Judson. I formulated and discarded countless arguments against Father's position, but I could tell it was hopeless. And I daren't broach the matter of the papers I'd found in Father's desk, because I wasn't ready to know what they meant. By the time we climbed silently into Magistrate Fox's carriage for the drive to his house, I felt as numb and defeated as a shipwrecked castaway.

To our surprise, Sally was at the Magistrate's house when we arrived, although I saw no sign of Mrs. Dudley. She was chaperoned only by Charley, who was distracted from his duties by the fawning attentions of the Magistrate's dogs, who had evidently adopted the elderly seaman as one of their own.

Sally rushed to greet us, wide eyes searching our faces. "How is your father? Have you learned who the dead man was?" But I knew she was really asking another question, and I wasn't at all sure how to answer it. *Do you know who I am?*

Once more, Magistrate Fox seemed delighted to see us, despite the solemnity of the occasion. "Sally, darling, we won't be a minute," he promised her, ushering us into a small enclave off the grand parlor with its huge fireplace and model ship. On closer inspection, this appeared to be the dogs' room, for it was full of soft, worn furniture covered in fur and blankets. Magistrate Fox retrieved a pair of spectacles from the arm of the chair—they were underneath an issue of

Tales from the Red Graves that claimed to have Charley's autobiographical* account of survival at sea.

I'm afraid I might have let out a less-than-approving sound.

Magistrate Fox chuckled. "It's jolly good reading," he said. "Even if there's not an ounce of truth to it."

"That's why we've come, sir," Miss Judson said. "We believe we now know the full story of the *Persephone*."

"Well, that's wonderful! Let's tell Sally at once."

Miss Judson forestalled this. "Mr. Hardcastle would like your opinion first." She handed over the letters, Father's first, then Mr. Pittman's.

If fidgeting could be fatal, I was having my second attack of the day, and I'd certainly have perished right there on Magistrate Fox's hairy old rug. (Which, all things considered, would not be the worst place to spend one's last moments. It would at least be cozy.) At long last, Magistrate Fox laid the letters down, removed his spectacles, and rubbed the bridge of his nose.

"I never did like Andrew Snowcroft," he said. "The man was a brute, if you ask me. Can't say I'm surprised to read this. Shocked, yes. But not surprised." Magistrate Fox tapped his fingers against the desk. "Julius Greeley, now . . . He's always seemed a fine man. Completely selfless. This business"—he waved a vague hand toward the papers—"terrible thing. Just terrible."

* pawtobiographical?

"What's terrible?" Sally's bright voice broke in. "Did you find out that I'm not Ethel Snowcroft? That would be a relief, actually." Before we could stop her, she thrust her way past us to snatch the letter right off Magistrate Fox's desk.

She was intercepted with cries of "No!" (me), "Miss Snowcroft—" (Miss Judson), "Wait, my dear—" (the Magistrate), and "Arf—" but she ignored us all. She stood rigid, suntanned hands holding the pages steady as she took in their bleak contents. But in the crushing silence, I swear I could hear her heart beating, like a hummingbird's frantic wings.

"Who wrote this?" she finally asked, tracing the mottled, tearstained ink. "It was him, wasn't it—the murdered man? The one who had the flag."

I stared back at her, unsure how to respond. Finally I nodded miserably.

"He could have told everyone who I was," she said softly. "He could have told *me*. But I suppose I know, now." She folded the papers, as if trying to hide the truth from herself again.

Miss Judson came forward and gently untwined Sally's grip on the letter. "Your father never wanted you to learn this."

"That they killed my real father?" Her voice was high and sharp. "Or that my real father was a—a—" Unable to bring up a word to describe him, she flailed a helpless hand.

"Exactly." Miss Judson met Sally's gaze levelly. I knew that look. It had steadied me in many a crisis, too. Charley, sensing something amiss, pattered over to his mistress and clamored to be lifted up.

"What about these other people? They're all dead now? Captain Snowcroft, Mr. Charles, Mr. Pittman . . . this Dr. Cutty, too, I suppose." Sally stroked Charley's worried eyebrows. "We're the only ones left now. We really are all alone in the world."

Magistrate Fox came to her side. "Oh, no, my dear. Not alone. Not as long as we've found each other."

Stiffly, she pulled away, composing herself. "You're very kind," she said formally. "You all are. But I need time—I need to . . . decide how I feel about things. I don't know what I expected to learn," she confessed. "Certainly not this."

Mr. Blakeney's take on the news came back to me now. "But this will help her case, won't it? I mean, some good should come from this . . ." I glanced to Sally, but she'd retreated into her own thoughts, twining the locket chain in her fingers. I could not begin to know what she was thinking, but a little of what she must be feeling had seeped into my heart.

Miss Judson took charge. She tugged the bellpull near the fireplace, summoning a maid, who arrived already carrying a pot of cocoa and lovely little dishes of rice pudding. As Sally sipped her cocoa, the discussion turned back to the case.

"What's next, sir?" Miss Judson asked. "The culprit seems clear." She gave me a pointed look as she said this, expecting me to speak up regarding the murder. But what did it matter now? Sally was devastated by what she'd just learned, and Father had shut me out of the Investigation. I sank against the furry armchair and stared at my cooling cocoa. A dog came from somewhere and laid a heavy head on my knee, sighing.

Magistrate Fox grew stern and serious—the face I recognized from court. "Well, speaking as a judge, I can't see moving forward with the case until after the Coroner's Inquest."

An Inquest was a time-honored English legal tradition, but—"Why do we need to wait?" I said. "It's obviously a homicide."

Magistrate Fox shook his head sadly. "The physical evidence so far also points to an accidental death. Mr. Pittman, a chronic drunkard, wandered into the laboratory, stumbled and struck his head, and accidentally knocked open the gas as he fell."

I frowned at Miss Judson. "But Matron Finch's account of hiding the body—"

"Only proves her desire to protect the hospital from embarrassment. An instinct, I might add, that I share." He held up a hand to overrule my next objection. *"For the moment.* Let the Police Surgeon's report come back, let the Coroner's Inquest proceed. Your father will need to testify, as he's the only witness who can corroborate that Mr. Pittman was in an altercation before his death."

"Sort of corroborate it," I mumbled.

Magistrate Fox put a kindly hand on my arm. "He's not going anywhere, Myrtle. There's plenty of time." He stood up—a signal that our evening had drawn to a close. But I seized the moment, while Miss Judson was otherwise occupied donning her coat and muffler.

"Father has those school brochures for Sally," I said to the Magistrate, but his eyes crinkled in a frown. "Didn't you ask for them?" That question came out more sharply than I wanted.

Now the crinkle turned to a smile. "Not me, Myrtle. No, no—those brochures must be for you. Clever girl like you won't need a governess forever." He cast a long—overlong, if you ask me—look at Miss Judson, and I had my third attack of Fatal Fidgeting.

"What do you mean?"

But the Magistrate just squeezed my shoulder and wouldn't answer. "I'm glad you'll be there for Sally tomorrow."

Sally heard this as her own cue to return, and she rose to fling her arms around me, squeezing me in a positively asphyxiating embrace. "I don't know how I could have done all of this without your family."

From what I could tell, all we'd done was ruin her last memories of the people she'd loved. When she finally released me, I made my cowardly exit. "I can't come to Hospital Sunday. My father won't let me."

"But how will I stand up in front of all those people and speak?"

"Charley will be there. And you've done dozens of lectures."

She twisted the locket chain around her finger until I thought it would snap. "That was *before*. It was easy to speak to them when I didn't know the truth. What will I say to them now? Myrtle, you *have* to come! Promise me you'll be there."

"I can't," I said. She gripped my arms.

"You have to."

23

HOSPITAL SUNDAY

The Medico-Legal Investigator is often called
upon to testify in court, and must be prepared to
speak in terms understandable to laymen who do
not share his technical expertise.

–H. M. Hardcastle, *Foundations of Legal Medicine*

Sally was right. I did have to be there—and not only
for her sake. Father might not realize it, but he was
depending on me, too. There were too many loose ends
to this case for one indisposed person to keep track of
by himself from a hospital bed.

I made one final, fruitless appeal to Miss Judson.
I would much rather proceed with authorization than
without it, but there was more to it than that. I needed
her to understand. When she came to see me settled in
bed (I am rather too old to be "tucked in"), Peony and
I were still sitting up. "I *have* to go tomorrow," I said.
"Sally practically begged me."

Miss Judson was unmoved. "Sally shall have Mrs.

Dudley and Aunt Helena. They won't let anything happen to her."

Would they squeeze her hand to give her the courage to face people after what she'd learned tonight? I didn't know how to put that in words to Miss Judson, though, so I didn't even try. "Good. Then that just leaves Father, Dr. Greeley, Matron, Squeaky Shoes, and Dr. Kinkaid for us to look after." Surely she could see that arithmetic didn't add up.

"I'm afraid they'll have to look after themselves," she said. "Since I will be here, looking after you."

I stared at her, my lifeboat sinking. "What? *You're* not going? What about Father? We can't possibly leave him on his own! What about Dr. Greeley? What about Dr. Kinkaid and the nitroglycerin?" How could he even think to keep both of us away from the hospital? He was even worse off than I'd realized. "That settles it. We're going."

"We are *not* going," she replied firmly. "I'm sorry, Myrtle. Your father was very clear on this point. You are not to return to the Royal Swinburne until Albert Pittman's killer has been arrested—and I am not to permit you to do so. I have been given very specific directives."

"Well, I'm countermanding them! If I can't be there, then you *have* to go." Arms crossed, I gave her my fiercest Look. "Father *needs* us. He needs you. You know I'm right."

She closed her eyes briefly with resignation—or relief. When she opened them again, her lips were pursed. "Without conceding your point, I'll admit I have my own doubts about the soundness of your father's orders."

"—" I didn't get a word out.

"Therefore I will attend Hospital Sunday—"

"!"

"—if you give me your word not to move *from this spot* until I return."

I make it a practice not to lie to Miss Judson, but there were lives at stake. Fingers crossed beneath the blankets, I met her gaze and nodded gravely. "You can trust me, Miss. Just—look after Father."

The next phase of my plan came the next morning, after Miss Judson's reluctant departure. I sulked about the kitchen, trying to look forlorn instead of impatient. Cook played her role well: she kept glancing at the clock, as if she had somewhere to be.

"It's not fair for you to have to miss the fete, too," I said, forcing a mix of sympathy and grumpiness into my voice. (One of those came slightly more naturally than the other.) "Father is being completely unreasonable!" I peeked beneath a towel covering a plate of buns, and Cook swatted at my hand.

"You know how Himself is." She set the buns on the hob to rise. "It can't be easy, him feelin' poorly and all. Still, I'd've liked to see Miss Sally's speech, I won't lie to you."

"We could both go. We'd slip into the crowds like anybody, and Father and Miss Judson would never even notice we were there."

"Don't think I don't know what you're doing, Young Miss. And it won't work." But she gazed around the kitchen, thoughts far away. At the hospital, I hoped. "I did make Charley some biscuits," she said. "It'd be a shame for them to go to waste."

"I'm sure Sally knows you didn't mean to disappoint Charley."

Cook turned to me, shaking her head. "Shameless, you are. Absolutely shameless." But I was already holding the tin of biscuits.

"I'll stay here with Peony and watch the dough rise, and *you* will go to Hospital Sunday with Miss Judson and keep an eye on Sally and Charley." I gripped her hands. "*Please*, Cook? Father's not thinking straight."

She softened, brushing a strand of hair from my forehead. "I'll be right back after Sally speaks, then, and had best find you in the schoolroom, with that cat o' yours, up to your ears in the Light Brigade."

Throwing my arms around her would have seemed excessive—not to mention suspicious—so I restrained myself. Barely. "Thank you," I said, with feeling. "Please don't let Father or Sally out of your sight."

❧

I waited a good fifteen impossible minutes, just in case either Cook or Miss Judson had second thoughts or forgot their gloves and returned prematurely. Peony kept time, no-ing reliably every sixty seconds. The Swiss could set their clocks by her. Finally, when I was certain the tram must have left by now, I ran through the house, gathering every supply I could think of: all the evidence, Albert Pittman's letter, the pomegranate flag, the earrings . . . Was it enough?

Peony paused before Father's study door, burbling a suggestion. "Should we telephone for reinforcements?" Not that I knew who to call.

"No."

"Make up your mind!"

Finally, I was as ready as I ever would be. I had scarcely ever been alone inside my own home, much less left it by myself. It seemed a strange and hollow place, and I felt a curious reluctance to leave it unattended. What if something happened while we were all gone?

That thought sent me on another anxious circuit of the house to check that taps were closed, drains were open, there were no open flames (or gas fittings!) anywhere, the hob was cool, and all the windows and doors were locked.

Peony, trotting at my heels, approved of my preparations. *"Now,"* she said. I found my own house key,* and

---

* I had insisted on receiving a copy when I was nine, despite the fact that no occasion to use it had ever arisen. I'd nearly forgotten where I kept it.

attempted to let myself out the door without Peony's accompaniment.

This was fruitless, and after several efforts to return her to the interior of the house left me sweaty, scratched, and disheveled, I gave up. She trotted purposefully to the carriage house, having deduced that I intended to take my bicycle. I hauled open the wide door, whereupon she sprang eagerly within, gave the space a quick once-over to forage for dead insects (it being time for a midmorning snack, evidently), then hopped into the basket on my handlebars.

I faltered. "You hate cycling," I reminded her.

"*No*," she said.

"It's *miles* to the hospital!"

With an impatient "Brrrb," she hunkered into the basket, only a narrow slit of eyes and the tips of her black ears visible. I sighed, wheeled the bicycle into the drive, shut the carriage house door, and mounted up.

There was no turning back now.

❧

By the time we arrived, the hospital grounds were crowded with everyone from Ladies of Quality wearing Hospital Committee rosettes to tradesmen toting their wares—armloads and cartloads of festive paper hats, sweeties, tambourines and whirligigs, marionettes and miniature ponies and roasted chestnuts—to families gathered for the festivities. The dreary Royal

Swinburne courtyard was transformed into a carnival of green-and-white banners, bunting, canopies, and flags. On a wooden stage that nearly hid the Anatomy Building and morgue from view, a brass band had staked their claim, horns blaring and tooting as they warmed up. The laundry where we'd found Mr. Pittman's body was artfully blocked by the tombola stall, with its heaps of prizes and gilded lottery cage. Nurse Pethwick was stationed there and gave me a cheery good morning, apparently unfazed that I had swapped Miss Judson for the chaperonage of a cat.

"Enter the raffle," she coaxed. "It's for a good cause." Hospital Tombola, it turns out, is no more interesting than regular tombola. The prizes included a disappointing lack of sphygmomanometers, Petri plates, or surgical specimens preserved in arsenic. "There's a lovely set of pen-wipers," Nurse Pethwick said.

"Put me down for twenty-five tickets." I turned to see Dr. Kinkaid fishing in his waistcoat pocket for a coin purse. "I rather fancy that Toby jug."

Nurse Pethwick showed off a hideous pottery mug shaped like a squatty man having a drink. "Me mum donated this!"

As Dr. Kinkaid paid for his tickets, I glanced about for Squeaky Shoes—and sure enough, he was loitering by the silhouette artist's booth, trying to hide in his oversized jacket. Was there dynamite concealed in that coat? Where were the police? That niggled at me again—the *something off* in Squeaky Shoes's appearance or demeanor—but I had no time to consider the matter or interrogate him, for just at that moment, I spotted Probationer Ling moving through the crowd, wheeling a sulky-looking patient in a bath chair.

Without thinking, I dug sixpence from my satchel and slammed it down on the tombola table. "You never saw me!" I gasped, and dived into the crowd. I could hardly count on Nurse Pethwick and Dr. Kinkaid to keep my secret, especially since Peony would abandon me for Father at the first opportunity, but panic got the better of me.

I squirmed and twined halfway across the courtyard before realizing I'd done the very opposite of what I'd come here for: left Father in the path of a bomber and his accomplice, with no sign of Cook or Miss Judson to protect him. I slumped against the stage.

"Myrtle, you came!" That accented voice was full of relief, and before I quite knew what was happening, Sally had thrown an arm around me. Her other arm, naturally, was full of Charley, who wriggled a gleeful, licky greeting. "I knew you wouldn't forsake me." She pulled away and waved heartily to Mrs. Dudley, who was deep in an animated exchange with Aunt Helena— apparently an argument over who would stand where upon the stage. "I'm so glad your father let you come after all."

"Er." I was sounding more and more like Father by

the day. Sally looked surprisingly serene, refreshed and composed, like she hadn't needed me here after all.

"Of course I need you!" she exclaimed. "Besides, I have to tell you something." She rummaged in her reticule, handed me the notes to her speech, and finally withdrew a slip of elegant notepaper. "I've been thinking about Mr. Pittman's letter—no, I'm all right. Pittman must have come to the hospital that night—when he was killed—to speak to one of the doctors. The surgeon from the *Persephone*—that Dr. Cutty."

I could only gape at her.

". . . And I figure, that must be who killed him, right?" Sally sounded eager. Too eager.

"I'm sure the police are looking into that," I said faintly.

"So I've made a list." She presented it proudly—in wobbly, girlish handwriting, a list of names, from *Julius Greeley, Governor* to *Alfred Stewart, House Officer.* "There are twenty-six doctors at the Royal Swinburne. We should be able to narrow it down to the one who was on the *Persephone*. And he'll be able to recognize me!"

"Sally—" She didn't seem to realize that confronting a murderer might not be her wisest course of action.

"My money's on that Dr. Kinkaid, since the murder happened in his laboratory, right?"

Where was she getting her information? "Er, Sally—"

"And he's the right age, more or less. He could have

been at sea with us ten years ago, couldn't he?" I was beginning to see why she was such a good hockey player: she just barreled headlong through the opposition.

"Well, no, actually." At least I could disabuse her of one notion. "We have his alibi for the time of your shipwreck." *Blowing up constables in Manchester.*

"Oh." Her face fell, but only momentarily. "All right, one down, twenty-five to go. I have to give my speech now," she said. "Tell your dad I'm sorry." On that cryptic note, she clambered up to take her place onstage between Aunt Helena and Mrs. Dudley, who appeared to have reached an amicable custody agreement for the young Viscountess.

As I turned away from the stage to scope out a spot in the audience—somewhere close enough to Sally, but with a clear view of the whole assembly—I found myself face-to-face with Dr. Greeley, who clutched a handful of notecards in white-knuckled hands. My blood curdled in my veins; there was no way he hadn't overheard every word Sally had just said.

He froze when he saw me, then managed a stiff "Good morning."

I might have managed a less-than-professional squeak. Fortunately, Aunt Helena intervened. "Julius!" she called out, voice carrying over the sound of trombones warming up. "Oh, Julius!" She clomped over, powerful footsteps echoing on the hollow wooden stage. "Have you been introduced to the Viscountess yet? Come here, your ladyship, and meet the Royal Swinburne's governor. Lady Ethel is a *tremendous* supporter of your cause."

Dr. Greeley stared at them. "No—I—it's not necessary. I must go—I'm needed at . . ." Mumbling something we didn't catch, he took his cards and his homburg and vanished into the crowd.

"Well, I never," huffed Aunt Helena, but it was too late. Where had he gone? And where, for that matter, were the police? D.C. Carstairs had assured us that there would be constables present today, but unless they were all undercover, they must be running behind. I scratched at my stocking with my other ankle; that annoying little niggle was back, like I'd noticed something but hadn't *noticed* it.

What I noticed next, however, was very clear indeed. A gloved hand caught me by the arm—not entirely gently. "*Explique-toi, s'il te plaît*," said a familiar, and rather piqued, voice. I winced, turning round to meet Miss Judson's gaze.

"Sally asked me to come?"

Miss Judson was not alone. Seated before her in a bath chair was a disloyal and judgmental cat, and beneath the cat, a glowering solicitor in pyjamas. And behind them, one Very Disappointed Cook.

For some reason, that made me bold. "Sally *asked* me to come," I said again. "She's our client. I couldn't abandon her."

"We dih't abadoh her!" Father's face had gone an unbecoming shade of pink. "We're righ heah."

I looked at him as steadily as I could. "I couldn't abandon *you*."

He didn't seem to know how to react to this.

"I suggest taking this discussion elsewhere, or postponing it for a more convenient moment," Miss Judson put in. "Miss Snowcroft's presentation is about to begin, and we are Making a Scene."

She wrangled Father's bath chair (not without some grumbling, which sounded like *I cad walg, you know*) to a spot within view of the stage, more or less. All I could see was the giant satin bow on the backside of the lady in front of me. The band stopped playing, and four loud bangs thumped out, demanding our obedient attention.

"Good day, Swinburne!" The stentorian* voice of Aunt Helena was perfectly audible. "On behalf of the Swinburne Ladies Hospital Committee, I would like to welcome you to this year's Hospital Sunday!"

A smattering of applause filled the pointed pause Aunt Helena left for it. "I remind you that the Royal Swinburne Hospital relies on these events to do its Good Work in our village. Please give generously, for this year the need is greater than ever. Now, I know full well that most of you are here for one reason only." She

---

* another splendid word with ancient origins: Stentor, herald during the Trojan War, had a voice as loud as fifty men. Or three Aunt Helenas.

gave another dramatic pause. "To see our special guest, a young lady we are honored to have lend her fame to our cause, who has promised to donate the proceeds of her appearance here today to the Free Surgery Fund! Please give a warm welcome to the Right Honorable Lady Ethel Snowcroft. And Charley, of course!"

Cheers erupted, which soon settled into a rhythmic chant of *"Snowcroft! Snowcroft!"* followed by *"Charley! Charley!"* Soon a heavy glass jar was making the rounds, coins plopping into it like raindrops.

I tensed, searching the crowd for ne'er-do-wells who might wish Sally harm. Sally came forward, Charley in her arms as always. Mrs. Dudley stood behind her, not at all ashamed of her duplicity, with Aunt Helena on her other side, scrutinizing the donors. Two peas in a mercenary pod, those two.

Sally had dressed for the occasion in a bright green dress with nautical flair. Her curly hair whipped in the wind. Even Charley wore a smart green-and-white striped scarf. Sally waved his paw, and applause burst up once more.

"You're all so kind!" Sally beamed at her fans. "Everyone I've met in England, and especially here in Swinburne, has been so generous and welcoming. Mrs. Dudley and the SWOBS"—that lady gave a gracious bow of her powdered and beribboned head—"and Miss Hardcastle and the Ladies Committee, and *everyone* here at the hospital." Her voice sounded sweet, but her eyes scanned the crowd—for the one person at the hospital who *wasn't* kind. "Thank you ever so much."

The audience roared with approval, but I felt tenser than ever. I craned my neck to Observe the spectators. Most were Swinburnians of Quality, turned out for the annual Charity Event, to see and be seen being generous. Matron had arranged her nursing staff in a green-and-lavender fence line along the perimeter. On the opposite side were the porters, sharp in their black uniforms and polished boots. One stocky fellow in a short dark coat shoved past me, disturbing the lady's giant bow, and she turned and gave me a nasty look. I'd have pointed out the true culprit, but he'd already vanished amid the press of bodies.

When Sally spoke again, her voice was soft and somber. "But something awful has happened." We were all silent now, every ear straining to hear each quiet word. "A man has been killed—murdered, right here in this very hospital." Everyone let out a collective gasp, turning to stare at one another. Father turned to stare at me.

"I don't know who committed this dreadful crime, but I do know the reason for it." Sally's voice broke. "Me. My presence here, my efforts to discover my true identity, to learn if I have family left . . . This is not what I wanted. I cannot bear to be responsible for such misfortune."

The crowd gave a sympathetic sigh, and I felt my

own heart squeeze with pain for Sally, for Mr. Pittman, for the whole sorry *Persephone* crew. But even I was not prepared for what Sally said next.

"And so I must be honest with you. I shall be withdrawing my suit at court, and with it any claim to the Snowcroft Legacy. If being Ethel Snowcroft is going to cause so much sadness, then I want no part of it. I was perfectly content being Sally Cooke of Melbourne, and to that simple life Charley and I shall return."

There was more to that speech, but no one heard it. After a moment of stunned silence, the audience began to react. Shocked whispers became murmurs, grumbles of confusion turned to cries of protest.

Father turned to us—to me. "Whah the devil dih you say t' her?" he demanded, but he did not wait for an answer. Abandoning the bath chair, Father stalked off toward the stage, shoving through the masses until we lost sight of his white dressing gown.

Miss Judson scowled in the direction Father had vanished. "Come along," she said crisply. But I lingered behind. I could see Sally's point, after everything. I wanted to give up, too.

Sally had likewise departed, but no one noticed. Aunt Helena, vainly attempting to salvage the event, barked out, "Now I should like to introduce the man we all have to thank for today, Governor Julius Greeley!"

Nothing happened. Aunt Helena repeated her

introduction, even louder this time. It didn't matter. Dr. Greeley wasn't there, and nobody was listening anyway—half of them were wandering away in stunned disappointment, their morning's entertainment spoiled. After a tense, bewildered interval, Aunt Helena signaled to the band. They struck up "Ta-ra-ra Boom-de-ay," and she stomped from the stage.

Where had Dr. Greeley gone? Why wasn't he here to deliver his much-anticipated Free Surgery speech? I could only imagine one thing that would convince him to give that moment up. Maneuvering through the crowd, I made my frantic way out of the fairgrounds and raced toward the main building.

Inside, the hospital was eerily deserted. My footfalls banged out louder than ever, echoing ominously as I thundered up to the Private Ward, dashed through the desolate corridors, past the unattended reception desk, and into the silent office wing.

Through all the wide-open windows in every ward, I could hear voices—Aunt Helena had evidently strongarmed Dr. Kinkaid into giving the speech instead. At least it would keep him from setting off his bomb.

Dr. Greeley's office door was open. I hesitated, then inched inside, breathing hard, my side cramping. Sally, having beaten me here, watched silently from the doorway, Charley cuddled at her shoulder. Dr. Greeley didn't notice us at first, intent on filling up a leather satchel, like a thief in a jeweler's shop. He swept his lovely wooden parrot and the furry drum into the bag, flung open a cupboard, and shoveled in an armload of warm clothes.

"It *is* you, isn't it?" Sally's voice was full of wonder. "I could tell—when you saw me."

Without turning, Dr. Greeley stiffened. "I don't know what you mean, young lady. Now, I'm very busy."

"Running away again!" I interjected. "In the middle of your big day. All those people out there are counting on you!"

Dr. Greeley's hand shook as he tried to latch his bag. "That's their mistake."

Sally stepped forward. "Can't you even look at me?" She reached a hand for Dr. Greeley's shoulder, and he jumped, startled, his arm knocking the engraved pocketknife to the floor.

For a moment nothing happened, as we all stared at the knife. The letters carved into the handle stood out in the shadows: *Cutty*. Sally kneeled down to retrieve it, and Dr. Greeley recoiled with a sound like a whimper.

"It's so small," she said, turning the blade so it caught the light. Slowly I rose, scarcely believing what she held in her hand.

"Go ahead," Dr. Greeley said. "I deserve it."

Sally's brow furrowed in confusion, and she tried to hand the knife back to him. He took a step closer, into its path. Sally's face paled.

I pushed her arm down. "She doesn't want revenge!"

I said. I hoped. "She only wants to know the truth."
I pulled the knife from her fingers, closing the blade
with a snap.

Sally put a trembling hand to her face, her troubled
eyes darting from Dr. Greeley to me. "I—I don't know,"
she whispered. Charley whined, squeezed too hard. "I
can't remember."

Dr. Greeley shuddered. "You don't want to remember. It was—we were—unspeakable things happened."

That was not exactly an admission of murder.
"It was a long time ago, and there were Exigent
Circumstances," I said. "Killing Mr. Pittman, though,
was definitely a crime."

He lifted terrified grey eyes to me. "No, no—don't
you understand? He came here to kill me! *She* sent
him."

"No," Sally said. "Never. I never would."

I'm not sure Dr. Greeley heard her. "I didn't mean
to do it. It wouldn't have happened, but I was sick, and
confused, and then he just fell—" With a broken sob, he
covered his face with his hand. "I should have let him
do it."

I didn't know what to do. I just stood there, holding
a murder weapon and watching a killer crumble before
me. "Sally didn't even know him. But he wanted her to
learn the truth. He just wanted to get it off his chest."
My heart squeezed again, for Albert Pittman this time.
"You didn't have to kill him, too!"

Dr. Greeley lunged for me. I squeaked and leaped away from him—but not before he'd grabbed the knife.

Now we were face-to-face with a killer—and *he* had the murder weapon. I backed away, pushing Sally behind me, heart banging louder than the crowd outside, who had burst into applause for Dr. Kinkaid.

Slowly, Dr. Greeley opened the blade on the knife, turning it so it glinted in the soft light. I squeezed my eyes shut, backing up and up—until I backed Sally straight into the door, closing it behind us with a horrible, final *click*. She moaned.

"It was so quick." Dr. Greeley's voice had an odd quality, grating and mechanical, that sent ice down my bones. "I didn't even know I had the knife until it was all over." For a ghastly moment we stood there, the unreal roar of applause behind him, the too-real solid door of oak behind us. Dr. Greeley's eyes were glassy and distant and terrifying. I clutched Sally's freezing hand.

Then it happened.

A crack from outside, loud as a thunderclap, loud as every window in the hospital breaking at once. Sally let out a little cry, I jumped out of my skin (not literally), and most importantly: Dr. Greeley dropped the knife. I turned and grabbed the doorknob, wrenching it desperately, but it wouldn't budge. I banged the flat of my hand against the wood.

"Help!" I cried, horribly aware that there was no one out there to hear me scream.

A hand reached from behind me and pried my fingers from the knob. I shuddered.

"That sounded like a gunshot," said a steady, reasonable voice at my ear. "We need to help."

"Myrtle, it's all right."

I twisted round. Dr. Greeley had another bag in hand, a medical bag this time. "I'm still a surgeon," he said—and I couldn't tell if he was reminding us or himself. Sally nudged me aside so Dr. Greeley could open the door, whereupon he broke into a brisk run toward the stairwell.

And I trusted him to head toward the danger, and not run away.

24

To Say Nothing of the Dog

> The sometimes gruesome and distasteful evi-
> dence produced by the Medico-Legal Investigator
> is nonetheless a vital part of jurisprudence, and of
> bringing the truth to light.
>
> –H. M. Hardcastle, *Foundations of Legal Medicine*

Outside, everything had erupted into chaos, and it was impossible to make out what had happened. What was happening. Shrieks heard while we descended the stairs had ceased, and the courtyard was a milling sprawl of people, all fleeing in opposite directions.

"Was it the bomb?" I cried. Where was Dr. Kinkaid? *Where was my father?*

Matron had mobilized her troops. Porters tried to keep order, directing the crowd to exit sensibly while nurses rendered aid to bawling children and fainting ladies. And one innocent fellow who had tripped over a cat and wrenched his knee. But amid the carnage of Hospital Sunday, no one seemed to be bleeding or dead. I stared about me in confusion. "What happened?"

Upon the stage, a swooning Aunt Helena was supported by a wide-eyed, white-faced Dr. Kinkaid. And down upon the deserted grounds below, flattened to the cobblestones in the remains of the tombola stall, lay a stocky man in a dark coat, who'd evidently been wrestled to submission by none other than Nurse Pethwick.

Probationer Ling stood guard, armed with a cricket bat that had been up for raffle. A pistol lay a few feet away, and a satisfied-looking Matron plucked it from the stones, as pleased as if she'd recovered it from a dyspeptic patient's gullet.

"What *happened*?"

Dr. Greeley, just as perplexed, was fitting the pieces together. "This looks like . . . an assassination attempt?"

"Not quite," said a new voice, harsh and unfamiliar—and American. I turned to see Squeaky Shoes heading our way, oversized coat thrown back to reveal his own brown suit. And a brass star pinned to his lapel.

"You're a policeman!" I cried. *That*'s what had been so strange about him: his clothes and mannerisms—especially those shoes—were constable-like, not hospital porter–like. I just hadn't placed him.

"That's right, little lady," he said. "Brody Jackson, on loan from Chicago P.D."

"Undercover," Nurse Pethwick huffed, hauling the assailant to his feet. "Been tracking this cove for six months!" She gave him a shake. "Patrick Paul Hanrahan, head of a group of Irish radicals, wanted for bombing a gasworks in—"

"In Manchester," I said with her. "In 1883. But—?" I was so confused I couldn't form a rational sentence.

"*And* suspected of plotting upcoming attacks on British and American targets," put in Officer Jackson. "We've got your whole operation now, Hanrahan."

Dr. Greeley came to my rescue. "Miss Pethwick is an inquiry agent for the firm of Sayers and Marsh in London. She and Mr. Jackson have been working undercover at the hospital, with the cooperation of Mr. Kinkaid."

"What?" My voice was painfully shrill. Like *I* had tonsillitis.

"Aye," said Nurse Pethwick. "Kinkaid's old crony here wanted supplies to build explosives. The good doctor strung 'im along until we could move in for the arrest."

"But ol' Patrick here must've gotten suspicious and double-crossed him," Officer Jackson said. Now I could hear that he had a slight Irish accent of his own. Matron handed him the pistol, and he tut-tutted. "This won't look good at all, Paddy."

Dr. Kinkaid had revived Aunt Helena, disentangled himself from her clutches, and dropped from the stage to join us. He looked pale, and some emotion I couldn't name. "Is it over, then?" He rubbed his beard, green eyes darting from the hospital staff to the surly Mr. Hanrahan, who had a spectacular bump rising from his temple. "You have the proof you need?"

"Wait!" I said, so sharply that everyone actually looked at me. "Then you *didn't* build the bomb that killed those constables?"

"Aye, I did, and I'd do it again, too," growled Mr. Hanrahan. Nurse Pethwick swatted him—right on his bruised face, silencing him.

Dr. Kinkaid let out a long, long breath. "No, I did not. But I knew who did. And he'll finally pay for what he did."

Mr. Hanrahan had not a word for his countryman.

"They think you're dead." I felt sluggish and stupid. How had this gone on, right under my very nose, and I'd missed *all* of it?

"It was my brother who died." Dr. Kinkaid's voice was very soft. "Michael. He was going to go to medical school, to be a surgeon. To save lives."

Now pieces started to click together. "You took his place!" I spun to Nurse Ling. "Is that the man he was arguing with?"

Nurse Ling nodded, a firm affirmation. "Should've set the porters on you after all."

"I think we're done here," said the American constable. "Miss Pethwick?"

She nodded. "Guv, might we borrow a porter to help us deliver this package to the police station?"

Matron finally spoke up: "I think Mr. Bentley could be of assistance," and set off to find him.

Nurse Pethwick—Miss Pethwick, I suppose—nodded at Dr. Kinkaid. "You come down and give us that statement when it's convenient."

"And no funny business with that nitroglycerin," put in Officer Jackson. "It's evidence."

Dr. Kinkaid reached out to shake their hands. "Thank you. I think."

"Thank *you*. You had the hard part." (Personally, I thought looking after Father had been the more challenging part of the operation, but I kept my mouth shut.) Pethwick gave one last businesslike nod, and she and Officer Jackson ushered Mr. Hanrahan away—none too gently, I might add.

I watched them leave, still confused. "But if there was no bomb, then who got shot?"

"Oh." That sheepish answer came from Nurse Ling. She scrounged around in the debris from the stall and recovered a fragment of broken crockery—a sturdy handle still attached to a shard shaped like a man's backside. "The Toby jug. Alas."

A breathless couple rushed upon us, looking disappointed. "Did we miss it? Robbie! I told you we were going to be late." Genie kicked one of the brick planters with her crutch.

"I'm not the three-legged one," Mr. Blakeney reminded her affably. "Stephen, you all right, then? Looks like it was quite the shindig."

I felt an irrational urge to check myself for injuries, patting down my coat and skirts. Dr. Greeley met my eyes, and I bit my lip. I didn't know what to say.

Aunt Helena, however, showed no such reservations. Having recovered both consciousness and dignity, she marched over to us. "I'll have you know, this man is a *hero*!" she announced to all and sundry. "Employing private detectives to ensure the safety of his patients and staff and foil a dastardly international conspiracy! And Dr. Kinkaid!" Her eyes shone dreamily. "So brave, to lure the criminal into the open like that."

Dr. Kinkaid's lily-livered pallor had not improved, and he looked like he might faint.

"Now, Helena, don't exaggerate," Dr. Greeley said, trying to recover some of his good-naturedness. "We were only doing our duty." I knew he didn't feel particularly heroic just then. With the immediate crisis over, he seemed uncertain what to do next. I felt exactly the same—a notion that left me more than a little off-kilter.

"Say," Genie broke in. "Where's Miss Snowcroft? I was hoping for an interview. Is it true she renounced her claim?"

Everyone looked around, but the erstwhile heiress and her entourage were nowhere to be seen. That awful little niggle came back, tugging at my chest. I spotted

Miss Judson and Father making their way to us, and—forgetting we were still quarreling—barreled straight into Father's arms. "You're not blown up!" I cried.

"Mmph," he replied, hugging me back just as fiercely.

"There now, Young Miss, don't smother 'im," said Cook, looking exactly like she wished to smother Father herself.

"Where's Sally?"

"Mrs. Dudley took her home," Miss Judson said. "She was a little upset." Her face held a question, but she did not give it voice. For now. I sighed, snuggling against Father, letting his solid, reliable, Fatherly presence calm my hammering heartbeat. Poor Sally.

"Do you think Sally meant what she said? About giving up the inheritance?"

Father, irritated, muttered something none of us quite got.

"I almost feel sorry for Mrs. Dudley," Miss Judson said. I almost agreed with her.

Genie snapped her fingers. "Myrtle, I nearly forgot. Robbie had me look that bit up about that ship for you."

I glanced to Dr. Greeley, who was still comforting—or being comforted by—Aunt Helena. Did I really need Genie's information anymore? I now had eyewitness testimony of my own to offer at the Inquest, but I felt nothing but compassion for Dr. Greeley. It would be a shame for his plans for the Free Surgery to collapse, when it would do so much good. Yet it wasn't fair, either, for Mr. Pittman's killer to go free. I didn't believe he'd come to the Royal Swinburne to hurt Dr. Greeley, but to unburden himself. Which was all, I think, that Dr. Greeley had wanted, in the end.

I could hardly say any of that to Genie, however, who was fishing in her pocket for a folded scrap of paper. "The captain of the *Gloria Mundi* was called Roger Dudley—if you believe it. That'll be easy to remember. Couldn't find anything else about him," she added, handing the paper to me. "Why'd you want to know?"

My Roge . . . went down in a coffin ship . . . somebody owes me. I stared, open-mouthed, heart plummeting to the bottom of the sea. I spun round and caught Dr. Greeley by the sleeve, before Aunt Helena could spirit him away for good.

"Yes?" he said, brow creasing.

"The *Gloria Mundi*—when it rescued you. *Was Velma Dudley aboard that ship?*"

Now that all his secrets were out, Dr. Greeley completely deflated, limp and weary as a windless sail. He nodded sadly, suddenly looking much older.

"She was blackmailing you. All of you." I wanted to sit down, but the facts spinning round my head kept me upright. "It was her. It was *all* her! SWOBS, the 'benefits club,' Mr. Pittman—good grief, when Sally renounced her heritage just now—!" I reached for something and found Dr. Kinkaid's arms.

"Buck up, Hardcastle," he said. "Take a breath, then speak your piece."

I shook my head. "There's no time. We have to go after them—oh, we'll never catch her!"

A new voice joined the conversation, unusually urgent. *"No!"*

We all looked down to where a small black-and-white cat and an aged seafaring celebrity stood together, tails twitching. Peony's was impatient, Charley's uncertain. The little terrier held something in his mouth—something slithery and glittering: a gold chain, which he dropped at Dr. Greeley's feet. Sally's locket?

A change came over Dr. Greeley. He crouched to the earth, fingers held out for Charley to sniff. "Hello, there, old friend," he said, and Charley squirmed with joy at the reunion.

I picked up the locket, still warm from Charley's mouth—or Sally's neck—and turned a stricken gaze to Miss Judson. "Sally would never have left Charley behind. Something's very wrong."

"Search the grounds," Dr. Greeley said. He waved to the nearest porters, giving crisp, calm orders. "We'll find her."

"They could be halfway to Upton by now!" I wailed.

"Stoff the trab," said Father, which Miss Judson had to interpret for the stumped porter.

"There are too many places to hide!" I said. "We'll never catch them!" What would Mrs. Dudley do now that her plan had failed? Sally would figure it out soon enough, just like she had with Dr. Cutty. I wanted to scream with frustration.

Then Mr. Blakeney did something daft. Regarding the small furry witnesses with utmost seriousness, he said, "Peony Hardcastle, do you know where Miss Snowcroft has gone?"

Peony yawned—and Charley turned to nip at her, letting out an urgent bark.

"Thas good eduff for me," said Father. "Lea' th' way."

We trotted as a group, Peony occasionally encouraging Charley with a pugilistic swat across the bow. She darted beneath the stage, forgetting that full-grown (and partially grown) humans could not navigate crowds or narrow spaces with quite such sinuous finesse, as we went the longer way round. It was a good thing we weren't trying to sneak up on anyone, as a cat, a dog, two doctors, a journalist on crutches, an unemployed law clerk, a solicitor in pyjamas, a nurse with a cricket bat, a governess, an off-duty house-keeper, and one small frantic Investigator do not a stealth party make.

I tried to explain, gasping out the story as we dodged obstacles I swear Peony was deliberately steering us *toward*. "It was Mrs. Dudley! She was black-mailing the *Persephone* survivors! But something must have gone wrong. Maybe Mr. Pittman decided to go to the police, or he was going to tell Sally—" I stopped, one more piece crashing into place. "He was Genie's source! That's why he never showed up—he was murdered before he had a chance to come forward. Mrs. Dudley had to kill him before it came out that she'd been blackmailing everyone for all these years."

"Blackmailing them about what?" Dr. Kinkaid asked, although somehow we all managed not to hear him.

Father picked up the recitation—or he tried to, anyway. "She vollowed Pih'man t' the hospi'al Mo'day nigh, t' keeb 'em froh seeig you, G'eeley."

Taking pity upon him (or everyone else), Miss Judson took over. "In the struggle—witnessed by Mr. Hardcastle—Mrs. Dudley either struck Mr. Pittman deliberately, or he fell and hit his head. She left him unconscious in Dr. Kinkaid's laboratory and turned all the gas valves on."

"Dih you fide a wigh coah, Muhrl?"

"Ivory," I panted, recalling the overcoat at Mrs. Dudley's flat above Swabs. Father gave a grunt of satisfaction.

We collected a morgue attendant on the way.

"Wotcher, Russ," Mr. Davis said, as Charley and Peony charged through the open doorway of the old Anatomy Building. "And, er, Guv. And . . . everyone . . ."

"Did you see anyone come past here?" Dr. Kinkaid demanded.

"Actually, yes."

"Well, who, man?"

Mr. Davis blinked at him. "That famous girl and some woman. The woman looked familiar, too, come to think on it. They've gone round to the theater."

"The Anatomy Theater!" I gasped. We sped through the dimly lit corridor to the old arched door, which ought to be barred tight against intruders.

It stood open, and some of the shadows within leaked out. Voices—one voice—rang from the lofty ceiling of the great amphitheater. "You ungrateful wretch! After *everything* I've done for you! *'No, I don't want the money—'* Well, some of us have *earned* that money, I'll have you know!"

"Velma, please—"

"That's Mrs. Dudley to you! I saved your life. Show some respect."

We burst into the theater. Daylight poured in from a huge multipaned skylight in the angled roof and the vast window overlooking the operating table. Row upon row of folding wooden seats, crammed tight together, soared right up to the ceiling, a dizzyingly steep swoop of stairs and tiers and not nearly enough railings. High at the very top balcony, Mrs. Dudley held Sally pinned against the wooden bars, a deadly drop behind her.

"Mrs. Dudley, then—just tell me what you want." Sally's voice was soft, but the superb acoustics bounced every word right down to us.

"What I *want*? I want my due! I've spent months on this plan—years!—and I will not see it destroyed by you."

"Mizh Duh'ley!" Father's voice was not strong, but he knew how to make it carry in a courtroom. "Izz over. We know ev'rythig. You've nothig to gaid by hurtig Sally."

She jerked up, trying to see us. Sally tried to jerk away, in an athletic twist, but Mrs. Dudley's barkeep's grip was too strong. "Please, we can talk about this."

"Like we talked about you deciding to give up half a million pounds?"

"That poor man died because of it—" Sally stopped, realization dawning. "Oh. He wanted to talk, too, I suppose."

"He betrayed me." Mrs. Dudley's voice was cold. "We had a nice thing going, but he had an attack of conscience! Decided *he* was going to come clean about all of it. Did he ever ask if I wanted our dirty laundry strewn all over England?"

I watched, horror spreading through me. It was too much for Charley. He let out a plaintive bark that burst up through the great room like a shot from a cannon and tried valiantly to mount the steps. But they were too tall for his elderly terrier legs, and he could only paw helplessly at the wood, whimpering.

Sally hadn't quite figured out what Mrs. Dudley meant, but she was trying her best to understand, to talk sense into the furious woman. "I'll speak to Mr. Hardcastle. I'm sure there's something he can do. The hearing's not for days yet . . ."

A flash of movement near the windows distracted me, and I glanced up to see Dr. Kinkaid slinking through the shadows. Several levels and rows below them, he inched his way up and along, like a cat stalking pigeons on a ridgepole.

Miss Judson, noting the same thing, moved to take up position from the opposite side—a flanking maneuver to make Lord Cardigan proud. But Father caught her by the arm. He shook his head, eyes pleading, and she relented, watching the scene unfolding above, her mouth a taut line.

What could we do? The more reasonable Sally was, the more hysterical it made Mrs. Dudley. She had Sally bent backward over the railing.

"Mizz Duh'ley, if you throw Mizh Sowcroff off th' balcody, ih will be the ehd of the Sowcroff fortune." Father's statement wore him out. He clutched his throat, wincing.

"He's right," I said. "If Sally dies, the Snowcroft estate will escheat to the Crown—and nobody will see a farthing of it!"

Father took a slipper-footed step up one stair. Two. A third. Mrs. Dudley and Sally had frozen, staring at him. Miss Judson looked like she wanted to hit him with something. But in the background, with all attention focused on Father, Dr. Kinkaid crept ever closer. I was afraid Charley would give him away: he watched, little white body stiff with hope, stubby tail a rigid flag.

"Theh's always room for degociatiod." In the vast theater, Father's weak voice sounded muddy and strange, but this was one word Mrs. Dudley understood.

"Negotiation? What sort?"

Father looked to me for support, and I scrambled to pick up the argument.

"Well, there's no physical evidence that you killed Mr. Pittman," I said. "And there's certainly no proof it was premeditated. The Magistrate's office might be prepared to let you plead guilty to a lesser charge." It was probably blasphemous to say a prayer to Magistrate Fox, but I sent him a quick telepathic plea-stroke-apology for my presumption in making deals for him.

"Plead guilty! I've done nothing wrong!"

"Kidnapping and extortion, however, will look bad to the judge."

"Come now, Mizzus Duh'ley—you aren' goig to gill Mizh Sowcroff in front of eleven eyewidnezzes."

Mrs. Dudley didn't seem convinced. (Nor did Sally, though she tried not to show it.) Hands still firmly on Sally, she said warily, "What are you offering?"

Father reached a hand to her, although he was still floors below them. He forced out a clear whisper: "A chance. An' opportu'ty to live out your life, not go to th' gallows for killig th' moz' famous heiress in Igland."

Mrs. Dudley seized Sally by the neck. "Not good enough!" she shrilled.

But *she* wasn't good enough. Sally—hockey champion Sally Cooke from Melbourne—had been waiting for her moment. She'd spotted Dr. Kinkaid at the side of the playing field, coming to her defense, and in an abrupt show of terrible sportsmanship, she elbowed Mrs. Dudley in the stomach and broke free. I heard the crunch of broken steel as the busk in Mrs. Dudley's corset snapped. She doubled over, gasping, and Sally made a mad, desperate move.

She swung herself—green ruffled nautical dress and all—over the railing and dropped to the next level down. My heart stayed fixed to the floor above, my breath with it.

"Oh, brava!" Genie applauded enthusiastically.

"Ooof!" Sally landed in a heap of petticoats, hitting the seats awkwardly, hip-first. Dr. Kinkaid dived for the railing, staring over the side with a mix of horror and admiration. Sally sat up slowly, gingerly—and little Charley overcame his doubts and with a mighty leap, bounded up the steps to his mistress.

Father made to run for her, but Miss Judson seized him in an iron grip. "Don't you *dare*," she said severely. Instead, Governor Greeley shuffled politely to the front of the anxious crowd and made his way, medical bag in hand, to Sally's side.

We'd all forgotten Mrs. Dudley. One level up, she surveyed the scene with the calculating gaze that had orchestrated a decade-long transcontinental blackmail scheme, and it was clear she had no intention of going down without a fight. She turned and pounded up the stairs.

"Where are you going?" The words leaped out of me, but Mrs. Dudley didn't look back. She dragged her skirts up through the tight aisles of seats and tottered along the very back row then down the next flight of steps over—neatly sidestepping Dr. Kinkaid, who had to turn back and rethread his way through the seats to catch her.

Mrs. Dudley reached the main balcony—the one with nothing below it but a sickening drop to the cold stone operating floor. Dr. Kinkaid lunged for her, but she dodged out of reach, feet slipping wildly on the Royal Swinburne's diligently waxed floorboards. She skidded right into the railing, unable to curb her momentum. With a cry of sudden panic, she pitched headlong over the edge and into the empty air.

"No!" I screamed, as the missile of purple taffeta frou-froued down thirty feet and hit the enamel operating table with a hideous sound—like a mast crushed beneath a rogue wave. I flung myself into Father and Miss Judson, unable to look. Firm arms held me tight, smothering me. I could feel the Tardieu spots forming, and I didn't even care. Something—someone—squeezed past us, soft boots padding over the stone floor.

A moment later, Nurse Ling said clearly, "Doctor—she's alive."

I peeled myself gingerly from Father's shoulder, just enough to peek. Mrs. Dudley was crumpled in a purple mound at the base of the operating table, her black hair a shambles, blood streaming down her forehead. Her eyes were shut, and her shoulder looked wrong.

Dr. Kinkaid slid down the handrail of the stairs and dashed to Nurse Ling's side. A quick consultation later—"Dislocated shoulder. Ripped the tendons clean through, most likely. She'll need surgery. Don't think her back's broken, though—plain daft luck, that"—he gave Mrs. Dudley's face a soft slap, semi-reviving her. Her eyes rolled toward him and she groaned.

"Now, madam," Dr. Kinkaid said. "That was just stupid."

Mr. Davis appeared next, toting a rolled-up stretcher, and the three of them got Mrs. Dudley aboard and carried away to the Casualty Ward. "The police can find her there," Dr. Kinkaid said. He paused only briefly to look up to the level where Sally was being tended to by Dr. Greeley. She lifted her fingers in a grateful wave.

The room fell silent after that, although I couldn't get the sound of Mrs. Dudley hitting that table out of my head. I closed my eyes and let out all my breath, then felt a soft warmth twining round my ankles. Peony bounded up to the arm of one of the seats, regarding me with concern. "*No?*" she asked.

I lifted her to my shoulder, where she dug in—hard—with her claws. "No," I agreed, and she bunted me in the chin, burbling and purring.

Above us, Dr. Greeley and Sally lingered together. "I'm not hurt," Sally was insisting to a skeptical Dr. Greeley. "Really. I've had worse on the hockey field."

I carried Peony to join them, Miss Judson and Father behind me. The others stayed below, although I could hear Genie cursing her own broken ankle. Charley had made it most of the way up, and I gave him a boost for the last few steps. He stopped at Dr. Greeley's leg and leaned, gratefully, stub of a tail moving too fast to see.

"There's my old shipmate," the surgeon said fondly, scooping him into his arms. Charley, used to being at the center of the action, clearly thought this no more than his due. "A good crewman," Dr. Greeley said. "Loyal."

Sally watched Dr. Greeley with serious brown eyes. "Yes, he was," she said, and we all knew she didn't mean her dog.

Dr. Greeley's breath caught, and he tried to speak, but Sally forestalled him. "Don't," she said gently. "You don't have to say anything. But I do." She pulled herself to standing and wrapped an arm around Dr. Greeley's neck. "Thank you," she whispered, and it was a long time before she pulled away.

When he was free once more, Dr. Greeley turned to Father, still holding Charley like he never meant to let him go again. "I did not kill Albert Pittman. I did ki—"

Father broke in. "No need t' say adythig elze, zir."

"But—"

Father looked at all of us—Sally, me and Peony, Miss Judson, the Blakeneys (only one of whom knew the whole story), even Charley. "I'b Proz'cudig Solizhtor for Swihburd," he said. "Weh you goig to codfess a crime thad ogurred id by jurisdigtiod?"

Dr. Greeley frowned.

I said, "Were you going to confess to committing a crime in Swinburne?"

"Oh." Dr. Greeley shook his head.

Father looked satisfied, and gave me a lofty cue.

"Only crimes that occur within Swinburne are of any concern to the Magistrate's Office," I said, and Father squeezed my hand. I thought we could count on Magistrate Fox agreeing with that. Let the Board of Trade or the Home Office or somebody else Investigate the *Persephone*, if they were so inclined. As far as Father and I were concerned, that case was closed.

Dr. Greeley's frown deepened. "But—"

"But *nothing*," Sally said.

"What about the Snowcroft Legacy?" I said. "Are you really going to give it up?"

Sally grinned. "I really am."

"No, you can't!" That protest, unexpectedly, came from Dr. Greeley. "Ethel—no. It's yours. You deserve it."

She shook her head. "I learned what I came here to learn. That money—it was always someone else's plan for me. I don't want it. Besides, with Mr. Pittman gone, there are no more witnesses to prove my identity."

"I can prove it." Dr. Greeley's voice was quiet but firm.

"But you'd have to tell everyone—"

He was smiling now. "I'd only have to tell them one thing." Holding Charley in one arm, he shifted aside the spiky white fur on his frail shoulder, revealing a pale pink mark shaped (not like a pomegranate) like a sickle. "See this? A scar from sutures. I put those in." He sounded proud. "Little Charley ran afoul of a broken bottle on the *Persephone*, and I patched him up."

Sally stared in astonishment. "I've never seen that!" she exclaimed, lifting Charley from Dr. Greeley's arms. "Oh, poor Charley!" Charley, for one, looked not the least bit pitiful, wagging his tail and wriggling, trying to kiss everyone at once.

25

Farewell and Adieu

Hard though it may be to believe, as a Medico-
Legal Investigator, you may find that your friends
and loved ones do not share your enthusiasm for
your field. Never let that discourage you from the
pursuit of justice.

–H. M. Hardcastle, *Foundations of Legal Medicine*

Two weeks later, the Hardcastles found ourselves back
at Magistrate Fox's house once more. Father had spent
another week in hospital, and I'd been sentenced to
a fortnight's hard labor for my spectacular display of
Wilful Disobedience. Miss Judson made me write an
entire history—in Latin—of the Siege of Sevastopol.
The pen-wiper I'd won at tombola came in handy, but
I was so grateful to have Father safe and on the mend I
didn't complain once. Well, twice.

This time the convivial party included Sally and
Dr. Greeley, but not, of course, Mrs. Dudley. After Dr.
Kinkaid fixed her shoulder, she'd been transferred

from the Royal Swinburne to the infirmary at the jail in Upton to await her trial for the murder of Mr. Pittman. She never admitted to her crimes—either killing Mr. Pittman or blackmailing the *Persephone* survivors—but she was only being charged with the murder.

"The story of the *Persephone* can be written by her survivors," Magistrate Fox assured us. "Some things can stay lost at sea." Dr. Greeley had twice more attempted to offer a formal confession for the death of Captain Snowcroft aboard the lifeboat, but neither Magistrate Fox nor Sally—nor Father—would hear of it.

"You've repaid your debt," Magistrate Fox assured the surgeon. Lost in his own thoughts, Dr. Greeley lingered before the model of the *Persephone* as it looked before the tragedy, handsome, stately, and whole. "I can't see any value in charging anyone associated with those tragic events with a crime."

Dr. Greeley still seemed troubled, and I supposed he would never quite recover from what had happened—what he'd done. But Sally planted a very forward kiss on his hollow cheek. "Besides," she said, "Dr. Kinkaid's darling wains need you." The darling wains of the Free Surgery, which was going forward, in large part thanks to a substantial endowment from a newly minted heiress.

Gallant Charley, ever the gentleman, was attempting to broker introductions between Magistrate Fox's dogs and Peony. Dr. Greeley had given us the full account of Charley's miraculous survival at sea, thanks to Navigator Charles slipping the pup portions of his own rations. Peony, being as stubborn as Dr. Greeley and Sally, had stationed herself atop the window cornice, hissing at anyone who approached. I sighed wistfully, knowing that Father wouldn't scold *her* for her behavior at his employer's house.

Today Sally had eschewed both her black crape and the childish frocks Mrs. Dudley had made her wear, and was dressed in a casual (but expensive) plaid day dress with dark velvet trim. She looked more her age, which somehow made her seem all the younger. She carried a stack of brochures—procured from an Undisclosed Source—and had asked Miss Judson's advice on choosing an English school with a good field hockey team. "I want to stay near family," she said, sounding shy. Magistrate Fox coughed, crinkly eyes moist.

In the excitement after Hospital Sunday, some days passed before I'd found my way back to Father's study—only to discover that the Secret File had vanished. Two more jewelry catalogues had appeared in its place, however, only deepening the mystery. Although I had begun to formulate a Theory of my own (after noting the dog-eared pages and a circle scribed round one particular item). It still gave me an unsettled, fluttery feeling—but of a very different sort now.

Father, for his part, was finally recovering. His mood and his color were both high since being released from hospital. His last week there had been surprisingly restful, despite the influx of paperwork caused by Mrs. Dudley's arrest. Matron Finch, overwhelmingly grateful for the service we'd rendered to her precious Dr. Greeley (if still foggy on the details), personally oversaw every aspect of his care. She was not exactly Nightingalian in her bedside manner, but the leather manacles remained packed away, and Father generously agreed not to bring charges for the "misplaced" property of the Private Ward patients, which had all been quietly returned (including Genie's fountain pen), provided she behave herself in future. "You are on a double secret probation," he'd warned her, though Dr. Greeley's disappointment appeared to be more than enough punishment to reform Matron Finch entirely.

Probationer Ling finished her training and was hired on as a full-time surgical nurse for Dr. Kinkaid, who suggested she start attending his medical lectures and train to be a surgical dresser. Matron gave her a demerit for acting above her station, but the hospital governor lent his wholehearted approval to the promotion. Dr. Greeley abandoned the study on starvation, and Dr. Kinkaid's subjects grew plump and sleek—definitely the luckiest rats in England.

Genie finally got her exclusive interview with Sally,

whose suit had been accepted by the probate court, and Father promised to let her cover every stage of Mrs. Dudley's trial. She knew we were all keeping some secret from her, and pestered Mr. Blakeney about it endlessly. Magistrate Fox might be able to keep quiet, but I feared Genie would eventually wear her brother down.

"Perhaps by then the publicity will have worn off," Sally said, rising from her seat on Magistrate Fox's plush settee (and half under a dog). "Mr. Hardcastle, did you bring those papers for us to sign?"

Father jumped forward. "Oh, yes. Here." He fumbled in his suit jacket and withdrew a creased folder—a very *familiar* folder, Dear Reader. I sat up sharply.

"Do we need to read this?" she inquired.

Father looked embarrassed. "Not really, you're only witnesses."

"Witnesses to what?" I demanded.

Sally took the file over to the table where we'd first examined the *Persephone*'s chronometer and removed its contents with great ceremony. The older gentlemen joined her there, pens in hand. Suspicious, I crept closer.

I, Arthur Hardcastle, Esquire, of the village of Swinburne, England, being of sound mind and body, do hereby make and declare this last Will and Testament—

"Your will! Why do you need a will?" I glared at Father—and at Dr. Greeley. "I knew there was something wrong!"

"No, no!" Father hastily bundled me into a hug. "It's nothing like that. I am perfectly healthy now. I promise. I can have Dr. Greeley write up an affidavit to that effect if you don't believe me." He smiled—a genuine, broad, Father smile, the kind he often gave to Peony. I softened. A little.

He continued, "It's just—well, after the Snowcroft Affair, I thought it would be a good idea to update my will. I haven't done it since your mum passed. We've all seen what can happen if an estate is left without clear guidance as to who inherits what!"

I tapped my foot, arms crossed, as Dr. Greeley signed the document and passed the pen to Sally. The law didn't specify the age of witnesses, and her status as a peer of the realm certainly wouldn't hurt her credibility. She inscribed her new signature upon Father's will, just one stately word:

$$\mathcal{S}nowcroft$$

"That seems so terribly *short*," she Observed, adding with a grin: "Maybe I ought to have Charley sign it too."

Father folded up the newly signed-and-countersigned document and tucked it into his jacket pocket. I would read it later, of course—if only to be certain he'd made proper provisions for everyone, not just me but Cook and Miss Judson, too. Father hadn't asked her to witness it, which I took to be another good sign he was considering her future: wills could only be witnessed by people who didn't stand to inherit.

Looking as placid as ever, Miss Judson sat on the arm of the settee, and Father settled beside her, Peony on his lap. It was as cozy a picture as the portrait of the Snowcrofts, and I crept in, squeezing between them. Father brushed the hair from my cheek, and Peony purred with contentment. Somewhere outside the Magistrate's sturdy brick walls, mysteries were afoot, but I supposed they could wait.

I sighed happily and leaned my head against Miss Judson's knee. "What about you?" I said. "You should make one, too."

"A will?" She looked bemused. "I don't own any property. I have nothing to worry about."

The Investigation Will Continue
in
Myrtle, Means, and Opportunity

A NOTE FROM THE AUTHOR

On December 5, 1872, the Canadian merchant ship *Dei Gratia* came upon a chilling sight: a deserted brigantine sailing along in the North Atlantic, in seemingly good condition but missing her entire crew—including the captain's wife and two-year-old daughter. The mystery of what befell the *Mary Celeste* has captivated imaginations for 150 years. What events caused Captain Benjamin Briggs to abandon his vessel, and what became of the ten people who simply vanished from the ship? What became of little Sophy Briggs?

The nineteenth century was rife with riveting true tales of seafaring misadventure. Newspaper readers gobbled up accounts of vessels like *Mary Celeste*; the whale ship *Essex* that inspired Herman Melville's novel *Moby Dick*; or the ill-fated survivors of the yacht *Mignonette*, whose infamous murder trial is still taught to first-year law students (*R v. Dudley and Stephens*, 1884). Victorian audiences thrilled to the most nail-biting details of life and death at sea. And more than a century later, these stories of mortal peril still fascinate.

The Snowcroft Legacy in this book was inspired by real-life inheritance cases of the age. The Tichborne Claimant, mentioned in the novel, was a global sensation in the 1860s, when an Australian butcher popped up in England and claimed to be Sir Roger Tichborne, believed lost at sea twelve years earlier. Despite possessing only the remotest physical resemblance to Sir Roger and lacking key elements of his personality and knowledge, Arthur Orton (or Thomas Castro, as he was also known) somehow convinced Mrs. Tichborne that he was indeed her long-lost son, going so far as to sue the family that had taken over the Tichborne property for his "rightful" inheritance. Tichborne mania gripped the English public, who were divided over whether or not the Claimant really was Sir Roger. After two sensational trials (Orton's lawsuit and his subsequent prosecution for perjury), English law was tightened to provide more serious penalties for "false personation," or impersonation of another for financial gain. Today we call this crime identity theft.

Return readers of the series may recognize shades of another famous Victorian inheritance case, namely the fictional "Jarndyce and Jarndyce" of Charles Dickens's *Bleak House*. According to Dickens, his interminable probate case, becalmed for generations in the morass of the antiquated court system, was inspired by a real trial, although he never specified which one. Historians have pinned down the likely source as the contested estate of William Jennens, a wealthy government official who died in 1798 without signing his will. In a bizarre twist, optimistic (or opportunistic) claimants to the Jennens fortune crawled out of the woodwork from all over England and North America *until well into the twentieth century*, before the vast fortune was finally exhausted by legal fees.

One more facet of this story deserves especial note. Matron Finch's macabre collection of oddments swallowed by patients is based on a real-life artifact that traumatized generations of Iowa schoolchildren. A similar collection assembled by Des Moines doctor James Downing during the early twentieth century is housed in the collections of the State Historical Society of Iowa. Although no longer on display, it lives on in many a nightmare. It has been included here by special request.

As always, my thanks go to Myrtle's incredible crew at Algonquin Young Readers: editor and champion-in-chief Elise Howard; production editor Ashley Mason; copyeditor—what was your name again?—Sue Wilkins; publicity and marketing moguls Kelly Doyle and Debra Linn; the spectacular design team of Brett Helquist, Leah Palmer Preiss, Carla Weise, and Laura Williams; along with Sarah Alpert and Adah Morales. And my apologies go to audio narratrix Bethan Rose Young for

Myrtle's father's dialogue in this volume, which will certainly require her Exceptional Forbearance.

Lastly, for always keeping our little vessel steady as she goes through fair and foul weather alike, my love and gratitude belong to Christopher Bunce, my co-captain of thirty-one years. *Quoth he, there was a ship . . .*